The Good Life

Kelly -
make it award-worthy!

♡ -Jodie Beau

Jodie Beau

This is a work of fiction. Names, characters, businesses, places, events and incidents are either the products of the author's imagination or used in a fictitious manner. Any resemblance to actual persons, living or dead, or actual events is purely coincidental.

Edited by Madison Seidler
Cover design ©Sarah Hansen of Okay Creations
Photography by Lise Gagne

For Ian, the little boy who turned my cup half-full.

PROLOGUE

It was late August. The air was warm and humid. Even at 3:30am it was still over eighty degrees. The young couple lying in the bed of the pickup truck threw their blanket off of them in an attempt to cool down. The move was a little risqué since they weren't wearing any clothes underneath.

They had come to the lot near the airport after the bars closed because they needed a place to be alone. She lived with her parents, and he shared an apartment with her older brother. There was a super-icky factor about being caught naked by any of those people. They preferred not to risk it. It was more fun to chance being caught by the police instead.

The lot was deserted; the restaurant it belonged to closed hours earlier. The girl had discovered the location about five years ago, shortly after she got her driver's license at sixteen. It was serendipity, she'd thought at the time, having just learned the word.

That was before the movie came out and everyone else learned it too. A happy accident it was.

The engine had been overheating on her old POS Buick and she'd pulled into an empty run-down parking lot next to a boarded-up restaurant to give it a drink. As she lifted up the hood, a plane flew right over her head after take-off. It was so close she felt she might have been able to touch it if she jumped high enough. She'd never seen a plane so close before and was amazed by its size and power. The best part of all was the blast of air she felt. It was only enough to mess up her hair and blow her skirt up a tad, but that small blast of air gave her a huge rush of adrenaline and she was hooked.

For the next few years she parked in the lot quite often. She would come after school and lie on the hood of her car while she listened to music and studied. Sometimes she watched the planes and fantasized about being on them, especially if they were going to New York City. She'd been fantasizing about New York City since the first time she'd seen the movie *Breakfast at Tiffany's* when she was nine. The city seemed so alive and the people who lived there so glamorous.

One day she would live there too. One day she would be glamorous. She would wear liquid eyeliner and big sunglasses and smoke cigarettes out of one of those long cigarette holders. She would attend the best parties, wear the best clothes, and make walking in high heels look easy. She would make it happen. One day. New York City was her soul mate. She knew they would eventually meet and live happily ever after.

It wasn't that she didn't like Michigan. It was fine. It had four distinct seasons, five Great Lakes and one fantastic hockey team. It was home to her family and friends and a perfect spot for watching planes land. Even if the abandoned restaurant was now reopened and the previously vacant lot was now occupied during business hours, she could still use it as a secret place to hang out with the boy late at night. Because Michigan also happened to be the home of one really sweet boy with a smile that made her heart do somersaults. And when she was lying under the stars with him in the back of his truck, she had no thoughts of moving to New York to flutter around the city in a tiara. As she watched the planes fly above them, she didn't think about where they could take her one day. She only thought about where they could go together. The only place she cared to be was in his arms. But she seriously needed to cut that shit out. It was totally cheesy. People all over the world would be swallowing their own vomit if they knew what she was thinking.

This was only a summer fling. That was the plan. They were only hooking up because he was her safety guy. You know, like a safety school was not your first choice but a sure thing? A safety guy was a guy who was sure not to hurt you. He was her safety guy because it was a sure thing she would *not* fall in love with him.

And that's not what's happening now, she told herself.

It didn't matter anyway. She was leaving for North Carolina the next morning to begin her final year of undergrad at UNC, and this – whatever it was – was over.

"I was kinda thinking..." he said. He had one arm under her neck and one arm under his head and looked as cool and laid-back as the Marlboro man used to look back when smoking was still cool. "It might be fun if I drove down with you tomorrow.

I've never been to North Carolina, and it's so long for you to drive by yourself."

A sunny 700-mile road trip with him sounded absolutely amazing to her. Since classes didn't start until Monday, they could take their time, maybe stop at a flea market, and eat lots of gummy worms and rock candy. She could show him the mountain that looked like a giant boob with a nipple on top. She could introduce him to her friends at UNC and spend just one more night in his arms. Yes, it sounded like the best frickin' idea ever.

"I don't think that would be a very good idea," she lied. "That's something boyfriends and girlfriends do, you know?"

"Yeah, I guess you're right," he said. "I don't know what I was thinking."

It was too dark for her to see the disappointment on his face. But when he pulled his arm out from under her and let her head hit the hard plastic of the bed liner, she could feel it, the difference.

He sat up and tossed over her Carolina-Blue tank top and they got dressed in silence.

CHAPTER ONE
Eight Years Later

I was sitting on the toilet when he told me he wanted a divorce. This wasn't the way I imagined it would happen. In fact, I didn't *ever* imagine it would happen, which is odd because I'm the kind of person who likes to be prepared. I consider myself a hardcore planner. Not the kind who takes a list to the grocery store or sticks a chore chart to the refrigerator. That's too easy. I'm more of a life planner. I don't sit by and idly watch life happen to me. I grab the wheel and let *me* happen to life. I imagine every possible scenario behind every corner and, by planning ahead, I make the ordinary moments extraordinary and the disasters more bearable. It's not because I'm a total control freak or anything; it's because, well, I guess I am a bit of a control freak. And if we're dissecting my personality here, I should probably admit to being a tad bit neurotic because you're going to find out anyway. But not in a crazy, spastic kind of way. I like to think of myself as more quirky than crazy.

As a film junkie, I had a habit of expecting my life to resemble a Best Picture nominee. Or maybe a Golden Globe or MTV Movie Award would be more my style. But nevertheless, I wanted a life filled with edge-of-your-seat excitement and the kind of comedy that made people shoot soda out of their noses. I wanted witty dialogue, romance and suspense in all the right places, and a perfect soundtrack playing in the background. It's a lot to ask for, yes, but we only get one shot at life. There were no second takes. If I found myself in a crappy moment, I couldn't just "fix it in post" or delete the scene like I could with editing software. So I simply didn't allow crappy moments. That was all.

This obsession with perfection started when I was a teenager. There are certain things little girls look forward to as they're growing up. For example, their first kiss. My big moment happened when I was fourteen. I was walking home from school with my brother, Adam's, best friend, Jake. Jake Odom had lived around the block from us for as long as I could remember. He spent so much time at our house playing Nintendo (the original Nintendo) with my brother he was practically another member of the family.

Adam and Jake were both juniors that year and I was a freshman. Jake and I walked home from school together nearly every day. We weren't exactly friends, but since we both went to the same school, lived in the same neighborhood, and he didn't have a car and I wasn't old enough to drive, we ended up walking together by default. I guess we ended up friends by default as well.

Adam did have a car, but he also had football practice after school in the fall, basketball practice in the winter, and baseball practice in the spring, so I never got to take advantage of that particular older brother perk.

There we were, two non-athletic high school kids stopped at a crosswalk, when he suddenly turned to me, grabbed my head on both sides by my ears, pressed his lips on mine and stuck his tongue in my mouth. I was so shocked and disgusted by the slimy violation that I gasped in shock and got my raspberry-flavored bubble gum caught in my windpipe.

It was the closest I'd ever been to death. I was unable to make a sound so I started flapping my arms around like a panicking penguin until Jake realized he had literally taken my breath away. Fortunately for me, he had taken a first aid class in middle school. He got behind me and Heimlich-ed the gum right out. Unfortunately for him, a lady who happened to be looking out her window at the time thought he was assaulting me and called the police. The cops found some rolling papers in his pocket and busted him for paraphernalia. Magic moment? Hardly.

Girls also think losing their virginity is going to be a sacred and special memory. I was sixteen and one of the last of my friends to take the plunge. After hearing the horror stories from everyone else, I knew better than to expect roses and candlelight. But when my boyfriend led me into his bedroom after school while his parents were at work, I *was* expecting something at least a little bit sweet, like maybe some Boyz II Men on the CD player. What happened instead is he never even took his shirt off. He dropped his pants and went at it looking like Winnie-the-Pooh in his red polo shirt. And the worst part of it all - he farted! Loudly and intentionally, at his moment of climax (about fifteen seconds in), he farted. He said later he thought it would be a good way to break the ice. *Break the ice!? Really? Your penis is in my vagina! We're like six months and three layers of clothing past ice breaking!*

I don't consider myself to be an unreasonable person. I could make do with a less-than-perfect moment every once in awhile as long as it was something I could laugh about later. The kissing scene, for example, was quite funny in retrospect. Jake and I have laughed about it on more than one occasion. And I can deal with a man being in such a hurry to get in there that he can't even take three seconds to get his shirt off. That kind of urgency can be sexy at times. I also understand that accidents happen and sometimes things just slip out. But a flatulent ejaculator is unacceptable. Fart jokes stop being funny to girls when we're about six. I understand boys matured at a slower pace, but farting should stop being funny for them by at least age thirteen. And farts are never funny when your penis is in my vagina.

After the fart fiasco I was determined to make sure I had no more blooper-reel moments on my DVD. That's when I became a bit obsessed with directing - I mean *planning*. I realized my experiences could not be put into the hands of others.

I can't always predict how the supporting cast will behave. Sometimes they forget their lines or decide to adlib. But I *can* be prepared to turn things around if they start to go sour and that's why I always had a trick up my sleeve. This girl does not like awkward silences or second act slumps!

I've been doing a pretty good job of keeping the pace so far. My life post-virgin has been better than I hoped for. I was voted "Best Laugh" and "Most Likely to be Seen Pushing a Car Down the Road" in my senior class superlatives. Both are less boring than "Most Likely to Succeed," if you ask me.

I went on to a pretty good university where I grabbed the proverbial bull by the horns every chance I got, as well as the literal horns on the mechanical bull at City Limits Saloon in Raleigh, where I stayed on for 5.3 seconds.

I changed my major three times (Film, Journalism and Social Work), wrote a popular column for the school newspaper, and was a DJ at the campus radio station during a primetime study hour slot. I never declined an invitation to a party and went somewhere tropical every year for spring break. I had lots of friends and lots of fun, which amounted to four years of great "footage" and ever-lasting memories. Isn't that what college is all about? I mean, except for the learning and never-ending debt.

It was the beginning of my senior year when I met Caleb Golightly during Speed-Dating Night in the Morehead Lounge. (Yes, that's really the name of the place. I am not making this up). I wasn't looking for anything serious, but I couldn't believe my luck when he introduced himself. *Breakfast at Tiffany's* was my all-time-fave! Holly Golightly was my hero! And when he told me he intended to move to New York City after graduation, I decided not to meet with any of my other "speed dates" that night. He was the one. *That's a wrap!*

Caleb Golightly was a dorky grad student with an ambitious goal of becoming an investment banker in New York City after he got his MBA. I liked a guy with goals, no matter how far-fetched they might be, and I'd always been turned on by guys who were smarter than me.

Speed-dating night was the beginning of a whirlwind romance with lots of roses and candlelight and even some Boyz II Men during flashback hour on 90.1. Our passionate courtship led to a (totally prepared for) proposal back in Morehead Lounge, complete with a bended knee from him and a dramatic exclamation of surprise from me (one I'd been practicing in the mirror for nearly two weeks). I had a Photojournalism student waiting in the wings, so not only was a picture of the proposal in the school paper, but I now had a canvas print of the perfect memory on our mantle.

I became Mrs. Roxie Golightly three months after graduation. The ceremony was held in my hometown of Ann Arbor, Michigan, in front of two-hundred of my closest friends, acquaintances, former classmates, coworkers and neighbors, and a few people that Caleb knew too.

I was a young bride, only twenty-two. I definitely showed my age when, after a little too much champagne, I stole the microphone from the DJ and burst into Frank Sinatra's "New York, New York." After my dazzling performance, I told all of my guests that Ann Arbor sucked and I was leaving and never coming back. I am not proud.

We moved to New York City after the wedding and spent the next few years living in a studio apartment in the West Village. A studio apartment in Michigan means you have a living room, kitchen and bedroom, but no walls to separate them. A studio apartment in Manhattan means you can cook your dinner on the stove, eat your dinner at the dining room table and then wash your dishes in the kitchen sink, without ever getting off the couch. It was tight, but I made the best of it by spending as little time there as possible. While Caleb's full time job was *looking* for a job, I worked as a cocktail waitress at night and stayed busy during the day by exploring the city in my big black sunglasses, occasionally drinking Starbucks in front of Tiffany & Co. New York City wasn't what I imagined it would be. It was even better.

What happened next is something I'd dreamed about, but never thought would really happen. I didn't think Caleb would get his Wall Street dream job. Or that he would be really good at it. Or that we would eventually move from our closet-sized apartment to a two-bedroom condo in Battery Park City complete with doormen, concierge services and the most incredible views of the East River and Midtown.

He wasn't an overnight success. He worked his butt off for several years before we bought the condo, and his hard work was worth it because every year he climbed higher and higher up the corporate ladder. And me, what have I been doing? Not too much. I watch a lot of ridiculous reality TV and cooking shows. I do a lot of shopping. I also take care of the condo. Granted, it's very small, only 900 square feet plus the terrace (we have a terrace!), but I keep it clean. I also take care of Caleb, even if he doesn't notice. I cook his dinners, pack his lunches, make sure his expensive ties match his expensive shirts, and the creases in his expensive pants are perfect. But the bottom line is that I do not have a job outside of the home, and this is why my friends call me a "kept" woman. I preferred the term "Trophy Wife."

Once we settled into our life together I started preparing for my next role: MILF. I wasn't pregnant yet, but I was planning. I had a list of baby names. I had a board on Pinterest filled with ideas for the nursery decor. I had an unpublished baby registry at

Pottery Barn Kids just waiting to go live. I'd even gone as far as making a big-to-us-but-small-to-them donation to a prestigious preschool. From what I heard, Manhattan preschools were a real bitch to get into, and I was hoping to get a leg up by making donations every year. Right now we were still considered middle-class compared to the crust of the Upper-East Side, but I figured by the time our baby was ready for preschool we'd certainly be sending the kid off to school in pinstripes.

A baby. *That* was supposed to be the next step. Not a divorce! Even during our nastiest arguments or the longest stretches of dullness, divorce was never an option. Not because we're the happiest couple on Earth, or because I'm super religious or anything, but simply because I don't like to admit when I've made a mistake. Especially when that mistake was made in front of two-hundred people, several of whom told me to slow things down and not get married so young. I figured if I had chosen to go against the advice of my family and friends, it was my own fault, and I deserved nothing less than to suffer in this gorgeous loft with breath-taking views!

So no, I hadn't taken the time to plan an ideal divorce, and now I was caught with my pants down – literally. As dumbfounded as I was by the morning's topic of conversation, all I could think about as I stared at the tile on the bathroom floor was Jennifer Aniston and Brad Pitt.

They were America's sweethearts. I was disappointed and crushed when they announced they were divorcing. Okay, maybe "crushed" is a bit dramatic, even for me, but there was a moment when I doubted if happily-ever-after existed outside of fairy tales. Then I saw a photo of them looking sweet and romantic on a Caribbean beach that was taken just one day before they announced their separation. Those pictures seemed to soften the blow a little. There was no better way to say goodbye to each other than by walking hand-in-hand on a warm sandy beach. At that time I told myself if ever I was to divorce, I was doing it up as classy as they did.

Is it too late to book a vacation? I wondered, as I looked at the grey sweatpants and old cotton panties that were pooled around my ankles. *This is definitely not Anguilla.*

CHAPTER TWO

I felt humiliated, unwanted and ugly, and I just wanted him out of the bathroom so I could wipe in privacy. As if reading my mind, he turned the faucet off (leaving little chin hairs all over the sink that I would have to clean up later) and said he was going to start breakfast, and I should join him on the terrace when I was finished.

Once he was gone, I stood up and looked in the mirror. I felt like someone slapped me across the face, and I kind of looked like it too. My face was blood red with a mixture of embarrassment and anger. I could honestly say I had never felt more betrayed in all of my life and that was saying a *lot*.

The first thing I needed to do was make myself look better. Maybe if I looked better I would feel better. They say that looking good is a girl's best defense, right? I didn't know if that was true, but I knew I could not go out there and face the man who didn't want me anymore while I was sporting bed-head, circles under my eyes and sagging boobs under my sleep cami. Don't get me wrong, I wasn't ridiculous enough to think that brushing my hair could save my marriage; but some time during the last ten minutes he had gone from being my occasionally loving husband to a total bastard, and I couldn't let a bastard see me in such disarray. Even if he did just watch me pee.

Working quickly, I sprayed some sea salt texturizing spray into my hair to create waves and applied mascara and lip-gloss. I put on sexy panties and a push-up bra under my pajamas and followed the scent of bacon out to the kitchen.

We have breakfast on the terrace nearly every morning as long as the weather allows. Usually something simple like bagels and lox because Caleb has to get to work. On Sundays, though, we go all out. I make the eggs. I can make eggs about three dozen different ways thanks to the Food Network. Caleb is always in charge of the bacon. I don't know what he does to make it taste so good, but his bacon is so tasty I can devour a whole plate even while watching *Charlotte's Web* (sorry Wilbur).

Mornings on the terrace were always my favorite part of the day. We'd drink our coffee and read the papers. We were the rare couple who still read real papers – you know, the kind that gets ink on your fingers – instead of those on electronic gadgets. Caleb would sit with the *Wall Street Journal* and me with the *New York Times* crossword puzzle I struggled with every morning (I even finished it a few times). We'd sit together in a comfortable and amiable silence before he'd kiss me goodbye and head off to work. I always thought couples who could sit quietly together were the good ones. Apparently I'd been mistaken.

It was a Thursday, but Caleb was making bacon anyway, which made the whole morning even more unsettling. Despite feeling sick to my stomach, I reached for a frying pan to start my eggs. He gently swatted my arm away.

"I'll take care of breakfast. You sit down," he said. "Your coffee is already outside."

I stepped out onto the terrace where my coffee sat on the bistro table. We bought the loft about four years ago and the view from the terrace still took my breath away on a daily basis. It was a beautiful morning in the beginning of June and the sun was shining, making the surface of the East River look like a bed of Swarovski crystals. I could hear the traffic on the street below. One thing I'd always loved about Manhattan was that I was never alone. The ambient sound of the city always surrounded me – taxi cabs honking their horns, police sirens wailing, car alarms blaring – all a 24-hour reminder that I was not alone.

I sat down at the bistro and took a sip of my coffee. *Yum – crème brulee creamer.* There are few things in life better than coffee with a great view. Coffee with a great view *and* a cigarette was one of those things. I quit smoking last year to get my body healthy for a baby. In typical Roxie fashion, I made a huge deal of it by throwing a Quitters Party. I hung up posters of Richard Nixon, loaded up the CD player with Paula Abdul and Jay-Z, and had my guests beat the crap out of a piñata that looked like Sarah Palin. The bigger the spectacle, the more likely I was to stick with it because you can't have a Quitters Party and not quit, right? But I could really have used a cigarette then. I was thinking about calling the concierge desk to see if they could send one up when Caleb walked out with a tray of bacon, eggs and toast. He set a plate in front of me but I didn't make any rush to touch it. *Am I really supposed to eat right now?*

Caleb sat down across from me and cleared his throat. "I know this must come as a surprise to you," he said gingerly.

I realized then that I hadn't spoken yet since I'd woken up. It was probably better if I remained silent. That was probably true in most situations. Less words = less to use against me later. But there was one thing I had to know.

"How long have you been wanting this?" I asked in my sweetest, softest voice, hoping it would make him feel guilty. You know, the whole kill-him-with-kindness trick.

"That's something I hope you can understand," he said. "I don't want this at all. What I want is for you to love me and for me to love you and for us to have a family and live happily ever after. That's all I've ever wanted."

I resisted the urge to roll my eyes. He sounded like a prince from a Disney cartoon. FYI - Disney movies weren't the kind I liked to emulate; too many damsels in distress and dying parents.

"I know you must love me on some level," he continued. "And I have love for you too. I'm just not *in* love with you. There's no magic here. We're more like roommates than husband and wife."

I was confused by this statement for two reasons. First of all, what's wrong with roommates? Roommates are fine, especially when you can have sex with them and they make good bacon. Second of all, who is to say that roommates and a husband and wife of seven years aren't one and the same? Did he actually go around asking married couples if there was still "magic" in their relationships? And which married couples would he ask? Surely not his coworkers and their asshole wives.

"If you want magic we can go see *The Quantum Eye*," I said, about the off-Broadway show. I was only joking to lighten up the mood a little. Divorce was way too serious of a topic for me.

He stood up, dusted toast crumbs from his shirt and set his napkin on the table. I knew he was angry even though he seemed calm and cool as ever. Caleb owned the ability to change his personality and demeanor according to his environment, like a chameleon of sorts. He was always very mild-mannered and polite when he was around me. But I'd seen him at work a few times, and he was completely different there. He was loud, fast and hungry. He treated his work like it was the last drumstick on the last turkey in the world and he was determined to sink his teeth into the meat before anyone else got to it no matter how much juice was left dripping down his chin. The transformation was quite scary to be honest. If I was the overly paranoid type, I might wonder if the guy was a total sociopath and moonlighted as a serial killer. But I'm just an average paranoid type, and I knew his hunger for success was the reason I lived such a charmed life, so I didn't question it.

"I guess you're going to make a joke of this like you do everything else," he said, as he tightened his tie.

I silently hoped he would strangle himself with it.

"I've got to head to the office," he said. "We'll finish this conversation via email."

And with that he walked back into the condo. A few seconds later I heard the door close.

I sighed and took another sip of my coffee. *This. Changes. Everything.*

I have always been prone to anxiety, but once I heard Caleb leave I was pretty sure I experienced my first real panic attack. At first I stayed on the terrace and waited for the punch line. Because this *had* to be a joke, right? Maybe someone at the firm dared him to play a trick on me. Maybe they were holding a *Punk'd* contest for a bonus check. Or maybe Caleb woke up today and felt like mixing things up a bit for a laugh. I tried to think of any possibility other than the truth. But deep down I knew it was real. Because, let's face it, Caleb doesn't joke around.

I slowly walked back into the condo and hoped he would pop out from behind a door and say, "Ha ha, got ya!" But it was quiet, super quiet. He really was gone. He really was ending this, us.

I stared at the door he had just closed, knowing that with it, he had closed the door on the last eight years of my life. He didn't even give me a say in it. My perfect little world was broken without my permission. The future I had been planning was never going to happen. All of that time, all of the planning, wasted! Decisions had been made outside of my control-freak hands, and I couldn't handle it!

I couldn't breathe. I felt dizzy. I felt sick. I dropped to my knees in front of the door, covered my head with my arms, tornado-style, and tried to talk my heart into beating a little slower. I squeezed my eyes shut, took slow, deep breaths and waited for it to be over.

When I finally got myself under control I didn't know what I should do next. Should I call the concierge for a cigarette and a Xanax and keep refreshing my email until I received further instructions? I decided to call for reinforcement before turning myself into a stereotype.

"What the eff?" That was Allison, my best friend since second grade, talking. She cut out swearing after she had her first kid in high school. She never cut out unprotected sex, though, and that's how she ended up with two more before we could legally buy beer. Her kids were now practically old enough to babysit the kids that I would almost certainly never have.

She probably wasn't the best person to call. She married her high-school sweetheart, had three well-behaved kids that preferred to eat yogurt and apples instead of chips and cookies, and actually had a picket fence separating her yard from her neighbor's. They started young, but they turned themselves into a near perfect little family and I doubted she could sympathize with me now.

"So he's seeing someone else," she said.

"He said he's just not in love with me," I said, defensively.

She snorted. "Of course he's not going to admit it. You probably get more in the divorce if he's cheating."

"I think New York is a no-fault state."

"You can't just think these things. You need to *know* them." She started giving me a list of tasks as matter-of-factly as if she were a divorce attorney herself. "You need a lawyer. ASAP. You need to know the laws and your rights. You might even think about getting a judge to freeze your assets before he starts hiding money, if he hasn't done so already. You need to make a list of all property acquired during your marriage, not just your condo but also things like jewelry, artwork, timeshares, 401ks, stocks and bonds -"

"You know we don't have a timeshare," I interrupted. "Where are you getting this from?"

"The internet!" she said. "The same place you can get it from. You need to be proactive about this. You need to act like your old self again. You can't just sit there and let it happen to you. It's time for you step up and take charge, or his lawyer will eat you up and spit you out!"

She must watch a lot of court shows on TV.

I let out a huge, dramatic sigh. The more this was sinking in, the worse I felt about it. And what did she mean about me acting like my old self again? Since when was there an old self and a new self?

Allison must have sensed my need for comfort because her voice was more soothing when she spoke again. "Honey, I'm sorry. I know you called for a friend and not a lecture. Everything is going to work out eventually. It might take awhile, but it will be okay. You just need to CYA, if you know what I mean."

"Thanks, Al," I said. "I'll start looking at lawyers now. I'll talk to you later."

I got out a pen and notebook and wrote down a list of things I needed to do.

- Google divorce lawyers.
- Google NY divorce laws.
- Choose a lawyer and schedule a meeting.
- Write down everything we own?
- Figure out where I'm going to live (since I can't afford this place on my own).
- Figure out how I'm going to start affording things on my own (ie: get a job)!

Oh gosh. It was all way too much to think about. I picked up my phone again. But I didn't call lawyers. I called Hope. Hope was my New York best friend. We met about seven years ago when we both worked as cocktail waitresses in the same martini bar downtown. The name Hope seemed so gentle and passive, but she was actually a hardcore chick. Allison tried to think reasonably and logically, and I knew I could count on Hope to do the opposite.

"That mother fucker!" she yelled. Hope does not have kids. "Where is this coming from? He must be fucking someone else."

Whoa, déjà vu. Does there always have to be someone else? "He said he's not in love with me, and there's no magic."

"That's a bunch of bullshit!" she was still yelling. "If he wants magic, I'll be happy to pull a rabbit out of a hat and shove it right up his tight ass! He'd probably love it!"

That is why we were such good friends. She said the things out loud that I kept in my head.

"I hope he knows you'll get half of everything," she continued. "You were the one serving drinks to support his ass when he was broke and jobless and living off a dream!"

"Really?" I kind of thought I'd be thrown out on my butt with maybe a few hundred a month in alimony.

"Oh yeah! You don't need to worry about a thing, girl," she said. "except which beach you want to have dinner on tonight."

"What beach?"

"It's a beautiful day and I've got the night off. Let's get the hell out, girl. Sounds like you need it."

I gasped when I realized what she meant. "Hamptons?" I asked, hopefully.

"ROAD TRIP!" she screamed. "I'll be there in fifteen minutes."

I hung up the phone and squealed like an eleven-year-old girl reading a copy of *Teen Beat* magazine.

See what I meant about Hope?

If we were going to the Hamptons, I needed to shower. I practically skipped to the bathroom. While I was in there I did something I hadn't done in nearly a week. I shaved my legs. I was going to have to start acting like a single girl again, one who kept an extensive daily maintenance regime. I needed to start plucking, waxing and exfoliating like it was my job. I needed to make sure my bras and panties were sexy and matching at all times because single girls never knew when they were going to be taking off their clothes. I couldn't ever leave the house without make-up, smooth, shiny hair and a pair of high heels. There would be no more yoga pants and ponytails! Speaking of shoes, I should probably buy myself a new pair of heels to commemorate the occasion.

I'd have to let Hope know we were stopping for shoes before we left the city. I needed some retail therapy, and it might be the last time I could afford the good stuff. Once I was poor and divorced I'd probably have to do my shopping on Canal Street. Even worse, I'd be buying shoes and handbags two aisles away from the produce section. I tried to shake the terror from my head as I pulled back the shower curtain and threw on my cashmere kimono-style robe. It had been a Christmas gift from Caleb last year. Maybe a robe for Christmas should be a clue that your husband doesn't want you anymore. He went to a lingerie store filled with bustiers and garter belts, and he bought a robe. At the time I thought it was a great gift. Now I had to wonder if I'd missed a huge neon warning sign.

Hope was waiting for me when I got out of the shower. She had a key to the condo in case of emergency. I have a tendency to lose, I mean, misplace things.

She was standing in my living room pointing at the notebook I had left on the coffee table.

"What is that?" she asked. Her face was scrunched up with disgust. You'd think there was a used condom on the table.

"Just a list I was working on."

"I can't believe you're writing in a notebook. With a pen even." She picked up the notebook and gave it a good examination like she'd never seen one before. "I almost feel like I'm in a history museum."

She was always getting on me about being "technologically challenged." She can't believe that I don't have an iPhone or an iPad or an iWhatthefuckever. I do have a Blackberry, isn't that good enough? Writing things down with a pen is a lot faster and more therapeutic than trying to type something on a tiny touch-screen keyboard.

I snatched the notebook out of her hand and walked away, towards my bedroom. She followed me.

"I get to pick out your clothes!" she said and headed for the closet. Ordinarily I would never let her pick out an outfit for me. Hope, with her pink and purple highlights in her blonde hair, had a very unique and eclectic style that seemed to work great for her, but I didn't think I could pull it off. I won't even wear black with navy, while Hope could wear orange plaid with blue stripes and make it look good.

In most areas of my life I was a rule breaker. But when it came to fashion, I took those taboos seriously. I did not want to be one of those people pictured in the *Don't* section of the fashion magazines with a black line across my eyes. But being in my room and looking at the bed, I suddenly didn't care about clothes anymore. I felt like I was caught in a tailspin of dread.

I grimaced and told her I was going to blow dry my hair. I needed to get out of that bedroom because I was starting to feel like my chest was caving in. To think I slept in that bed with my husband only hours before and had no idea he didn't love me anymore; it didn't make me feel so hot. I tried to be strong about all of it and not fall onto the floor in a big heap of patheticism (hey, it's in the Urban Dictionary – look it up if you don't believe me). But I couldn't face the room. Not yet. So if Hope wanted to dress me up like a homeless vagabond, I'd let her – as long as I didn't have to go back in that room.

Hope appeared at the bathroom door just as I was finishing with my hair and handed me a black and white polka-dot bikini and a yellow bandeau sundress. I would *never* wear a halter under a bandeau top. It's a conflict of interest at best and a tan line disaster at worst. But I could probably put up with that minor discrepancy if she had picked a bikini that actually fit me.

"I haven't worn this bikini in years," I told her. "There's no way it'll fit."

She put her hands on her hips. "Why is it still in your drawer then, hoarder?"

Sometimes I had a hard time getting rid of things, especially clothes. I seemed to develop a sentimental attachment. The bikini in question was special to me because I bought it for my college senior year Spring Break trip to Cocoa Beach. That was the last trip I'd taken without Caleb and the bikini represented freedom, fun, youth, and pina coladas. I bet the fact that I saved this particular bikini for all these years, but couldn't even tell you what swimsuits I wore during our honeymoon in Cabo, would prove quite interesting to a psychotherapist.

I smelled the bikini top to see if I could catch a whiff of suntan lotion. Nope. It was long gone, along with my twenty-one year old boobs, tongue ring, and delusional optimism.

I shrugged sheepishly. "Sometimes I like to pull it out and reminisce about being young and skinny." I handed it back to her.

"It's stretchy." She pushed the bikini back into my hands. "Put it on." It was an order, not a suggestion.

Ten minutes later I was prancing around in front of the full-length mirror in the bathroom. It fit! There was some extra softness around my hips and a mini-muffin top above the bikini bottom, but it fit. What a boost to my self-esteem!

"How's it going in there?" Hope asked from the other side of the door.

"Great!" I yelled back. "I'm Rebecca Dunbaring!"

Rebecca Dunbar was the wife of one of Caleb's coworkers. She had been a cheerleader for an NFL team back in the nineties and couldn't seem to let go of it. She had a gigantic picture in her living room of herself in her cheerleading uniform from back then and she thought it was cute to burst into cheers at company get-togethers. Her husband told Caleb that she wears her uniform around the house and literally cheers him on during foreplay. And rumor has it that she showed up to her son's first t-ball game in full uniform, pom poms and all, and did a complete routine on the sidelines. Basically she was the joke of the entire firm.

I've told Hope all about her; about how I actually feel sorry for her. She's got a good husband, two cute kids, and a home in Greenwich, Connecticut, but she's so desperate to hold on to her past that she's clinging to her cheerleading uniform as if it's the only life jacket left on a sinking ship.

I guess you could say the polka-dot bikini was my new lifejacket, but that was okay with me. Unlike Rebecca Dunbar, I actually *was* on a sinking ship, and I was just glad I had something to keep me afloat.

CHAPTER THREE

When Hope finished packing my overnight bag and reserved us a rental car on her iPad, we hopped into a cab and headed straight for my haven – also known as Barney's New York.

I didn't always feel this good about shopping. I'll never forget my first time in a top-of-the-line designer store (which shall remain nameless, as I don't need a lawsuit on my hands on top of a divorce).

We'd been married about two years. Caleb was still a newbie junior banker at the firm. We were invited to the housewarming party of one of the senior bankers who had bought a home in a wealthy neighborhood in the Town of North Hempstead. Yes, the word Town has a capital T. At this point in his career, Caleb was still doing a lot of minute tasks such as making coffee and going on lunch runs, and I was still serving martinis to "suits" during Happy Hour. We were basically your average struggling young couple, but that didn't mean I wanted to look the part.

I bought a dress from Victoria's Secret that cost $90. This was the most expensive piece of clothing I had ever owned up to that point. I felt amazing when it came in the mail and I put it on. I looked like a goddess in the short, shimmery, backless number. I put on black thigh-highs, the kind with a seam up the back, and black stilettos and splurged on a manicure and a blow-out at the salon. Caleb looked at me like I was the most beautiful girl in the world. He told me how proud he was to have a trophy wife as he linked his arm with mine, and we walked into the elegant, sprawling home in Manhasset.

To make a long story short, I'll say I learned some important lessons in Manhasset.

Lesson #1 – There is a big, HUGE, difference between the Town Of North Hempstead with a capital T and plain old Hempstead, and one must never make the mistake of using the shorter form. Because, you see, the Town of North Hempstead was a wealthy area filled with the kinds of houses that had their own parking lots. And apparently, Hempstead, on the other hand, was a completely separate town in Nassau County where there was gang activity, government-funded housing, and an Old Navy.

Lesson #2 – There was no lower scum on Earth than a waitress. I probably would've earned more respect from Caleb's coworkers if I had told them I was contributing to the household expenses by hiding our neighbor's dead body in my closet and cashing in her social security checks. Can you believe one of the wives asked me if I could grab her a drink from the bar? "To make you feel more at home, dear." It was after this party when Caleb told me it would be a good idea if I quit my job because he would hate for one of his colleagues to show up at the bar while I was working. After feeling mortified at the party, I had to agree with him.

Lesson #3 – The shoes were everything. The dress was not important. I could have worn a dress from Goodwill and claimed it was vintage couture and no one would have known the difference. It was the shoes that mattered. Shoes were the topic of several conversations: the shoes at the party, the shoes on the runways, the shoes in the tabloids, the shoes on the red carpet. Then someone asked me who I was wearing. Who! Not what, but who! Apparently Payless was not a designer. I decided then and there that I would never be out-shoed again. From that point on, I would have the best shoes in every room I stepped into, and that was a promise.

A week later I took the subway to the Upper East Side for some shopping on Madison Avenue. This was where the situation occurred.

I went into the designer-who-shall-remain-nameless' store. The sales associates were a bunch of girls around my age who wore cardigan sweaters and geek-chic glasses. They all had their boobs pushed up to their chins and had very thick, golden highlights in their dark hair, the kind of highlights that made it look like their heads were striped – a trend I am so glad finally went out of style.

The fact that none of them would meet my eyes made the whole scenario a bit creepy. I began to wonder if I was on the set of *Bitches of the Corn Part V*. Or that I'd accidentally walked in on a top-secret cloning experiment. I decided to make my selection quickly before I, too, was kidnapped and cloned. I could do the glasses and cardigans, but I'd honestly rather die than have striped hair.

I decided on a pair of shoes I wanted to try on. I picked up the floor model and looked around for help, but the sales associates wouldn't help me. They wouldn't make eye contact with me. They acted like I was invisible, but I knew they weren't blind because as soon as someone else walked in the door there were boob-on-boob collisions as they fought to see who could greet the new customer first. I knew for sure it was intentional when I spoke to one and she stared at the wall behind me for a few seconds before she deliberately turned and walked away. All right fine, so maybe Pollyanna-style pigtails and an American Eagle hoodie wasn't the best way to dress for a shopping trip with the big dogs, but I was still a person and didn't deserve that kind of treatment. I felt like Julia Roberts in *Pretty Woman* when the salesladies were mean to her.

I left, discouraged. With the lyrics of Reba McIntyre's "Fancy" running through my head, I cried all the way to Dylan's Candy Bar. This definitely called for gummi bears.

Once I managed to get myself together, I headed back out there. I didn't want to, believe me, but those girls at the Manhasset party made me feel like trash and the clones at designer-who-shall-remain-nameless made me feel even worse. I needed to get on the same playing field before everyone in Manhattan was laughing at me and I was on eBay looking for pig's blood.

I stood outside Barney's, took a deep breath, touched the extra stash of candy in my pocket for reassurance, put on my bravest face and walked in ... to heaven on Earth! Everywhere I went, from handbags, to shoes, to the make-up counters in the basement, I encountered happy, helpful people. This time I felt like Julia Roberts in the "Pretty Woman" scene of *Pretty Woman*. I walked out of there with both hands filled with shopping bags, and my very first pair of Christian Louboutins (which are worth every penny, by the way).

When I was out on the street I threw my hat into the air like Mary Tyler Moore and hailed a cab home. Just kidding. I wasn't even wearing a hat. But it would have been pretty cool, huh? Looking back, I really wish I had worn a hat that day.

In case you're wondering – as I'm sure anyone would be – no, I didn't go back to the designer-who-shall-remain-nameless to wave my bags in their faces because the bags were heavy and I'm quite lazy. But I never did go in there again.

"Roxie!" Yes, they know me by name in the shoe department. I know it's totally cliché, but when I said I'd never be out-shoed again, I meant it!

"Carly!" I replied. No, we didn't do air kisses or anything preposterous like that.

"We need some FMPs," Hope told her.

I guess being married for so long I was a little out of the loop on the sexy acronyms. "What are those?" I asked.

"Fuck Me Pumps," Hope whispered.

Carly gave Hope a knowing smile. "Those are very high heels," she told me. "Higher than your 120s." She was referring to the height of the heel in millimeters. For me, 120s were as high as I could go without moving into drag queen territory. Higher heels might be fun for dress-up, but if I was going to spend hundreds of dollars on a pair of shoes, I needed something more practical, something that didn't make anyone wonder if I was packing a penis in my skinny jeans.

Carly showed us a pair of FMPs in red satin. They looked more like DQPs if you asked me. I tried them on just to pacify them, but I decided to buy hot pink patent peep-toes in my usual 120mm heel instead. Yes, hot pink stilettos *are* absolutely practical, but I appreciate your concern.

As I headed up to pay for the shoes, I got the worst feeling in my stomach. *What if Caleb cancelled the credit cards?* The scene flashed before my eyes. Me at the counter. Carly telling me the credit card declined. Me pulling another card out of my wallet. Declined. Another one. Declined. Declined. Declined. Carly with a pair of scissors, cutting up all of my cards and calling security over to escort me from the building. All of the other trophy wives taking pictures of me on their iPhones and posting them to Twitter and Instagram – Hashtag:pathetic.

I felt my face burning, my brow sweating, my breaths were becoming fast and shallow, and I thought I might pass out.

"You okay, Roxie?" Carly asked from the cash register. She looked concerned.

"Um, yeah," I said. I sounded weak. I handed her a credit card, held my breath and closed my eyes while the blood drained from my face.

"You gonna sign, hun?" she asked patiently.

I snapped out of it and saw the signature line on the credit card screen. It went through. I finally exhaled with relief. My husband wasn't a total scumbag after all. I mean, yes he was. But he wasn't a scumbag who cancelled my credit cards.

We picked up the rental car when we were done at Barney's. Hope had reserved a convertible because "Why the fuck not?" Right?

I sent Caleb a text to let him know we were headed to the Hamptons for the night.

My phone rang almost immediately.

"Hi," I said softly, a little scared he was going to

yell at me for running away from our problems. I had a little nagging voice in the back of my head already doing as much. But he didn't.

"Hello, darling." He sounded totally normal, like the whole divorce discussion had never taken place.

"You got my text?"

"Yes. I think it's a great idea for you to get away. I'll reschedule the papers to be delivered tomorrow then. You two have a nice time."

"Um, okay. Thanks." It felt so awkward.

"Just be careful with the money, Roxie," he warned. "Once it's divided up, it doesn't replenish itself anymore."

Hmm. What the hell did that even mean? For some reason his comment made me think of lizards and how they can supposedly grow back their tails if they ever fall off. Why their tails would fall off in the first place, though, I'm not sure. "Okay."

"Have a nice time, dear. I'll send you the email with the details as soon as I finish and we'll talk more when you get home."

This whole thing was just too weird.

I hung up the phone and got into the passenger side of the convertible. I resisted the urge to hop over the door without opening it because I'm not eighteen.

We wrapped Boho scarves around our heads to protect our hair from the wind, put on our huge sunglasses and took off – *Thelma and Louise* style.

CHAPTER FOUR

I'd say we picked a great day for a ride to the Hamptons, but that would be like saying my husband picked a great day for a divorce, and I don't want to go that far. But the sun was shining, traffic was light and the A/C was kickin' (we put the top up about ten minutes into the ride). Hope put on her beach playlist and "Summer Girls" by LFO helped me find a brighter disposition.

"Now tell me what happened," Hope said. "Start from the beginning."

I sighed, reluctant to be ripped out of my LFO-induced reverie to relive the crapfest that took place in the bathroom this morning (no pun intended). "Caleb was in the bathroom shaving, and I woke up and had to pee," I started. "So I went into the bathroom and, as I was peeing, he says-"

She held up her right hand and interrupted me. "Wait! You mean you were peeing right in front of him?"

"Um …" I paused as I questioned the behavior. "Yes?"

"Oh hell no!" she said, looking disgusted. "Do you always pee in front of him?"

I shrugged my shoulders. "No, not always. But he was in the closest bathroom."

"So!" she yelled. "We only have one bathroom, but we don't use it at the same time!"

She shared her apartment with a roommate, J.D. J.D. was an aspiring actress who was working for a chauffeur company until she got her big Broadway role. She'd been an aspiring actress since Hope met her about ten years ago. We sometimes joked with her about how long she would continue to call herself an "aspiring actress" before she started saying she was a chauffeur. But we were just teasing. I respected people who refused to give up on their dreams.

"You guys aren't married," I said in my defense.

"We do hook up sometimes when we're both single," she said with a smirk. This did not surprise me. Hope was not a lesbian, but she was very open about her sexual adventures, of which there were many. It's not that she's sleazy, but she's perpetually single and that's just what single people do. They have a lot of sex. With a lot of different people. If this was 2002, I'd describe Hope as the Samantha to my Charlotte.

"Hooking up sometimes is totally different," I told her. "Hooking up sometimes means you still shave first."

She looked at me in horror. The car swerved a little. "You *don't?*"

I crossed my arms in front of my chest, suddenly feeling very defensive. "I do. Sometimes. When I remember."

"Do you wax?"

"On special occasions."

"Do special occasions happen at least once a month?"

"No. More like once a year. Maybe."

She shook her head slowly. "I'm a little disappointed in you. Do you think Holly Golightly went around sporting a cooch afro like she was doing seventies porn?"

I did my best to stifle a giggle but it snuck out as a squeak. "I do not have a cooch afro!" I squeaked again. "Nobody has a seventies porn cooch afro anymore. Didn't you hear? Cooch afros were done away with through evolution, just like the human tail." I was no longer able to contain my laughter, so I let it all out.

She didn't look amused. "Is that so?" she asked, rhetorically. "But on a more serious note, I do hope in your future relationships you will try to maintain some of your dignity. No man needs to see you pee, and no man *or woman* should have to light a flare to find their way around your hoo-hah. Now go on. You were peeing ..."

"Right. And without even turning off the razor or looking at me, he says he started the process for a divorce and I would be served papers this afternoon. Just like that!"

"Hmm ..." she rubbed her chin in thought. "Have you guys been fighting lately?"

"No! This is totally out of the blue."

"Has he been doing anything suspicious? Working later than normal or anything?"

"No. I mean, he always works late. I don't think he has time for an affair because he barely has time for a wife."

"Has your sex life changed any?"

"No. We had sex during ovulation week, just like

every month."

"Oh. I guess it didn't work."

I looked down at my hands and started pushing my cuticles back. This was a sensitive subject. "No." It didn't work. Again.

At first, we had taken the casual approach to baby-making. I stopped taking my birth control pills about two years ago thinking *if it happens, cool.* When it didn't happen, I started a more serious approach. And then it still didn't happen.

Most couples would have seen a reproductive specialist after a year but Caleb was against any help in that department. He said it was unnatural and creepy, and he kept giving me that ever-popular line of bullshit called, *"If it's meant to be, it will be."*

That was when I started researching Old Wives Tales (OWTs). Some were based on mystical beliefs, like when I bought a Native American Kachina doll on the internet. Some were based on new studies, like the one that prompted me to track down an authentic African yam at a Ghanaian market. And some were minor things, like standing on my head for an hour after sex, which isn't that bad if you lean against a wall. I did poses much harder than that in yoga class.

Every month during ovulation week, we had sex dates. In the TTC world (TTC means Trying to Conceive) this kind of baby-making sex was called FWP (Fucking with Purpose). I know scheduled sex doesn't sound very sexy, but unfertilized eggs only live for a few hours. There wasn't time for spontaneity.

For a few weeks after the FWP, I stayed hopeful. I would daydream about sippy cups and chubby thighs and work on my baby registry while wondering if a boy named Anakin would be taken seriously.

Every month, exactly four weeks from the last, I would get my period. I would spend the whole day crying, moping around and commiserating with all of my fellow TTCers on internet forums. And the cycle would start over again — literally.

TTC was a bit like a full time job. I guess you could say I was now being laid-off. I actually smiled at the irony of the term. But then I realized what that really meant. It had been hours since the D-word had first been mentioned, but it wasn't until then I realized I wasn't only losing my husband. I was also losing my future children.

That was when I felt it – the pain in my heart. Some people say heartbreak is a myth, but it was real as ever to me. I touched my chest and reminded myself to breathe. I wished then that I hadn't left for the beach. *Whose idiotic idea was this?* All I wanted was to be home in my bed under our down comforter so I could cry in privacy. Instead I was blinking back tears while on my way to the Hamptons, wearing a bikini that was one size too small and creeping up my butt crack.

The Hamptons were pretty quiet since it was only Thursday, which was fine with me. I preferred to visit in the off-season because the beaches were more beautiful without all of the pompous assholes ruining the views. I know, I was supposed to learn to mingle amongst them but I was never going to fit in with that crowd and I knew it. They were old-money, I was new-money. I could learn to walk the walk in my red-soled 120s, but I would always end up being a sheep in a bear's costume or a wolf dressed as a sheep or however the saying goes.

They grew up eating caviar with silver spoons. I grew up eating neon orange macaroni and cheese with a flatware set my mom bought on clearance at Kmart. Maybe one good thing about a divorce was that I could stop pretending to be someone I wasn't. And I could eat all the Kraft mac and cheese I wanted without any shame.

Hope leaned her head back on the headrest and turned to me while we were stopped at a light in Southampton. "What sounds better?" she asked. "A glass of wine or Cooper's Beach?"

"A whole bottle of wine," I said dryly.

"Even better."

"*At* Cooper's Beach."

She thought for a moment. "I don't believe alcohol is allowed on the beach."

I shrugged. "Then we'll have to do it guerrilla-style."

"I love gorillas," she said with a wicked smile.

When I was in high school, my friends and I thought it was cool to sneak in drugs and alcohol. We would come up with different methods, more for the thrill than anything else, because it's not like anyone really wants to multiply fractions with a buzz. At the time, we thought we were pretty clever. A few years later, when a decent amount of my friends were watching our commencements from the bleachers, they probably didn't feel quite as good about it.

Now, here I was, a grown adult, pouring wine into a plastic cup I got from a gas station's soda fountain. I had to admit, the thrill was still there.

I thought it was best to check in to our hotel before I drank too much. That way, if I got sloshy drunk, Hope could take me directly to our room and minimize my opportunities to make an ass out of myself. Hope had no qualms about getting wasted but I don't usually get drunk. As I've mentioned before, I am a bit of a control freak, and it is hard to control anything when I feel like my head's on backwards. I also have a tendency to get pretty stupid, as witnessed by my wedding guests all those years ago. But if ever there's a good time to lose control and get stupid it's the day one's husband tells her he wants a divorce, right?

Cooper's Beach was named the "Most Beautiful Beach" in the country a few years ago. I have seen a lot of beaches in my life and there are definitely prettier beaches out there, but for New York, yeah, it's not so bad. We rented a few chairs, laid our towels down and relaxed in the sun with our fountain cups.

At first, I was a little nervous. I had forgotten to pack sunscreen and my average amount of paranoia had my imagination running wild thinking of all of the cancerous cells that would undoubtedly be multiplying by dinnertime. I was also thinking about Caleb, the quality and quantity of my eggs and the fact that I hadn't worked a day in six years and was suddenly going to have to find a job in a weak economy and try to support myself, *by* myself.

But the more I sipped, the less I cared about any of it. *This is why people drink,* I thought as I relaxed into my beach chair, suddenly feeling more optimistic about starting a new life.

I could be a waitress again. It was about the only thing I knew how to do anyway. I'd gone from serving coffee and Grand Slams at Denny's when I was in high-school, to serving Jaeger bombs and buffalo wings in college, to serving overpriced martinis and tapas to the overconfident business class of NYC. So bring on the apron and the short shorts! It's not like a Bachelor's degree in Social Work was going to get me anywhere better.

It would be a lifestyle adjustment though. I can't

speak for all servers out there, but in my experience, being a server in a bar meant staying up until the sun was shining and sleeping all day. If I was feeling particularly reckless (which only happened *very* rarely), it also meant doing lines of cocaine off the toilet paper dispensers in the bathroom and hooking up with coworkers and customers, sometimes both in the same night. Being able to do shots at work could make for a very interesting life, and I had a lot of fun in those days. It was certainly a lot more fun than playing June Cleaver for Caleb. But could I really do it? Just jump back in there at my age? Or am I too old to do things like that now? There comes a point in everyone's life when it's time to grow up. Just because I decided to do my growing up a little earlier than others did not give me a free pass to act like a strung-out floozy eight years later. Or was that exactly what it gave me?

"I wonder if Wes would give me my job back," I said to Hope, who was reading a book on her Kindle in the chair next to me. Wes was the owner of the martini bar we used to work at together.

"Of course he would," she replied, without looking away from her Kindle. "But you won't need to. Caleb is going to have to pay you some big bucks. No doubt about it."

But not forever. I had researched a little bit on my phone, and it seemed pretty likely he would have to give me enough to maintain my lifestyle for a certain amount of time. Apparently, this is now called "maintenance" and not alimony. But he wouldn't have to pay me forever. I needed some kind of income coming in. Oh yeah, and a place to live. Gosh, what a mess I was in!

Hope set her Kindle down and looked at me. "So I'm just gonna go ahead and say it," she said.

Oh gosh, what does she know? I looked at her with fear in my eyes. If this was a movie it would be the perfect time for the supporting actress (in this case, Hope) to reveal the details of a sordid affair Caleb had been having that everyone in the audience already knew about.

"I think this is great news," she said.

"Huh?" I definitely wasn't expecting that and I gladly let my breath out.

Hope swung her legs over to one side of the chair and took off her sunglasses so she could look me clear in the eyes. "When I met you, you were different. You were happy and fun, and you were optimistic, and you had plans to do good things for the world."

I vaguely remembered something like that.

"And now," she continued, "your life revolves around impressing people."

Is that true?

"Throwing the best parties, going to the best salons, buying the most expensive jeans." She put a hand on each of my shoulders to make sure I was listening to her. "Roxie, you're already trying to get your unborn, not-even-conceived-yet child into the best preschool in Manhattan. I'm sorry if I sound like a major bitch right now, but don't you see what a waste that is? I mean – it's preschool! It doesn't even count!"

Her words were a bit harsh, but if they were true, I needed to hear them.

"None of that stuff is for you," she told me. "Even though I haven't seen my old friend in awhile, I remember her, and I know she would be much more comfortable coming to the beach in a pair of Old Navy flip-flops than whatever expensive and complicated contraption that is you're wearing now."

I looked down at my turquoise patent leather platform espadrille wedges with the buckled ankle straps. They were gorgeous. Hope may have some valid points, but she was wrong about the shoes. I wasn't wearing them for anyone but myself ... right?

"I don't know about that," I said. "These are Brian Atwood. And they're pretty amazing." Hmm, I guess I did kind of sound like a douche.

Hope laughed. "You're right. They're perfect for the beach."

I nodded in agreement and took another sip of my wine, smugly.

Hope stood up and kicked off her flip flops. "Let's go stick our feet in and see if it's warm enough for swimming."

I set my fountain cup in the sand and, while Hope ran off to the shoreline, I arranged my body in contortionist positions while trying to unbuckle the ankle straps.

"Come on!" she yelled. "Hurry up. The water feels great."

"I'm trying," I yelled back as I struggled with the strap. The girls in movies always made this act look so graceful, but I'd never quite mastered it and usually ended up falling on my face or giving everyone around me a view usually reserved for my gynecologist.

"I just saw a dolphin swim by!" Hope yelled from the shore.

OMG! A dolphin! And I was missing it because I couldn't get my ... oh. I realized then what she was doing. Very clever. "Okay, smartass!" I yelled. "I get your point."

She laughed as she plopped back down on the seat next to me. "What were you saying about those shoes again?"

"Maybe they aren't beach shoes," I reluctantly admitted.

"They aren't *you* shoes."

I was still hesitant to agree with her. This *is* me now. And these are "me" shoes.

"And this life you've been living with Caleb," she continued, "is not you either. You sit in an apartment all day planning all of these things you want to do. But you never do them."

"Like what?"

"Like you watch all of these cooking shows but you hardly ever cook anything that doesn't come out of a box."

"Caleb's a picky eater," I explained. Ugh, it was true. He had a list three pages long of foods I was not allowed to serve to him; mostly veggies and spices. And what could I cook without veggies or spices?

"And the vacations you plan that you never take."

"You know he doesn't get a lot of vacation time!" I argued in my defense.

"He doesn't get a lot of *any* time!" she said. "He doesn't have time for you, and if you did have kids, he wouldn't have time for them either. Sometimes I think the reason you want a baby so bad is because you're lonely and I don't blame you for wanting some companionship. You're like Rapunzel locked up in a tower. Instead of hair, I bet you could tie a bunch of expensive shoes together to make a rope."

I was glad I had sunglasses on so she couldn't see how much her words were hurting me. I wished she would stop, but she didn't.

"Whether you think so or not, this divorce is your opportunity to get things right. You have the time and the money. So take the vacations, make the rosemary lamb chops, even have a baby on your own like the celebs do if you want. But as far as Caleb goes, run away and don't look back because the guy is a tool and he's turned you into one too." She stood up and grabbed our fountain cups out of the sand. "I'm going to the car to refill these."

She walked away then and left me alone to think about all of the mean things she'd said. It was good to have a few minutes alone to let it all sink in. I knew she didn't mean to hurt me, and I figured this was a tough love tactic, but it still sucked to hear those things. Was she right? *Am I really a tool?*

By the time Hope got back with the refills, I was sobbing into my sundress. She didn't look surprised. She set the cups down in the sand, sat down in front of me on my beach chair and hugged me while I cried. It was pretty embarrassing, but not any more so than my love handles. Who cared anyway? I didn't need to impress anyone anymore.

"Come on," Hope said. She stood up and held out her hand to me. "Let's go back to the hotel and get dressed for dinner. I packed you something fabulous."

CHAPTER FIVE

"Don't beat yourself up over it," Hope said. We had just been seated at an outdoor table at a restaurant on Main Street. I looked fabulous, as promised, even if I felt like shit. "You were just morphing into your lifestyle. Like a 'when in Rome' kind of thing."

"Except I didn't know I was in Rome," I said.

"The good news is that you're leaving Rome, and you can go anywhere you want and be anything you want. You get a fresh start. Or, in Roxie terminology, you get to rewrite your script."

I wished I was as perky about it as she was. The idea sounded all right on the surface. But I had failed at marriage, and I'd failed at being a trophy wife, so what if I failed at my new life too? And what would I do with my new life anyway?

There were three things a woman could be – a career woman, a mom, or a wife. Some overachievers juggled all three and still had time left to bake cupcakes, make their own wreathes for their front doors, and always look like they stepped out of a salon. But I'd never heard of a woman who dropped all the balls. Except me. No career, no husband, no kids. What the hell was I supposed to do?

As the waiter dropped off a few glasses of water, I noticed the light blinking on my Blackberry, signaling the arrival of a text or email. Ordinarily I wouldn't check my phone at dinner, but I thought, under the circumstances, it was a forgivable offense.

And there it was. An email from Caleb that said 'Divorce' in the subject line. It had been hours, and he still wanted a divorce. It was really happening.

With a shaky thumb, I opened it.

TO: GoRoxie@dmail.com
FROM: alwaysbeclosing@dmail.com

I know this seems sudden to you, and I'm sorry for that. I thought it would be best to make a clean break so we can stop wasting time and get on with our lives.

For the past year all you have cared about is getting pregnant. Every month, while you were disappointed to get your period, I felt more and more relieved, but I didn't know why.

Then I decided to surprise you on our anniversary. I was going to get one of those bungalows in Bora Bora that you're always going on about. I booked a week at the resort and was about to purchase flights when I realized that the idea of going on this trip was filling me with dread. I wanted you to have a vacation because you deserve one after all of your hard work. But I didn't want to take that vacation with you. That's when I realized I am not in love with you anymore.

You've been a good wife to me and I'm not trying to hide anything or take anything that you deserve. The papers detailing my offer will be delivered to you when you get home but I've attached an unofficial copy for you to look at now since you're out of town. You have 20 days to agree to my offer, dispute my offer or make a counteroffer. If you agree to everything, we can settle this quickly.

You have been very supportive of me while I was getting my career off the ground and, as a result, your career was put on the back burner. My lawyer and I took this into consideration when we came up with the numbers. We think the monthly maintenance amount is fair, and I think two years gives you an ample amount of time to establish a career of your own. You may think this amount seems small, but you need to realize that after paying off our student loans, buying the condo, and living above our means for the last few years, we are basically living paycheck-to-paycheck.

One thing we need to discuss is the condo. I don't know if you realize how much of my (our) income is spent on the mortgage payments, association fees, taxes and insurance. I can't afford to buy you out of it, and I know you can't afford to buy it from me, either. Luckily for us, the housing market in Manhattan has gone up a little recently, and we should be able to make a small profit from the sale. The bad news is that it could take months, even a year, to find a buyer and we still need to maintain the payments until then. I've already spoken to a realtor, and he thinks it will sell faster if we move out and he has someone stage it. So it's best if we both start looking for another place to live ASAP.

I have set up a separate account to cover your legal fees. Go ahead and hire a lawyer, and have them contact my lawyer to discuss the information on the documents. Have them send all bills to my office.

I have booked a room at The W for a week. I'm hoping to have a new place within that time frame. If you are on board with selling the condo, you might want to make that your goal as well.

Don't hesitate to contact me via phone or email if you have any further questions or concerns. Enjoy the rest of your time in the Hamptons. We'll be in touch soon.

Both Hope and I were quiet for a few moments after I finished reading the email out loud. My thoughts were flying around inside my head like a bunch of balls being juggled by a circus clown. *Bora Bora! Happy face. Establish a career. Scared face. Sell condo. No, not my beloved condo. Find lawyer. Move out. IN A WEEK? I need a new luggage set. Bora Bora! Sad face. Why would he even mention that just to take it away? Start over. What the hell am I going to do? Scared-as-hell face. A WEEK? Is this what ADHD feels like? Do I need Ritalin?*

Hope finally broke the silence and my panic-attack-in-the-making when she started laughing. She was pretty loud. I looked around to make sure no one was staring at us before I remembered I wasn't supposed to care anymore.

"I'm glad you're finding my crisis entertaining," I spat out.

"Lighten up, Rox," she said with a smile.

"I'm pretty sure he told me I have to move out within the week. Where *is* the light?"

"He thinks you're his employee!" she said between giggles.

I didn't say anything. I just glared at her across the table.

"You deserve a vacation," she mocked. "Don't hesitate to email if you have any further questions. That guy is a real piece of work. It's hysterical!"

She was right. His email sounded like he was talking to a business client, not his wife! That's what I was to him, wasn't I? When I'd called myself a

Trophy Wife in the past, I'd always thought of it as a cutesy term. It wasn't until I read the email that I realized it wasn't cute at all for your husband to think of you as an employee or business prospect. All this time I'd thought he loved me, but I was just his maid, his cook, his personal assistant and his call girl!

"Open up that document so we can get a look at these numbers," Hope said.

Oh yeah. I'd forgotten about that attachment. I clicked a button on my Blackberry to open the document. Hope and I put our heads together from opposite ends of the table and both watched and waited while the hourglass spun around and around and then, finally, the document opened. It was a bunch of legal mumbo jumbo, so I scanned quickly looking for numbers.

It was right about the same time when we both saw it, the "offer," so to speak. Her mouth was hanging open in shock. My eyeballs probably looked like they were about to fall out of my head and onto the table. *No, no that can't be right. There must be a mistake!*

Hope ordered a bottle of red wine while I tried to remain composed, even though my world was crumbling around my feet like the debris following a natural disaster. But this wasn't a hurricane, tornado or earthquake. This was just my greedy, arrogant bastard of a soon-to-be ex-husband ruining my life!

Breathe in, breathe out. Slowly. Blow it out like cigarette smoke. Try not to hyperventilate. Feel your body relax with every breath.

I had seen a hypnotist in my quest to quit smoking, and I tried to practice the calming techniques she taught me. I also tried to channel my inner yogi, whatever it took to get my composure back, so I could figure out what the hell I was going to do with *that*.

I felt dizzy and sick again. Was it possible for someone to have two panic attacks in the same day? I prayed the waiter hurried with the wine. And if he brought a shot of tequila with him, too, that'd be great.

The waiter arrived and I tried to stop the restaurant from spinning while he opened the wine bottle and poured us each a glass. I kind of heard Hope order a few appetizers, but her voice sounded like I was hearing it from under water. I wasn't at all hungry either. At least not for food. More so for revenge.

"Let's not panic," she said.

I looked at her and blinked a few times, trying to make her less blurry. I must have had tears in my eyes. I took a drink of my wine. A big drink.

"We now know," she said slowly, "without a doubt, that he is a complete ass, and this divorce is the best thing for you."

I now agreed with her that this was for the best because the only way I could imagine putting my arms around Caleb again would be if I were squeezing every last bit of life out of him.

She had my Blackberry in her hand and was reading over the documents as she spoke. "He is giving you half of his 401k. It's not much."

I reached down into my beach bag and pulled out my trusty notebook and pen to take some notes as she continued. "He's paying for your health insurance for two years, so that's good."

Bless his heart, I thought, in that snide insulting way I'd picked up when I was going to school in North Carolina. In my notebook I wrote *Access to Drugs*.

"He's paying all of your legal fees, including

transportation to and from consultations and court proceedings, and he's offering to pay a quarter of the tuition costs if you choose to go back to school."

I wrote *Apply at Columbia and NYU* in the notebook. If he was paying then I should go to the most expensive school around, right? Oh, wait, I had to pay the other 75%. I scratched out Columbia and NYU and wrote *CUNY or Berkeley*.

"That's all the good stuff." She stopped and took a big drink of wine, and I did the same. "Now for the bad stuff."

I closed my eyes. I knew what was coming.

"Half the costs to maintain the condo will come out of your monthly maintenance until it is sold or rented."

I nodded.

"Which is total bullshit," she said, "because it doesn't look like you're getting half of his monthly income. Definitely ask your lawyer about that."

I nodded again.

"And half of the credit card debt is your responsibility, too. Forty thousand *dollars*, Roxie? And that's only half? How the hell?"

I shrugged. I'd developed expensive tastes throughout the years – hair salons, pedicures, spas, shoes, handbags, 7 For All Mankind and Citizens of Humanity jeans – that stuff all adds up and so do the payments. I wouldn't have racked up that much in credit card debt if I knew my husband was planning a divorce, but there was no point in crying over it now. I was lucky he was going to cover the other half.

"And the maintenance. I don't know if he's hiding money or if he just doesn't make as much as we thought, but it's a pretty small amount."

"Yeah, I got that."

The waiter dropped off our appetizers and Hope

ordered entrees for both of us. I was glad she was here. It felt good to have someone taking care of me for a change. I guess that part had been missing from my marriage because I couldn't remember Caleb ever making me feel like I was taken care of. He kind of ordered me around a bit, but he never made sure I was eating. I wasn't hungry, but I would go ahead and eat a few stuffed mushrooms to make her happy since she actually seemed to care.

"So the way I see it," she said between bites, "you can move to another borough, look for someone who has a room for rent and use the 401k money to prepay for an apartment for as long as you can afford, maybe a year, depending on the neighborhood. You can get student loans to enroll in grad school, use your alimony to pay your credit card bills and utilities and serve drinks at night for spending money. I know Wes would hire you back."

"But what would I do when the prepaid lease was over?"

"Hopefully by then the condo would be sold and you'd have more money."

"And I can't work in the Financial District," I said while shaking my head furiously. "What if one of Caleb's coworkers came into the bar? Or even worse, one of the wives. I would be mortified! I can't be the new laughing stock of the firm."

We munched on our appetizers in silence for a few minutes while we thought of a plan. It probably seemed petty that I was basing my future life choices on the chance of running into one of about fifty people in a city of eight million, especially since I wasn't supposed to care what they thought of me anymore. But, well, I *was* and I *did*.

Just the thought of one of those horrible, wretched women coming into a bar where I was working to laugh at me and then stiff me on a tip was too much to bear. They'd run home and laugh about it with their husbands, who would go to work the next morning and laugh about it with Caleb, who would go home that night and laugh about it with his new girlfriend who was probably skinnier and prettier than me and loved anal sex. NO. FREAKING. WAY. Was that EVER going to happen.

"He's probably got coworkers living all over Manhattan," Hope said, sounding disappointed.

I nodded. "They're all over New York, period."

"So what are you saying? That you need to work in Jersey?" She shook her head vigorously. "I understand you're feeling a little embarrassed right now, but I think it's silly to go all the way to Jersey to make less money than you would here just because you might possibly run into someone who knows your ex."

"I think I should go farther away than Jersey," I said thoughtfully.

"Like where?"

"Somewhere new where I can get a fresh and cheaper start. Maybe back home to Michigan. I've been gone over ten years, so it would really be like starting over."

"What would you do in Michigan?" She said the name of my home state like it was an undeveloped Third World country; a common misconception actually.

The waiter brought over another bottle of wine for us, and I used the interruption to think about what I *would* do in Michigan. My intention back in the day had been to get my Master's in Social Work and work with underprivileged teenagers. I'd wanted to help them achieve success in their lives and get out of the "system." I could do that in Michigan for sure.

The whole Metro Detroit area was in a disgrace at the moment and the underprivileged were many. Plus, my money would go a lot further there, especially if I moved in with my brother. Yes! It was definitely possible. I could make do on the measly amount of money my loving husband was "paying" me if I moved back to Michigan.

"I'm going to do what I was supposed to have done all along," I told her. Now where was our food? I was suddenly famished.

I got back into the city by noon the next day and went straight to the lawyer's office – (I had used Hope's iPad at the hotel the night before to get the scoop on divorce lawyers. Maybe this technological overload actually had some relevance). The lawyer looked over the papers and said as long as Caleb was being honest about his finances, the offer was on the lower end of fair. She was going to send over a counteroffer asking for the higher end and do a little bit of research to see if she could find any hidden assets. I told her to do as much research as she wanted since Caleb was paying for it.

She said I didn't have to move out of the condo until it was sold, but I already had it in my head that I was going to Michigan and it was too late to change my mind. I told her to let me know anytime she wanted me to come to New York to meet with her again since the transportation expenses were taken care of, wink wink.

The moving expenses were also taken care of. When I told Caleb I was moving back home, he had a moving company lined up within minutes. He told me to go ahead and pack a carry-on because he had booked me a flight to Michigan for Monday morning. The movers would have all of my stuff packed up and driven to Ann Arbor by Wednesday. Except for the furniture. The realtor said the condo would sell faster with the furniture in it so we were leaving it for now.

And that was it. That was all it took. Thursday he told me he wanted a divorce and Monday morning I was on the first flight to DTW. I left behind Hope, my amazing condo, and a city I loved as if it were a family member. But I was also on my way to gaining back my independence and all of the things that made me, me, before I met Caleb. I was gaining the ability to think for myself and make my own decisions and make my own flight arrangements, when needed.

The funny thing about it, though, was that I had no idea what the hell I was doing. The one who planned everything, in a borderline-OCD kind of way, was doing something unplanned. I didn't know what was before me, but I had faith that whatever it was, it was better than what I was leaving behind – somebody cue the soundtrack guy, please. I think something uplifting would be suitable here.

Once the plane had taken off and the fun part was over, I reached into my tote bag for a magazine. A white envelope fell out of a copy of *Self*. First, I thought it was a heartfelt apologetic goodbye letter from Caleb, but since I didn't see any pigs flying outside of my window, I knew that couldn't be the case. I opened it up. It was from Hope. She must have snuck it into my bag when she came over to say goodbye.

It was written on two pieces of college-ruled lined notebook paper stapled together. I looked out the window again. Nope, still no pigs. She must have borrowed some supplies from the American Museum of Natural History. That or she made a special stop at Duane Reade. I definitely appreciated the effort. A handwritten letter to a friend was better than any email, text, Facebook message, tweet or any other form of technological correspondence.

Dear Friend,

*I'm really proud of you for taking this leap of faith. And even though I'm going to miss you <u>like crazy</u>, I understand why you have to go. My only concern is that you are going to be building a new life without my wisdom and guidance, which I think we both agree is an influence you really shouldn't be without. No offense, Rox, but you don't have the best track record when it comes to making decisions on your own. I mean, you **are** the one who married that jackass to begin with. And I'm not sure if I can trust these Michigan people either. If I leave your summer activities up to them, you might end up wearing denim overalls and shooting beer cans off a tree trunk while eating deer jerky with the three teeth you have left.*

That's why I'm volunteering to act as your sponsor. I've done a lot of thinking this weekend, and I've come up with a way that I can keep you moving in the right direction from several states away. It's called the Good Life List and it's your new syllabus. Remember when I threw that bachelorette party for Lindsay and everyone had to complete tasks in order to win a free day at the spa? This is kind of like that, except I'm not handing out hits of ecstasy and there aren't any bonus points for performing oral sex in public. I created this list with you in mind so it's meant to be more classy than trashy.

On the next page you will find your Good Life List. You need to complete each challenge on the list by the end of the summer. I know you are always saying that there are no dress rehearsals in life, but I disagree. Since you're thinking about going back to school you'll probably have figured out what the hell you're going to do with your life by the time fall semester starts. But right now you have no one to impress – (except me ;), no one to answer to – (except me ;) and no one to please – (except me ;).

This is your in-between. This is your dress rehearsal. So go on now and make me proud, little one. Oh, and please, for the love of all that is holy, if you even think about marrying someone because his last name sounds good with Roxie, you call me first so I can smack some sense into your pretty little head! Love you! Muah XOXO

By the time I finished reading the letter I was laughing out loud while dabbing tears from my eyes. That girl is crazy, but I love her.

I flipped over to the second page. On the top line she had written *The Good Wife*. Then she crossed out the word *Wife* and wrote *Life*. *The Good Life*. Underneath the title was the list of challenges she wanted me to complete this summer.

The Good ~~Wife~~ Life

1. Sunbathe in the nude.
2. Get thrown out of a bar.
3. Do something nice for a stranger.
4. Go skinny dipping in someone else's pool without their permission.
5. Have sex for fun and not to make a baby. You should probably use a condom too. Remember, classy not trashy.
6. Get your picture taken in a photo booth … topless.
7. Give that picture to someone.
8. Wear a miniskirt in public without underwear.
9. Tell somebody (preferably somebody

you're attracted to) that you're not wearing anything under your skirt.
10. Pee in the shower.
11. Wash a car while wearing a bikini.
12. Go into a toy store and use a hula hoop for at least one minute.
13. Watch a sunset.
14. Watch a sunrise.
15. Take a nap in a park.
16. Start a food fight.
17. Play in the rain.
18. Burst into song in public like you're the star of a musical, and get at least one other person, a stranger, to sing along.
19. Sleep outside overnight.
20. Get drunk!
21. Swing on the swings at a playground.
22. Go into a department store and make a divorce registry.
23. Mail out divorce announcements.
24. Make out with a stranger.
25. Volunteer at a homeless shelter.
26. Host a party and serve at least ten recipes you've never made before.
27. Drive around in your car until you find someone who is jogging and then follow the person while blasting the song "The Final Countdown" by Europe. (Just kidding about this one. But if you do it, please make sure you get it on video).

Wow. That was quite a list. Some things were disgusting (peeing in the shower – gross). Some things sounded kind of fun, like skinny dipping. I could probably play in the rain and nap in a park without a problem. But there were some that really pushed my boundaries. Going commando under a miniskirt! Washing a car in a bikini! Bursting into song like I'm on *Glee*! Those things took guts – guts I didn't have. I may have had such guts about ten years ago, but while my literal gut got bigger, my proverbial gut seemed to disappear.

I was starting to realize what Allison meant when she said I needed to act like my old self again. She had a point. And Hope had been right-on with her Cooper's Beach assessment. It sucked that it took so long for them to get through to me, but I couldn't dwell on time wasted. All I could do now was look forward. I was ready to be fun and happy again, even if it meant peeing on myself.

CHAPTER SIX

I called Allison when the plane landed so she could head over from the waiting lot to pick me up. All I had on me was my carry-on and large purse/tote so I was able to skip the luggage area and walk right out the door into the beautiful, warm, sunny day.

The passenger pick-up lane was a no-bullshit, hurry-the-fuck-up kind of place that's heavily enforced by big bouncer-type security guards. For that reason, there wasn't any time for squeals and hugs when Allison pulled up. I ran to the back of her minivan and saw the decals on the back glass; a stick-figure family of five, plus one stick-dog and two stick-cats and what looked like a stick-hamster, or possibly rat. I popped open the hatchback, threw in my as-big-as-the-airlines-allowed carry-on and hopped in the front seat in a matter of about two seconds. She pulled away before I even had my seatbelt on. *Then* she squealed.

You know that sentimental saying about how you know you have a great friend when you can go months or even years without speaking and as soon as you see each other again it's like no time has passed at all? That's Allison and me. There's never any stiff handshakes or awkward silences between us. There's no reason for me to pretend around her either. She is not impressed with money or anything that it can buy.

Allison hadn't changed much since I left. It had been over ten years since I'd lived in Michigan full-time and, while I felt twenty years older, she never seemed to age a day. With her naturally blonde hair in a messy ponytail (not the fake-messy look that takes an hour to achieve, but the actual I-don't-give-a-crap ponytail which still managed to look just as good as the premeditated kind), and her hot pink sweatpants and white v-neck t-shirt, she was the same laid back, low-maintenance girl I'd known all my life. In New York, people spend so much time trying to achieve the look of someone who doesn't care, but in Michigan, and with Allison especially, it's genuine. She really doesn't care. And it's not in an arrogant way either. She just thinks, or I guess I should say, she *knows*, there's more to life than designer jeans.

After spending the better part of a decade trying to keep up with the Joneses, Allison was just what I needed to rehabilitate. I was ready to take a whole glass of her nonchalance and pour it all over me.

"The kids wanted to skip school today," she said. "Since school's almost over and they haven't missed very much this year, I said it was okay." She said it in a whisper, like someone outside the vehicle might overhear and call CPS about the neglectful mom in the minivan who let her kids skip school just to pick someone up at the airport. "They're so excited to see you. We all are."

I kind of got that idea by the way the van was bouncing up and down from all of the excited antics going on in the back. The kids – Kayla, 12; Kenzie, 10; and Drew, 9 – all said hi to me and acted excited to see me for a good minute before their "normalness" kicked in. This included yelling, whining, physical abuse, arguing, kicks to the back of my seat and that really annoying game kids play where they repeat everything a person says. Ugh, it's bad enough with one kid playing, but three at one time was the closest to torture I'd ever known. It was even worse than that Geology class I'd taken at UNC for an Earth Science credit. By the time we made it to Ann Arbor I couldn't wait to bust out of the van. I was happy to be back in their lives full-time, but I was going to have to start with part-time doses.

"We'll be hanging out in the backyard all day, and we're gonna grill some steaks and ribs for dinner," Allison said. "We'd love for you to come over, but I know you're probably anxious to get settled in."

"Yeah," I said, sounding less than enthused as she pulled into the driveway of my childhood home. "I should probably go in and get this part over with."

She nodded and gave me a sympathetic smile. She totally got me. Hope is a great NYC friend to me, but there's really nothing like a friend since childhood who knows every version of you. Allison knew the smart me, the silly me, the adventurous me, the married me ... and she loved all of them unconditionally. It's good to have someone who knows every important event in my life, the good and the bad, the triumphs and heartaches, the bad decisions and great times and just ... everything

"Call if you change your mind. I'll come get you," she said.

"A barbeque sounds good," I said, truthfully. Caleb and I never cooked on a grill at home. Unless you counted the George Foreman. "Come get me before you start cooking."

"Great! I'll see you tonight then. Invite the guys, too, if you want. It can be like a welcome home party!"

I hopped out of the minivan, grabbed my bag from the back and waved goodbye as Allison and her clan pulled away. Then I turned around and looked at the house I grew up in.

After our dinner in Southampton Thursday night, I had gone back to our hotel and called Adam to find out if he'd rented out the third bedroom yet. See, my dad, who had been a science professor at the University of Michigan for like, *ever*, had seen some research that made him believe he and my mom would live longer, healthier and happier lives if they moved to a warmer climate. At least that was the excuse they'd given to us. It could just be that they wanted to live in the sunshine on the ocean, and I can't blame them for that. Either way, three years ago my dad gave up his tenure at U of M and transferred to a school in Fort Myers, Florida.

They were very happy there. Dad said the school was a lot more casual than U of M. He taught his classes in Bermuda shorts and Hawaiian print shirts and spent his weekends fishing and golfing. My mom had started yoga classes and met with a group of senior women several times a week to play Just Dance on Xbox Kinect. It's funny because they are in their fifties and aren't even old enough to qualify for some senior discounts, but they're already fully embracing the lifestyle. Maybe that's just the cycle of life. When you're younger, you want to be older. When you get around my age, you want to be younger. And apparently when you are their age, you're in a rush for your AARP membership.

Since the housing market in Michigan had been so crappy lately, and my parents didn't want to lose a butt load of money by selling their house for dirt cheap, my brother, Adam, agreed to move in and handle the mortgage until the market picked up. Since Adam was a third-year surgical resident with an alarming amount of student loans to pay off, he couldn't afford to make the mortgage payments on his own. What's a guy to do in that situation? Rent out the other two bedrooms. In Ann Arbor, there was always someone looking to rent a room and they were willing to pay a nice amount, too, especially since the house was so close to campus.

I knew that one of his roommates had just graduated and moved out a few weeks ago so this divorce really came at a perfect time. Adam thought it was a great idea for me to move back and, compared to NYC, the rent was cheap enough that I'd be able to cover a whole year's worth, plus utilities, with my 401k settlement. And I'd still have some left over for a used car.

I intended to get a job to save up enough money to start grad school next fall. Not this fall, but *next* fall, over a year from now. I'd done my research and gotten some information on the MSW programs at every university within fifty miles of Ann Arbor. And guess what – you're supposed to apply for those things a year in advance. I missed the deadlines by a long shot. But I didn't let that get me down. I would just register for some Continuing Education classes in the fall to freshen up my smarts a little. Or not.

Whatever. I was trying hard to be carefree about this... kind of an oxymoron, huh?

I walked up the driveway and through the gate of the privacy fence to enter the backyard. Adam had hidden a key under one of the cushions of the patio chairs and I found it easily. I unlocked the French-style patio doors that led to the kitchen a bit apprehensively. I hadn't been in the house since my parents had moved out because we'd spent the last few Christmases in NYC. I took a look around to see what my brother had done to the place. It was actually kind of impressive for a bunch of guys. The décor was modern and the place looked clean ... and empty. I was glad there wasn't anyone home. I kind of wanted a few minutes to settle in before I was forced into any uncomfortable reunions. No, Adam didn't make me uncomfortable – he's my brother. But the other roommate was another story. A long one.

Remember Jake? The Heimlich guy? He was the other roommate. And I should probably let you know that the bubblegum disaster of a first kiss wasn't the last encounter between us.

During my junior year at UNC I fell hard and fast for a guy named Jim. He was a quiet and enigmatic kind of guy that drove me crazy in a good way. At least I *thought* it was a good way at the time. I was young and stupid and believed that trust was something a person was given automatically until they broke it, when really it should have been the other way around.

Jim was also a junior at UNC but he was a "local" who lived with his parents and commuted. Once we started dating, he spent the night at my apartment with me probably three or four nights a week. He had space in my closet and a toothbrush in the bathroom. We were practically living together. It was my first adult relationship. I thought it would last forever.

Looking back, I've realized it was lust and not love that made me so crazy about him. Or just plain crazy, period. I felt like I needed him, like I was an addict and he was my methadone. It was unhealthy at best, but I didn't know any better at the time. I thought all of the drama and fighting was normal. I thought I'd found something spectacular. In my head I had already planned our wedding, named our children and found us a house in Ann Arbor on a cozy cul-de-sac with a swing set and a sandbox in the backyard.

One night, during finals week, we were in my apartment. He was helping me pack for the summer and I was wondering how the heck I was going to live without him for three months and distracting myself by anticipating lots of passionate goodbye sex during the next few days.

Instead, passion came in the form of a pregnant chick nearly tearing my door down demanding to see her boyfriend. Long story short – on the nights he wasn't with me, he wasn't sleeping at his parents' house. He was living with his girlfriend and her parents. She was eight months pregnant. And a senior in high school. And her name was Destiny. Oh, and he wasn't even a student at UNC. He'd been making up a bunch of lies about his classes and even pretending to do homework. Truth was, he was a high-school dropout who worked as a custodian for the school – and NOT in a *Good Will Hunting* kind of way.

I was devastated. And I was angry. But even worse, I was embarrassed and ashamed and I felt like it was my fault for trusting someone without question like that. I was young and I didn't know then how cruel people could be. But I learned. And that was one lesson I wouldn't need repeated.

A few days later I drove myself home to Michigan in a rental car, and that was the beginning of the summer that will always be referred by me as *The Summer of Jake and Roxie*.

I got a job as a cocktail waitress at a hip bar that was popular with the college-aged crowd. It was called The Bar, as in Raising the Bar. It was supposed to be a classier version of a college bar. Anyway, Jake, who shared an apartment with my brother at the time, was a bartender there. Every night after my shift, I would sit at the bar to count my money and Jake would pour me a drink or two and then drive me home since my parents had finally given my POS Buick to the POS graveyard.

I would go home after work, cry myself to sleep over Jim's betrayal, sleep in until past noon, mope around for a few hours and then go to work to start the cycle all over again. I was too depressed to even go shopping! I was making hundreds of dollars a night and wasn't spending a dime. It was a sad excuse for a life, and I was growing tired of it. I needed something to keep my mind off of my battered ego and wounded heart. And just like having a drink in the morning when you wake up with a hangover eases the pain for a bit, hooking up with another guy after one guy hurts you is a bit of a heart bandage. So one night, when my brother was in Cleveland for the weekend with some of his friends, I got into Jake's pick-up truck and asked him to take me to his place after work instead of mine.

"Are you fighting with your parents?" he asked curiously.

"No." Leave it to Jake to need this spelled out for him.

"Did you leave your sheets in the washing

machine? I've done that before."

"No, Jake." I stared straight ahead through the windshield and started to wonder if this was a bad idea. "It's not that I don't want to go to my house. It's that I want to go home with you. Get it?"

"Umm ..."

"Oh jeez," I said, exasperated. "You're being a buzz kill. Never mind. Just take me home."

"No. We can go to my place."

"Forget it."

He turned to go toward his apartment instead of my house.

"I said forget it. Take me home."

"I don't want to," he said. "You said you wanted to come home with me so that's where we're going."

"It's pointless now. You've ruined the moment." As he turned onto his street I crossed my arms and stared out the passenger window feeling mortified that this conversation was even happening.

"You can't blame me for ruining a moment I didn't even know we were having. Let's start over. Tell me to take you home with me again."

He pulled into his apartment complex, found a parking spot and put the truck into park.

"I feel really stupid," I said. "Can you please just forget this ever happened and take me home? There's really no way to make the moment sexy again."

He turned off the ignition. "I can make this sexy again." He sounded confident, and he had good reason to. With his gorgeous brown eyes, messy-on-purpose dark hair, a body that spent just enough time at the gym without going overboard and a smile that could bring a girl to her knees, he could make anything sexy. But he didn't *know* it, which made him even hotter to me.

He looked over at me, and I met his eyes for a

second. He knew what I was coming over for and the look in his eyes let me know he was ready and willing to give me exactly what I wanted. That look alone was enough to make the moment sexy again.

"Will you take me home with you?" I asked again, suddenly feeling shy.

Jake got out of the truck and walked over to my side. He opened my door and met my eyes again, then reached across my waist to unbuckle my seat belt without ever looking away. He put his hands on my hips and turned my body towards him.

"I've been wanting to get this uniform off you all summer," he said.

"Then what are you waiting for?" I asked.

Then he kissed me. And he was right. He could make it sexy again. It was a wonder we even made it into his apartment with clothes on. Hooking up with Jake was something I'd been fantasizing about since I was a teenager, and I was ready to get started right in the truck as not to waste any more time.

What happened when we did get upstairs to his apartment turned out to be the hottest night of my entire life up to that point. I woke up in the morning thinking he'd give me some blow-off and blame it on the alcohol, but instead it turned out to be the hottest morning of my life. And after a few more hours of sleep and some leftover pizza, we went ahead and made it the hottest afternoon of my life too.

I intended for it to be a one-time-thing, and that was why I didn't mention it to anyone. We didn't really need our coworkers or families trying to interfere. But there's something about having a secret with someone; it really turns me on. And even though I was still wounded, I needed to have some kind of fun, and he seemed the perfect candidate for a rebound summer fling. I'd known him forever, and I knew for certain he was a good guy and not a total douchebag. I knew my heart was safe with him. I figured if I was going to fall in love with him, I would have already done so sometime in the last fifteen years. That's why I called him my "safety guy." The whole point of a safety net was to catch you when you fell. I fell. He caught me. But he wasn't going to let me fall any further, which was exactly what I needed that summer.

Jake and I were great together. He was so different from Jim. Jim was a tortured soul who suffered from un-medicated bipolar disorder and needed to be babied all the time. He loved to live dangerously, and I liked to take care of him. I liked feeling needed. Jim was also super jealous and loved dramatic fight scenes so it seemed we were always having make-up sex.

Compared to that disaster, Jake was a breath of fresh air. There was no drama or jealousy or arguing (unless it was done on purpose, because let's face it – make up sex *is* pretty fun). We just liked being around each other. It was really that simple. And we didn't need to fight to have good sex. Have you ever worked with someone who you were sleeping with? It's like eight hours of foreplay. And with him living with my brother, and me living with my parents, we really had to get creative to spend time alone, and that put the hotness factor off the charts. We'd sit at the dining room table and have dinner with my parents just fifteen minutes after he'd had his head up my skirt in the garage, and all we could think about was when we'd be alone again. And while I said that first night was the hottest night, it got even better every time. *The Summer of Jake and Roxie* – it was the best summer of my life.

We both knew it was just a summer thing. I

figured as soon as our families, friends and coworkers found out about us and we were no longer keeping a secret, things wouldn't be as hot anymore. And once you took the hotness factor out of the equation, what would we have left besides something that would die a slow death in front of the TV and ruin a lifelong friendship? I didn't want to stick around to find out and watch the best thing that ever happened to me turn into something bad. So even though I could have probably happily spent an entire lifetime in his bed, we cut things off cold turkey at the end of the summer. He said he didn't think a long-distance relationship would work. I agreed with him. Then I went back to school, met Caleb a few weeks later and never looked back.

We didn't leave things on bad terms or anything, but there was really no reason for us to keep in touch. I'd been back home to visit several times since then, but our paths just hadn't crossed. I did invite him to my wedding because, like I said before, he was practically a member of the family. It would have been a lot weirder to *not* invite him. But he had other plans that night and couldn't make it, which was a shame because I really would have liked him to be there. I looked for him the whole night, hoping he'd change his mind and show up. I don't know why I cared so much. Maybe I was secretly hoping for him to run in all out of breath in typical rom-com style, tell me he loved me and hadn't stopped thinking about me since last summer, and I shouldn't marry Caleb. Or maybe it wasn't a secret hope, but a very conscious one. Either way, it didn't happen, and it was probably for the best because I might have told him I loved him, too, and ran into his arms and spent the rest of my life in fear of the day his teenage pregnant girlfriend would knock down our door. If anyone could hurt me more than Jim, it was Jake. And what a life that would have been, to be so happy, yet always looking over my shoulder and waiting for the rug to be pulled out from under me. Ugh.

"Roxie."

The sound of his voice behind me caused a stir in my belly like someone had lit a stick of dynamite in there. Or make that *two* sticks of dynamite. One burned upward toward my heart, the other burned down. It's funny how a sound can work like a time machine and take a person back to the past.

I stood in the kitchen next to the island, still holding my carry-on bag. He must have come inside the patio doors behind me. Though where he was coming from this early in the day I did not know. I probably didn't want to know.

I figured I was as prepared for this moment as I'd ever be, and it was best to get it over with as soon as possible. I turned around.

There he was, no longer a punk kid in a baseball cap who looked like he might crush a beer can on his forehead, but a grown up. He had the Adam Levine stubble look going on, and his hair was shorter and no longer had that slept-in look. But there was still enough there for me to tangle my hands in – not that I had any reason to do that and not saying I wanted to – just saying I could.

He had on faded jeans and an un-tucked short-sleeve button-up shirt that hid all of his tattoos except the ones on his forearms. He had a fancy DSLR camera hanging from a thick strap around his neck. Is there something about a guy with a camera that is incredibly hot? And how about tattoos on the underside of the forearm? And how bad of a person was I to be thinking anything was hot just four hours after leaving my marital home?

Just because we hadn't seen each other or spoken in years didn't mean I hadn't kept tabs on him. I was his Facebook friend so I did know a little about what went on in his life. I knew he was still tending bar part-time at The Bar. I knew the owner had tried to make him manager several times but Jake didn't want to give his whole life to the place because he needed time to pursue a career in photography. He had established a pretty successful company over the last few years doing every kind of portraits imaginable … except weddings. Adam told me it was because he didn't have the patience for that Bridezilla behavior, and who could blame him? Even the nicest girls turn into some crazy ass bitches on their wedding days. By the way, I know everyone who can afford a good camera was starting a photography business these days, but let me be clear about one thing – he was legit. His pictures have been published in magazines and websites, and his business page on Facebook has over 3000 fans.

He stood there, his face expressionless. Not angry, not happy, not bored – a complete poker face. I had a feeling he was waiting to see how I would play this. My intention had been to wait on *him* to make the first move. But somebody was going to have to show their cards before this standoff became uncomfortable for both of us.

What's it gonna be? I could give him a casual shrug of the shoulder and an "Oh, hi. I forgot you lived here." I could go one step further into idiocy and say, "Oh, hi. Jake, right?" I could give him the cold shoulder and make sure he never went out of his way to speak to me again. Or, instead of playing games and worrying about what he was thinking, I could do what I'd normally do when I ran into an old friend who had at one time meant a lot to me. I could smile and be happy to see him. So I did.

"Jake! It's so good to see you!" I said. And I meant it.

He smiled back at me and looked relieved. Wow, that smile, it had gotten better with age. I almost fell right there onto the kitchen floor.

"Roxie," he said again. "How are ya, Little Girl?" He'd been calling me that since I was actually a little girl. I hadn't heard him say it in so many years I'd forgotten all about it.

"Um, okay," I said. What a brilliant conversationalist I was! Of all the things he could possibly say to me, *"How are you?"* was on top of the list. I'd been on a plane for two hours imagining this very moment, and I thought I had written a line for every comment he could possibly make, but for some reason, the answer to a simple *"How are you?"* had slipped through the cracks. I was definitely losing my touch. I would never make it in Hollywood.

He took his camera off his neck and set it on the kitchen island – the same kitchen island we'd had sex on one night after work while my parents were sleeping upstairs. I wondered if he ever thought about that night when he was in the kitchen, or if he even remembered. Probably not. I doubted I had made the kind of impact that would have him remembering any part of that summer after all this time. To him, I was just another girl.

"From what I hear it's probably for the best," he said. There was a softness to his voice that sounded empathetic. Sympathy would have been humiliating. Smugness would have been aggravating. But empathy I would take.

"I just came by to change before work," he explained. "I have to work open to close today at The

Bar. I usually only go in on Friday and Saturday nights, but they've got someone down with mono so I'll be filling in all week."

I smiled and nodded. The smile and nod. Works in almost every situation. Except when you're being interrogated by the police and they ask if you're guilty.

"I know you don't have a car here so if you ever need to use my Jeep you can just drop me off at work. And don't go looking for a car without me, okay? I'll come with you to make sure you don't get screwed over."

That was nice. Some women would have been insulted and gone on a feministic rant over the last comment. But he was right. If anyone was going to be screwed over by a used car salesman, it was me.

"Wow, thanks so much," I said. "That's so nice of you." Like totally. Oh Em Gee, I sounded like some bimbo on an eighties sitcom! What a disgrace.

"Do you need it tonight?" he asked. "We don't usually keep a lot of groceries around. Adam is hardly ever here, and he eats most of his meals at the cafeteria." He ran his fingers through his hair – a habit I knew meant he was nervous. "I picked up some mac-n-cheese and Cinnamon Toast Crunch last night. I don't know if you still like them, but I wanted to make sure you had something to eat if you were here without a car."

There goes that stick of dynamite making my heart burn. Cinnamon Toast Crunch was not only my favorite cereal, but my favorite food period. I didn't pause to think about it. I didn't mentally go over any and all possible results of my actions. I just did it. I hugged him. I wrapped my arms around his waist, pressed my cheek against his chest and breathed in his familiar smell that was like a mixture of dryer sheets and Tide.

"I still love them," I said about the foods he'd picked out for me.

He clearly didn't have any dynamite in his chest because he kind of held his arms out in front of him like he didn't want to touch me and then patted me on top my head.

I pulled away, embarrassed, and mentally scolded myself for acting before thinking. "Thanks," I said, "but I'll be fine. I'm having dinner at Allison's tonight."

"Okay. I'm gonna go change and then head out. I'll see you later."

It wasn't my best and brightest moment, but I was glad it was over.

I walked upstairs to the spare bedroom – the bedroom that had been mine for the first twenty-two years of my life – and found it completely empty. That was fine with me. I liked a fresh, clean start. I had ordered a bedroom set online over the weekend that would be delivered this afternoon sometime between noon and four.

I peeked through the blinds at the pool in the backyard. It looked so welcoming. Too bad I didn't think to pack a swimsuit in my carry-on. I remembered the Good Life List then and pulled it out of my handbag to review my quests. Skinny-dipping in your own pool was not on the list but nude sunbathing was. Maybe I should go ahead and work on my tan *and* the GLL. I looked at my Blackberry to check the time. It was 11:10. I had fifty minutes before the earliest my furniture would arrive. Those people never showed up in the beginning of the time slot anyway.

I stripped, wrapped myself up in a towel I found in the linen closet and headed downstairs quickly. I knew I needed to hurry before I lost my nerve. There was a privacy fence in the backyard so the only way anyone could see me would be if a neighbor was looking out of an upstairs window, and I figured that was probably unlikely. The kids were at school this time of day and the adults were at work.

I sunbathed in the nude! I did fifteen minutes on my back and fifteen minutes on my belly. I had carried my sundress down with me in case of emergency and kept it within arm's reach at all times, but I never even reached for it. I felt really proud of myself. Proud and hot! It felt like it was at least ninety degrees out – (Yes, it does get hot in Michigan).

I figured I still had time for a quick swim to cool off. Since the pool was only two steps from my chair I stood up and jumped in. And, in case you were wondering, it felt great! I'd been here less than two hours and already crossed off one quest on the GLL. This was going to be the best summer ever!

I laid back and floated in the pool with my hands behind my head, smugly. Roxie Golightly, living the good life.

CHAPTER SEVEN

"Hello? Anybody home?"

I was startled by the sound of a man's voice coming from the front of the house. I jumped up and covered my chest with my hands. Before I could decide on my next move I heard a knock on the back gate.

"Roxie?" the man called out. "Are you back here?"

In my head it seemed to happen in slow motion. First, I looked toward my chair and saw that neither my towel nor my sundress were within my reach. Then I looked at both of the pool's exits: one, an attached metal ladder in the deep end, and two, the cemented steps in the shallow end. I knew there was no way to get out of the pool via either of those exits without showing *something*.

A man's head peeked over the top of the fence and I crouched low in the water.

"Roxie? Is that you?"

Shit! He saw me. What the hell do I do now?

"Roxie? It's Phil. Phil Barnaby. From high school."

Phil? The name wasn't ringing a bell, but how unbelievable was it that my ears were still popping from my flight, and I'd already run into someone I went to high school with? And I was naked! Ann Arbor is not a small city! Can the universe please give me a break here?

"We have your furniture. Is it okay if we go on in?"

"Yes!" I shouted. "Please put it all in the empty bedroom upstairs."

"Gotcha."

His head disappeared from the fence. I knew I shouldn't let a bunch of delivery guys in the house unsupervised, but I was willing to take the risk. Then I remembered that Jake left his camera on the kitchen island, and it probably had his memory card in it. I couldn't very well let his camera and photos get stolen on my first day in the house. Damnit!

I had no choice but to get out of the pool and get to my towel as quickly as possible. I hoped and prayed that no one was looking out any windows during those few moments. And I prayed even harder that if anyone *was* looking out a window, they weren't recording it! Just my luck my boobs would be viral within the hour.

I made it into the house, braless but covered, made sure the camera was safe, signed for my furniture, thanked Phil who I still didn't recognize and wondered if every quest on the GLL was going to turn into such an adventure. To be honest, I kind of hoped so.

I could definitely get used to this new life!

After spending the afternoon (seriously, a whole four hours!) putting my bedroom set together and proving to myself that I could make it on my own, I had a great time over at Allison's. Adam had a rare few hours to spare and came over for a little bit too. We had dinner, drank some beer, started a bonfire, made s'mores for the kids, and chased fireflies around the yard. You just can't *do* stuff like that in Manhattan.

I wasn't sure what to expect out of Jake when he got home from work that night. He used to be a real party animal back in the day, like a lot of people who work in that industry. I was half expecting him to bring a slutty cocktail waitress home after last call and bend her over the kitchen island. I definitely would have been annoyed by that. And not because I was still harboring feelings for him. I'd be annoyed if *any* roommate of mine was partying in the middle of the night or having sex in communal areas where we eat. Believe me, if I was a cast member on MTV's *The Real World,* I would be having conniption fits in the confessional on a daily basis.

Either his chick was a very quiet lay, or he came home alone because I didn't hear a thing. I slept very well on my comfy new pillow-top bed. I would have slept a lot longer, but I was awoken by the sound of someone banging on the front door just after nine.

I jumped up in bed thinking it was probably someone delivering a package for me. I had done some internet shopping over the weekend and bought new summer clothes and interview clothes to cheer myself up. I knew I had a serious credit card debt problem and should take a break from shopping for a while, but I thought I deserved just *one* divorce shopping spree. Besides, I shopped at H&M for practically pennies.

I knew Adam was already elbow-deep in surgery by that time, but I didn't want Jake disturbed after working so late. I knew he wasn't much of a morning person.

I got out of bed, threw my robe on over my cami and sleep shorts, and headed down the hallway toward the stairs. I stopped when I heard a woman's voice.

"I don't know who she was, but I would really appreciate it if you boys did not leave your girls here unsupervised. I have a thirteen-year-old and an eleven-year-old, and they do not need to look out their window and see naked women in your pool!"

I gasped, put a hand over my mouth and hid behind the wall upstairs to eavesdrop.

"I'm really sorry about that, Mrs. Kemp." It was Jake's voice!

OH. MY. GOD. *Is this is a joke?* Maybe Hope called and told Jake about the Good Life List and he set this all up as a prank? I could only hope.

"You know," the woman continued, "she's lucky my boys were still in school. They probably would have recorded it on their phones and showed it to all their friends. But you let her know they'll be out of school in a week, and I would really appreciate it if she would wear a swimsuit from now on."

"I'll make sure it doesn't happen again."

I heard him close the door and head up the stairs. I pressed my back up against the wall in the hallway as hard as I could, like I thought I could actually disappear into it. I see people doing that in movies *all* the time. And I'm always thinking, *What a dumbass. Do you really think people can't see you if you lean against a wall?* But there I was doing the same thing.

It turns out people *can* see you. Jake definitely saw *me*. He stopped, looked at me for about two seconds, gave me a dirty look and then went into his bedroom and slammed the door. If ever there was an appropriate time for me to do the slide-down-the-wall-and-put-my-head-in-my-hands move, it was now. But that move was a bit overplayed. Instead, I got back in bed and vowed never to leave my room again.

A half an hour later I was about to die of boredom. There was nothing to do in my room. No computer, no TV, no books. A person can only stare at the walls for so long. Jake was sleeping so there was no reason for me to hide out all day. I was trying to put my humiliation out of my mind and gather the courage to leave the room when I heard the sound of a truck's brakes outside. Could it be a UPS or mail truck? Could it be my new clothes? I had paid extra for express shipping, so it was possible.

I left the room, ran downstairs and intercepted my package from the mail carrier before she even had a chance to knock. Then I took the box upstairs to try on my new clothes. I was used to more expensive fabrics, but for the price I paid, I couldn't complain. Even the bikini I bought looked pretty good. It was one size bigger than the infamous polka dot one I wore last week and the extra room made a big difference. The fact that I had hardly eaten anything in almost a week was helping the situation too. No more muffin top. I guess that's what they call the Divorce Diet.

It was just a plain turquoise bikini with an underwire top. They didn't have a huge selection, but for $20 I didn't care. At least I wouldn't have to horrify the neighbors with nudity anymore.

Then I got an idea. One of my challenges on the GLL was to wash a car while wearing a bikini. I had a bikini now! And Jake had a car! Or a Jeep. Whatever. Same thing. Maybe if he woke up to a shiny clean Jeep he'd forgive me for the rude awakening this morning.

Look, I am not Paris Hilton or the 2005 version of Jessica Simpson. I'm not even the sweet and innocent girl-next-door who is hot without knowing it. Trust me. I'm all right but I'm not music video or hamburger commercial-worthy. The car wash was pretty much just that – a car wash. I didn't put my pink sparkly lips to the hose water to give my pretty little tongue a drink. I didn't squeeze the sponge over my chest to make soapy water drip down my cleavage. I didn't rub my butt up against the car to scrub it with my bikini bottom. I didn't have stilettos on. And Def Leopard's "Pour Some Sugar on Me" wasn't playing anywhere (except maybe in my head). But I was still embarrassed when I noticed Jake standing at the back door watching me. Creeper!

He opened the door and stepped out when he realized he'd been busted. He crossed his arms and leaned against the brick house. I set the sponge on the hood and crossed my arms, too, which just so happened to make my boobs look freaking amazing, if I do say so myself.

"You spy on people often?" I asked.

"Sounds like I missed a good opportunity yesterday, huh?"

I scowled and tried to act like I wasn't embarrassed about both incidents. "Yeah, well, my suit didn't arrive until this morning."

He nodded. "I see. And what's this little show about?"

"It's not a show," I said defensively. "I felt bad about this morning. I thought it would be a nice gesture is all."

"Not that I don't appreciate the gesture," he paused and tilted his head in my direction, "or the uniform. I just didn't know you were such an exhibitionist."

I almost laughed at the absurdity. "I'm hardly exhibiting anything. Just working on my tan and washing a car. No. Big. Deal."

I didn't want to tell him about the GLL. He'd probably think it was dumb. Plus, I didn't want him to know I'd gotten so boring since my wedding day that I now needed to follow a list just to have a semblance of a personality. Maybe I *wanted* him to think that skinny-dipping in the middle of the day and washing cars in a bikini was just part of my regular routine.

"I'm sorry about earlier," he said. "I'm not really into mornings."

"It's fine. I'm sorry I caused you trouble in the first place."

He shrugged. "I guess if you're gonna cause trouble you should do it naked, right?"

I hoped he thought my cheeks were pink from the sun.

Jake told me he'd be editing photos on his computer for the afternoon and to take the Jeep if I needed it. I decided to take him up on the offer because there was no way I wanted to hang around there and experience any more embarrassing and awkward run-ins with him. Two in one day was more than enough.

After spending a few minutes on Craigslist and Monster, I put on my new interview outfit from H&M and headed out to look for a job. My first stop was an Italian "ristorante" that had posted an ad on Craigslist looking for servers with immediate availability. The restaurant, er, ristorante, didn't open until four so I rang the doorbell per the instructions in the ad.

NOOOOO! No, no, no, no, no! Caroline Ganier answered the door. Caroline Ganier, AKA the bitch who stole my boyfriend during our senior year of high school.

CHAPTER EIGHT

His name was Riley. He was the star goaltender for our champion hockey team. You may remember the story about Winnie-the-Pooh, the guy who took my virginity. That was Riley. He was a master in the net, but a bit of a bore in the bedroom. Not that I minded. I was a high school student, not a porn star. I didn't have anyone to compare him to anyway.

I liked having a hometown hero as a boyfriend. I felt that his popularity raised my worth as a person. During my freshman year, I just kind of blended in. I didn't play any sports. I wasn't in any clubs or the band. I didn't shop at Abercrombie & Fitch. And even though I was really smart, I was too quiet to speak up in class, so no one knew it. No one really knew I existed.

After working on a Social Studies project together at the beginning of our sophomore year, Riley took an interest in me. Suddenly, everyone knew my name. People said hi to me in the halls. I went from being one of the last girls picked when we divided into teams in gym class, to being one of the first, even though I had the athletic ability of a tree slug. I was invited to every party, went to every game, and there was always a seat saved for me at the hockey team's table in the cafeteria – a seat many other girls were dying to sit in, including the Skank Queen, Caroline Ganier.

Go ahead and call me superficial if you haven't done so already, but I liked having friends. I liked being social. I liked having fun on the weekends instead of reading *Sweet Valley High* in my bedroom. When you're in high school, that kind of stuff matters.

We were the royal couple for the next two years. I was in the bleachers cheering him on at every game, including the away games. We went to every dance together and were both on Homecoming court during our junior and senior years. We were totally on our way to the coveted "Cutest Couple" spot in the yearbook.

It was the end of January, the morning of his 18th birthday, and I woke up bright and early and headed over to Riley's house with eighteen helium balloons in the trunk of my POS Buick.

I made a list of seventeen things I loved about him and then cut each item on the list into a little strip of paper about the size of the fortune in a fortune cookie. I put one strip of paper in each of the first seventeen balloons. In the last balloon, the big one that said *Happy Birthday*, I put two tickets to the Incubus concert the following weekend. I filled the balloons using the mini helium tank I'd bought at the party store. Once they were filled with helium I'd tied a string and one of his favorite candy bars to each balloon to weigh it down. It was a lot of work, but I loved every minute of it because it made me feel good to do nice things for people.

My intention was to get into his bedroom before he woke up and set the balloons around his bed so that when he woke up he'd be surrounded by balloons. I'd already made arrangements with his mother to let me into his room that morning.

It was 7:30am when I arrived. I knew nobody who'd been hitting the beer bong with the guys the night before would be up that early. I unloaded the balloons from the car carefully as not to get the strings tangled together. I lightly knocked on the front door. His mom answered right away since she knew I was coming.

I quietly walked up the carpeted staircase to his room, gently turned the knob and pushed the door open softly.

Then I screamed.

Skank Queen herself was in MY boyfriend's bed, tangled up in his sheets with mascara all over her slutty, ugly face and a major case of bed head in her ratty-ass, over-processed, yellow hair. They both sat up when they heard me screaming, and she didn't even attempt to cover herself up. She just sat there in his bed, boobs hanging out in the open, and smirked at me. Not just at me, but also at both of his parents, who had come running upstairs when they heard the commotion and now stood there horrified.

"HAPPY FUCKING BIRTHDAY!" I yelled as I dropped the balloons before running down the stairs and out the door.

Not only was she a ho-bag, but she had a big mouth as well. My phone was flooded with phone calls almost immediately. People were willing to get out of bed early to hear that kind of gossip. I ignored the calls. It was too embarrassing. I couldn't face anyone from school, but there was no way I was going to sit home and sulk while everyone I knew was celebrating that bastard's birthday at his party later. So I packed an overnight bag and headed to Mount Pleasant.

Mount Pleasant is a city a few hours from Ann Arbor, and home of Central Michigan University, where both Adam and Jake were sophomores. Adam decided on Central because they offered him a full scholarship to play for the basketball team. He wasn't really into the sport anymore, but he was good at it and figured it was the best and cheapest way to get his Bachelor's degree so he could move on to med school.

Jake had decided on Central simply because he didn't have the grades, the ambitions, or the money to go to a more scholastic school, and he wasn't ashamed to admit it. Jake was all about the party scene and made no attempt to hide it. He joined a fraternity right away and had been telling me how great their parties were. When he was home on winter break he told me to come hang out and party with him whenever I wanted and I thought a college party was a good way to celebrate my newfound freedom. A one-night-stand would be the best revenge I could get. My goal was to meet a guy who would fuck me senseless and make me forget all about Winnie-the-Pooh and his stupid, skanky honey pot.

I didn't even think to call first. I just got in my mom's car and drove off. When I arrived at the campus a few hours later I used my cell phone, my very first cell phone that I had gotten for Christmas a month before, and called my brother's phone for directions to his apartment.

"Shit," he said when he answered, "I've got a

game in Buffalo tonight. I won't be back on campus until tomorrow."

I gulped in embarrassment as my heart raced with anxiety. Had I driven all this way just to turn around and drive right back?

"Do you know the number to Jake's room?" Adam asked.

Jake didn't have a cell phone yet. It took a few phone calls back and forth with Adam and a few calls to Jake's frat brothers, but I was finally able to reach him. Once I told him where I was he said he'd be there to get me in a minute, no questions asked.

As I sat in my car trying to stay warm, I saw him walking towards the visitor's parking lot. He wore a burgundy baseball cap with a gold letter "C" on it, a navy blue zip-up hoodie with some white Greek letters sewn across the front, and loose fitting jeans. He looked like a typical college frat guy. To a high school senior whose boyfriend was just caught fucking the town tramp, there wasn't a whole lot more enticing than a typical college frat guy. My heart raced again, but it wasn't embarrassment or anxiety this time. I turned the heat off and fanned my face to stop the blush I felt creeping onto my cheeks. *When did Jake get so hot? And why didn't anyone tell me?*

I stepped out of the car when he approached.

"Where's your coat?" he asked.

I shrugged and rubbed my hands up the arms of my wool sweater to keep warm. "I left in a hurry," I explained.

He unzipped his hoodie. "Get in here," he said as he held his jacket open for me.

I put my arms inside the hoodie and wrapped them around his waist. He pulled the jacket around the back of me and held tight. I didn't mean to lose it, but with that one move, he made me feel safe and protected and loved, and I can't explain why, but it made me cry.

He rested his chin on the top of my head and held me tighter. "What did he do to you, Little Girl?" he asked.

I shook my head inside his jacket. If I talked about it, I would cry even harder.

He rubbed his hands up and down my back on the outside of his hoodie, and I let him hold me for a minute (and enjoyed every second immensely, by the way) before I let go of him.

He pulled off his coat. "Here, take this," he said. "I'll get you one for yourself when we get to the house, but wear mine for now."

All he had on underneath was a long sleeve white t-shirt that said Central Michigan Basketball on the front. Aww, he supported his friend. And took care of his friend's little sister too.

I felt bad taking the hoodie from him, but it was so soft and warm and I really was cold; plus, looking at the size of the campus, I had a feeling we were in for a long walk.

He told me there was a visitor's lot closer to his house so we drove there first and then Jake carried my overnight bag on our walk to the frat house. He also took my hand since there was some snow and ice on the ground. It seemed perfectly normal that we would walk across his campus holding hands.

What if? I wondered. I had never before thought of Jake in any romantic kind of way. But what if I did? And what if he thought of me the same way? What if Jake and I were more than just friends? What if I came to Central next year? Would he be this sweet to me then? In case you haven't figured this out yet, I have a tendency to get a little ahead of myself. For a minute I had a montage of images flash through my mind: Jake and I walking to class together hand in hand; Jake and I studying in the library and sneaking kisses in the empty aisles; Jake and I cheering for Adam at a basketball game; Jake and I cuddling on the bed in my dorm room and watching movies; Jake and I doing lots of other things in my dorm room; Jake doing lots of other things with some skanky blonde who wore too much eyeliner and whispering to her, "Please don't tell my girlfriend about this …"

Insert sound of screeching record – this fantasy was over. I let go of his hand and put it to my chest, trying to comfort the heart that had broken for the second time that day. Just the idea of Jake being another Riley was enough for me to know that I could not survive heartbreak like that in real life. Because Jake wasn't Riley. Riley was a fun guy with a good future ahead of him, but I'd never been delusional enough to think I was a part of that future. I'd always known in the back of my mind that Riley was just a high school boyfriend. I was devastated by what he had done, but I knew I could live without him. Jake, on the other hand, was way more important. He wasn't something, or someone, I was willing to lose.

I gave him a quick glance and tried not to look angry. I wasn't crazy enough to be mad at him for something I'd only imagined him doing. But I wasn't dumb enough to let it ever happen either. There were a lot of other guys in this world and a lot of other guys at this school. Jake was off-limits. Not just for tonight. Forever.

My cell phone rang. It was my mom calling. I flipped the phone open, pulled up the antenna (yeah, this was a long time ago) and put the phone to my ear.

"I just talked to Adam," she said hurriedly. "He

said he's in Buffalo!"

"Don't panic, Mom," I said, "Jake's here."

"Is he there right now?"

"Yes."

I heard her exhale the breath she'd probably been holding for awhile. "Put him on."

I handed Jake the phone. "Hey, Mom," he said. He'd been calling my mom "Mom" for as long as I could remember. "Yeah, don't worry about a thing. I've got this."

His fraternity was having a party that night called Get Leid. It was a summer-in-winter themed party where they intended to crank up the heat and give everyone a flower lei at the door ... but that was it. Theme parties were definitely my forte and those boys clearly needed help. I pushed my cheating boyfriend to the back of my mind and made it my personal goal to make sure this was the best party of the year.

Jake and I went to the party store and bought drink umbrellas and frozen daiquiri mix. We got a few beach balls and an abundance of cheap grass skirts and coconut bras for the guys. I made an excellent summer playlist for the DJ including DJ Jazzy Jeff and The Fresh Prince's "Summertime" and "School's Out" by Alice Cooper. I convinced the guys to uncover the gas grill on the back porch and cook up some hot dogs. I dug out a few tiki torches from the shed and lit them in the snow. I even put up the volleyball net in the backyard hoping a few people might drink enough to play. I was right. They did play.

It turned out to be a great night for everyone. Everyone except me! Jake was so worried I'd end up hooking up with one of his fraternity brothers he never let me out of his sight. He knew if that happened he'd have to deal with the wrath of my brother. He followed me around the whole night. Every time I tried to dance with someone, he'd pull me away. Every time I grabbed a drink, he'd dump it out. He even escorted me to the bathroom and stood outside the door to make sure no one came in after me. It wasn't until after 2am when the guests had left and everyone was cleaning up that I was able to sneak in a few drinks.

When we were done cleaning he took me upstairs to his room and locked the door behind us.

"Are you sure you don't wanna put the baby gate up?" I asked sarcastically.

"Huh?"

"You know, since you're my father, and I'm just a child?"

"You're kinda acting like one," he said in an arrogant, unapologetic tone of voice that I immediately hated.

"Well you're *kind of* an asshole!" I said loudly. I looked at his roommate's bed to make sure I didn't wake him and saw that it was empty. Jake must have asked him to stay somewhere else, probably because he was worried the guy would try to have sex with me in the middle of the night. Because apparently every single guy within a ten mile radius was trying to get into my pants, and it was his duty to ward them off.

"What's gotten into *you*?" he asked like he had no idea.

"Nothing, Jake!" I yelled. "Nothing has gotten into me or even near me! Why did you keep telling me to come hang out with you at school if you weren't going to let me have any fun?"

He sat down on his bed and started untying his tennis shoes. "I know how you are. You think everyone is filled with rainbows and glitter. But people around here can be pretty shady. You've seen the after-school specials about frat guys, right? And the Lifetime movies?"

I rolled my eyes at his lame attempt to be funny. "If these people are so bad, why did you tell me to come visit you? What did you think I would do here? Tour the library?"

"I thought you'd have some friends or your boyfriend with you, and I thought your brother would be here. I couldn't send you out there alone. You would have ended up in one of these beds, outside throwing up in the snow or, in the worst case, passed out somewhere with guys jacking off on you."

Okay, that was a gross visual. "Ending up in someone's bed might not have been *that* bad," I said after a moment. "Maybe it's what I wanted." I sat down in his desk chair, crossed my arms and tried to make a mad face.

He laughed.

"What's so funny?"

"The look on your face. It's so funny when you try to look mad. And would you want to be in one of these beds if I told you no one in this house has washed their sheets since September, and there's a different girl's DNA left on them pretty much every week?"

Eww. Maybe not. These people are sick!

"Whatever," I said, rolling my eyes again.

"Is 'whatever' what you say when you know you've lost an argument?"

I didn't answer. He had me. I couldn't very well tell him I would love to contribute my DNA to his dirty friends' bed sheets. That was just sick.

"My roommate is staying at his girlfriend's tonight. He said you could sleep in his bed."

"Ew! Not after what you told me!"

He laughed again. "You can sleep in mine then. I'll even change the sheets for you."

He went over to his dresser where he pulled out a folded sheet from the bottom drawer. "Your mom washed these for me over Christmas break," he told me. "I can still smell the Tide."

My mom was very motherly towards Jake. She always had been. She felt bad for him because his own mom wasn't very, well, motherly. She was a bit of a party animal. She was the kind of person who started drinking as soon as she woke up in the afternoon. She didn't do a lot of laundry.

Jake's parents were teenagers when he was born. They broke up when he was a few months old and had been fighting over him ever since. They didn't fight over him the way most separated parents fought over their kids, though. Most of the time the parents both wanted *more* time with the kids, but in this case, they both wanted *less* time. The fights went like this:

"What do you mean you can't take him this weekend? You promised you'd be here! I have plans!"

"Oh give me a break! I had to keep him two extra days last month and still had to pay you child support! Unless you want to give me some of my money back, you can keep him this weekend."

The reason why I knew about these arguments was because they would often have them in front of other people, including my brother and even Jake.

Jake always acted like such a tough guy and pretended it didn't bother him, but I knew the truth. I'd never forget the first and only time I'd seen him cry. It was Father's Day. I was about eight, which would have made Jake about ten. He had spent both

Friday and Saturday nights at our house which was pretty normal, especially during the summer. His dad, who had gotten married by this time and had two more children that he actually seemed to love, was supposed to pick Jake up from our house on Sunday afternoon to take him to the zoo with his brother and sister. But he never showed up. My mom tried calling him for hours and kept getting his machine. She finally called his mom to come pick him up. I'm not sure what Jake's mom said on the other end, but we could all hear what my mom said on our end, and we knew Jake's mom wasn't coming to pick him up either. It wouldn't have surprised me any if his mom said something along the lines of, "This is Father's Day, the one day a year I'm guaranteed my freedom."

We had a table in our living room back then that was covered in my dad's plants. Some had vines that hung down over the edge of the table and some of the vines nearly reached the floor. That table was a great dark place to hide under during hide-n-seek. It was under that table where I saw Jake that night while my mom was on the phone.

He hugged his knees to his chest and cried; the Father's Day card he'd made for his dad ripped up in pieces on the floor at his feet. It was a quiet cry and he had his face pressed down into his knees, but I could tell he was crying by the way his shoulders shook. I'd seen my brother cry plenty of times as a child, but Jake seemed tough and strong, and even though I should have moved on and acted like I never saw a thing, I was so surprised that I froze for a minute and gawked. That was when he lifted his head up and saw me looking at him. He stared at me for a minute with his big, brown eyes bloodshot and wet with tears. I couldn't just walk away after that so

I crawled under the table with him and held his hand. "It's okay, Jake," I whispered. "I can ask my mom to take us to the zoo next weekend if you want."

He didn't say anything or even acknowledge that he'd heard me. He just cried even harder. So I let go of his hand, put my arm around his shoulder, pulled him toward me and let him cry.

My mom found us a little while later and she, too, crawled under the table.

"You know you're always welcome here," she told him as she patted his knee. "Now let's get out from under here, you two. Dad wants pizza!"

It's funny how certain memories stay with a person. I didn't remember a whole lot about my life as an eight-year-old, and Jake and I never spoke of it, but I didn't think I'd ever forget that Father's Day. It was the first time I'd ever felt real love for someone that wasn't related to me.

Even at his frat house ten years later I still had a soft spot for Jake, and it was hard to stay mad at him, especially when he was willing to make a bed for me at almost four in the morning. I sat at his desk and watched him pull the old DNA-covered sheets off his bed and put the clean ones on. When he finished, I yawned, stood up and stretched my arms over my head.

And that was when he walked over and kissed me. It was so unexpected and happened so fast. One second he was at his bed, and the next second he had crossed the room and his lips were on mine. It's hard to make a move like that and get it just right. Usually the guy ends up missing the target or smashing teeth to teeth. Or the girl ends up choking on bubblegum and needs life-saving maneuvers. This, though, was *just right*. It was the perfect amount of sexy mixed with the perfect amount of sweet. Since my arms had already been over my head at the time, he put his hands on them and gently pushed them against the wall behind us. I don't know if it was all the crying I'd done earlier, or the fact that I'd been awake for almost a whole day, or the two plastic cups of beer I'd stolen from the keg when no one was looking, but I suddenly felt weak and dizzy. It was like I was falling. When he ran his tongue along my bottom lip I felt like I was falling off a cliff and never hitting the bottom. In two years Riley had never, ever made me feel that way.

But then Jake pulled away. and it felt like a crash landing. He put his hands to his head and grabbed onto a few clumps of his hair like he was frustrated. "Shit, Rox," he said. "I'm sorry. You're just so cute when you try to look mad."

I was still so dizzy from his kiss that I couldn't figure out how to form words. I just stared at him with what was probably a deer-in-the-headlights look.

He took a deep breath and let it out slowly, his hands now clasped behind his head. "I'm gonna sleep downstairs. Make sure you lock the door behind me, okay?"

He walked out the door. I was pretty disappointed he didn't stay, but when I remembered the pain I'd felt earlier when I imagined him betraying me and breaking my heart, I knew he did the right thing by leaving. Because if he had kept kissing me like that, there was no way I could have said no to him.

The next morning Mom called and woke me up bright and early. There was a winter storm on the way and she wanted me to leave early so I'd be home safe and sound before it started snowing. I was headed out the front door of the frat house when Jake called to me from the couch in the living room.

"Roxie?"

I turned around. "Yeah?"

He sat up and yawned. His blanket fell down and exposed his tattooed chest. I'd never been a huge fan of tattoos before, but he really made them look good. Think Justin Timberlake in *Alphadog,* but with darker hair. Smokin'!

"Are you leaving?" he asked.

"No," I said, my voice dripping with sarcasm. "I'm going outside to build a snowman." I smiled to let him know I was only teasing.

He stretched his arms and yawned again. "Let me buy you a coffee first. You can't get on the road without caffeine."

I could have gotten my own coffee, but I didn't argue. We walked to a coffee shop on campus. It was kind of weird. The silence between us seemed to magnify the other sounds around us, like the sounds of our feet crunching into the snow.

When we got into the café he ordered two coffees and we sat down in a booth. He looked tired. His eyes were bloodshot and he had his hood pulled up on his head because his hair was a disaster, but he still looked damn good to me. Seriously, when did he get this hot, and how did I not notice?

"So what do we have to do to make this not weird?" he asked.

I smiled at him. I love a guy who gets right to the point and doesn't bullshit. "In the movies we'd probably go outside and get into a snowball fight to cut the tension. There would be a montage of scenes of us falling into the snow and laughing together ..." I paused as I thought about it. "But it's too cold for that shit."

He grinned.

"It's not weird," I told him with a shrug. "Shit happens. People get drunk and make out sometimes. It's fine."

"I didn't have a single drink last night."

"Oh," I paused, surprised. "That explains a lot."

"Explains what?"

"Why you were so annoying. A few drinks would have done you some good."

"Yeah, probably."

"But really, it's not weird. I'm glad you kissed me."

"You are?"

"Yeah. I was hoping to get laid at the Get Leid party. I thought it would make me feel better about Riley. So I'm glad I got at least a kiss. I kind of think you owe me a lot more than that for twat-blocking me all night."

He actually choked on his coffee. "I can't believe you just said twat-blocking."

We both giggled.

"I guess I'll have to take a rain check," I told him with a wicked grin.

I could tell he thought I was kidding, but I wasn't sure I was. A relationship was out of the question … but maybe, just maybe, we could pull off a one-night-stand someday. A girl could dream.

CHAPTER NINE

Caroline Ganier stood in front of me in her stupid, ugly cardigan sweater with a nametag that said "Skank Queen, Ristorante Manager." Okay, it didn't really say that. The Skank Queen part anyway. And if they were going to use the Italian word for restaurant, why didn't they also use the Italian word for manager? I hated the place immediately.

There was no way I could tell her I was there to apply for a job. That would be a ten on the mortification scale. Standing there and shitting my pants in front of her would have been less embarrassing than asking her for a job. Yet, there I was ringing the doorbell before hours wearing a nice pantsuit and holding a manila folder on the very day a wanted ad was listed on Craigslist. What the hell else would I be there for?

"Roxie Humsucker," she said (Yes, that's my maiden name. Can you see why I was in such a hurry to change it?). With a smirk on her face not unlike the one I saw when I caught her in my boyfriend's bed more than ten years ago, she leaned on the doorframe, crossed her arms and raised her chin up. She looked seriously entertained, and I wanted so badly to punch her in her stupid, ugly face!

I am known for my quick-thinking skills. But it's a total fake-out. The reason people think I'm a quick thinker is because I prepare so extensively for every situation I can think *of.* I make it seem like I'm a quick-thinker, but really, a lot of thought goes into nearly everything I do. But this, this I was not expecting in any part of my imagination. I have to say, though, that for being put on the spot like that, I was impressed with the way I handled the situation.

"Hey there ... *you,*" I said, purposely not using her name so she would think I forgot it even though it was on her nametag. "I'm so glad someone's here. I just ran over on my lunch break because I heard you guys do catering for large groups."

She gave a sly grin like she didn't buy the story. "Yes, we do catering. You didn't have to come in person though. We have the menu and prices on the website. You can order it online too."

"Yes," I said, thinking fast, "but this is kind of last minute so I wanted to do it in person. I'm in a jam and I need it this Thursday. Will that be possible?"

"Of course. For how many people?"

"Thirty," I said quickly.

Damnit! Why didn't I say twenty?

Several hundred dollars later, as I was walking back to Jake's Jeep, the only positive thing I could think of was that this would make a really funny story someday. Oh, and that she's not aging well.

I got back into the Jeep and blasted the A/C. That incident was a serious blow to my self-worth, not to mention my dwindling bank account. My overall outlook on life took a major nose dive. I couldn't continue to job search after suffering such a blow. Job applicants needed to be oozing with confidence, not pouting over a bad memory and a mean girl.

I was starting to think moving back here had been a bad idea. I'd only been home two days and already these people and events from my past were trying to bring me down. What happened to the last ten years I'd spent maturing into a classy and confident woman? All it took was an old rival with bad hair and suddenly it was like I was back in high school again with a head filled with silly, childish insults. I mean, yes, her hair could use some serious professional help, and that turquoise eye shadow didn't work with her skin tone whatsoever, but that's no reason for me to call her a stupid, ugly face. It was her personality that made her ugly, and if I stooped down to her level, I would be just as bad.

In one of the classes I took in college, we discussed the problems criminals faced once they were released from prison after an extended period of time behind bars. I don't remember the exact wording of this theory, but it was something about how their minds stopped maturing when they entered prison. If they went in at twenty and were released at forty, their minds were still mentally age twenty. They ended up socially inept and were unable to develop mature relationships with people their own age. This usually resulted in them returning to their lives of crime. Or looking like total pervs trying to date women twenty years younger.

Now I wondered, was this similar to what happened to me? Was my marriage a prison? Am I now being released from incarceration with the maturity level and mental capacity of a twenty-two year old? Am I socially inept?

I had a lot to think about. I needed to go somewhere where I could find some clarity and peace of mind and do some serious soul-searching, which is how I ended up sitting at the water fountain in the mall sipping on a frozen Coke. I know how bad sodas are but I wasn't concerned with calories anymore. First, a brutal I-don't-love-you announcement from my husband, followed by memories of several breakups from the past coming back to haunt me, all in a few days time. I was done. Over it. It wouldn't bother me one bit if I got all bloated on soda, filled my closet with unshapely muumuus, grew a beard and adopted a dozen cats.

Oh, speaking of the boyfriend … after Riley took Skank Queen to the Incubus concert *I'd* bought him tickets for, he was recruited by a Big Ten college hockey team and given a full athletic scholarship. He spent most of his freshman year on the bench as the back-up goaltender. Rumor had it he was destined to be the starter the following year once the current starter graduated, but the rumor never had a chance to turn into reality because he got in a car accident that summer and suffered a career-ending injury to his knee. I'm not proud to admit this, but Allison and I threw a killer party the night we found out. Karma had come back around and smacked Riley on the butt real good. Now I was starting to wonder if Miss Karma was after my ass, too, probably because we threw the party in the first place.

I didn't go to the mall to shop. I thought I could people-watch for a bit and maybe see some people who had it worse than I did to help put things into perspective. It was always easy to do that in New York where there were less fortunate people all over the place. But everyone looked pretty happy to be in a suburban shopping mall in the middle of a weekday. The teeny-boppers were giddy as they walked past me, proudly carrying tiny pink bags from Victoria's Secret. These girls were like junior-high age. I know it's off topic, but my daughters, if I ever have any, will NOT shop at Victoria's Secret until they have graduated from high school!

The couple who looked to be in their sixties looked pretty happy, too, as they slowly walked hand in hand. Even the group of three middle-aged ladies in full-out exercise gear who were walking swinging-arms-style looked happy.

Once the frozen drink started to make my teeth hurt, I was about to give up and go home. And then I saw a Sephora!

This was the part of my movie where the clouds parted and a beam of light shone down on me.

I just *had* to go in and try on some turquoise eye shadow to see if I could rock that color with *my* skin tone. It looked pretty good on me, and I really wanted to buy it, especially since there was a free gift with purchase. Ahhh, the free gift with purchase had gotten me so many times in the past. But I was supposed to be different now. I didn't know who I was without Caleb just yet. I didn't know who the Michigan Roxie would become or even if I wanted to be a Michigan Roxie at all. But I knew I couldn't be the New York Roxie and only a New York Roxie would spend $20 on one eye shadow color.

Then I remembered the Good Life List. One of the tasks was to go to a department store and create a divorce registry. I shrugged and headed towards Macy's. It was as good a time as any.

The young salesgirl looked seriously confused when I asked.

"We have a wedding registry and a baby

registry," she told me. "But no divorce registry. I've never heard of such a thing." She scrunched up her face like she thought a divorce registry was a bad idea.

Oh, what do you know anyway? What are you, like fifteen? Wait until you're in my shoes before you judge, you little bitch!

She pointed me in the direction of the registry kiosk and told me to come back for a scanner when I was ready.

I hit the wedding button on the screen since I wasn't going to be registering for baby bottles and bibs. When it asked for the groom's name I typed in Dick Microphallus at 123 Douchebag Avenue. I believe I just proved a theory – a person coming from a failed marriage really was like a newly released prisoner. I was now basically twenty-two again. Hmm, that might not be so bad!

I spent the next hour and a half registering for everything I would need to build a new home for myself. I registered for kitchen appliances, bath coordinates, wall art, candles. Nothing overpriced and extravagant either, just the basic stuff. I didn't expect anyone to buy me a divorce gift, but it was a good way for me to keep track of what I still needed to set up a home of my own. And it was also a good way to remind me that being single meant being able to make all the decisions, and that wasn't such a bad thing.

When I was done picking out stuff for my future home, I decided to have some fun with it. I took my scanner to the lingerie department. I didn't think anyone would ever see the registry anyway – unless Hope did a search to check up on me. And in that case, I should make her proud, right?

I had a pretty good time in there. It was a relief

being able to pick things out on my own for a change. When Caleb and I had done our wedding registry, it had been one argument after another.

"No rubber duck décor in the bathroom. We're not Bert and Ernie."
"Why do we need eight towels for two people? How often do you plan on doing laundry?"
"I don't care if proceeds go to breast cancer research. We are not getting a pink toaster."
"What do you need a stand-up mixer for? You're not exactly Betty Crocker."

Ugh. He really knew how to suck the fun out of everything.

Good thing I had a friend like Hope. She knew what she was doing when she made the Good Life List. I came to the mall feeling miserable, but by the time I left I had some pep to my step.

When I got home I saw Jake sitting at the patio table with his laptop. I figured he was editing photos, and headed out there to tell him his Jeep was home. I was about halfway out the patio doors when I saw his laptop screen and realized he wasn't editing pictures after all. On his screen I saw a picture of a woman wearing nothing but black fishnet thigh-highs.

Seriously? Stop the madness! Reverse the curse! Why must I stumble upon one mortifying moment after another like I'm stuck in some terrible slapstick comedy? I didn't know who was in charge of this mess, but I was starting to get really pissed off! If I was on some kind of hidden camera show, it was time for the reveal already.

"I'm sorry," I said quickly. "I didn't mean to …

um, interrupt." I put my head down to avoid eye contact and tried to escape back into the house but he called after me.

"Hey!" he called. "You're not interrupting anything."

I shrugged and avoided his eyes. "It looks like I am."

He looked puzzled for a few moments until he glanced at the computer screen and realized what I was talking about. Then he burst into laughter. He laughed so hard he could barely even speak.

"You (snicker) thought (giggle) I was (snort) ... Oh God. That's great, Roxie. Thanks for the laugh."

I just stood there like a dumbass. I didn't know what the hell was going on.

"Hey," he said. "*I'm* not the exhibitionist here."

He doubled over in laughter. It took him several minutes to compose himself, and then he motioned at the patio chair across from him for me to sit. I sat.

"This," he said, pointing to the picture on his screen of the woman in fishnets, "is a boudoir photograph." He sounded like a professor giving a lecture. "It's a style of photography that shows women in various stages of undress. It's supposed to be elegant and tasteful, not pornographic."

"I see."

"It's gotten pretty popular lately. Women have been getting these done to give as gifts to their husbands and boyfriends. I'm hoping to start doing some boudoir work myself so that's why I was looking at these. To get some ideas."

Yep. I felt like an ass. But what else was new? "Gosh, I'm so sorry," I practically stuttered. "I feel so stupid." I could literally feel my cheeks burning.

He sighed, closed the laptop screen, crossed his arms on the table in front of him and leaned forward like he had something important to say. "I think we need to throw some snowballs around, Rox."

"What do you mean?" I asked.

"All of this weirdness and tension and excessive apologizing. If we need to hash something out, let's do it and move on."

All this time I'd thought he might not remember anything about *The Summer of Jake and Roxie* – like maybe he drank so much that summer that it was a three month long blackout. I know that sounds silly, but sometimes when something goes unmentioned for so long it seems like the other person forgot about it. But the comment about the snowballs told me otherwise.

Back then I kept things inside. When my feelings were hurt or I doubted myself and felt inadequate, I kept those feelings and insecurities inside, which sometimes caused me to do things I shouldn't do. When someone hurt me, I would either withdraw from them completely or do something to hurt them in return. This usually left the other person confused since they didn't know they'd hurt me to begin with and didn't understand where my behavior was coming from. It was all very immature – I knew this now. But I didn't think it was all that uncommon, especially for people that age.

The first time we "threw some snowballs" was shortly after we started hooking up. We were at work, and I saw some girl at the bar give Jake her phone number. Jake smiled and looked at her appreciatively and I didn't like it, especially being so fresh out of a relationship with a guy who had been lying to me the entire time we were together. I had some issues, that was for sure.

Instead of just saying to Jake, "Dude, that is not cool," I started serving lemons to one of the guys in my section with my mouth. Once the bar closed, I told Jake I didn't need a ride home because the guy was taking me to an after party.

"Dude, that is not cool," he said, as we both sat at the bar counting out our banks. "Instead of getting a ride home from one of the girls and pretending you went to an after-hours just to piss me off, how 'bout we throw some snowballs around right now?"

Jake is different than me in that way. He's not afraid to say what he thinks or what he feels or what he wants. And he has a way of completely taking control of a situation with his bluntness. There I was thinking I was the one in charge, and I was really going to show him to flirt with other girls. And then he called me out on it and knocked out my whole plan. Typical.

"What are you talking about?" I asked with an eye roll. "There's no snow."

"It's an expression. One that you made up a few years ago, remember? When things get weird we're supposed to have a snowball fight. So let me hear it. What's the issue here?"

"There's no issue," I said quietly. My anger started to melt away. How many guys remember something that was said one time like five years ago? Not too many.

"We will talk about the issue when *I* drive *you* home tonight."

"Fine."

It took a little while, but he eventually broke me down and got me to admit that seeing him flirt with that girl bothered me, and I'd only been trying to get him back by doing some flirting of my own. He nodded like he completely understood. That's one thing I always liked about him. Even though he was different than me, he tried to see things from my perspective. He didn't make me feel like an annoying, psycho, jealous girlfriend.

"I work for tips," he said patiently. "If a girl is tipping me well, even if a *guy* is tipping me well, I'm gonna flirt a little. That's what bartenders do. You need to get it in your head that it's just part of my job. I know you're doing the same thing out on the floor."

I nodded.

"This can't turn into anything messy," he said. "We've been friends too long to screw it up over some dumb shit. I'm telling you right now that my intentions are not to hurt you, piss you off, screw you over, or anything like that. I just like being with you, Roxie. And I'm not gonna like you any less if you tell me what's on your mind. If you ever have something to say, say it. If there's something you want to know, ask me. If you're mad about something, tell me. It doesn't have to be complicated."

"Okay."

"No mind-games, no secrets, no lies. Promise me."

"Promise," I said.

From that point on, there wasn't any drama between us – unless we created it on purpose, which we did on occasion just to spice things up. Like the one time he caught me in the beer cooler.

One of the guys in my section that night had asked if he could do a shot out of my cleavage. Since he was drunk, and giving me $20 for each shot, I let him. Then his whole group of friends decided they wanted a body shot, too. I knew Jake was watching from the bar, but I figured it was okay since we'd already had the conversation about flirting for tips.

When the group left and the crowd started to thin out, I went into the beer cooler. I liked to stock the bar for Jake at night so we could get out earlier.

I was about to grab a case of Miller Lite when I heard the door open and felt him come up behind me. He pushed me up against the boxes, not forcefully, but firmly. He put his hands on my hips and his mouth really close to my ear.

"Are you trying to make me jealous?" he asked. His voice sounded rough and a little jaded, nothing like the sweet and patient tone I was used to. And I kind of liked it. More than kind of, really. It was hot.

"Maybe," I answered playfully. "Is it working?"

"I don't care what you do out there," he whispered into my ear, "because I know I'm the one who gets to fuck you when we get out of here."

He pulled my hips back into him and kissed the back of my neck.

"Do I have to wait that long?" I asked innocently. "Can't you fuck me right here? Just like this?"

I heard him gasp. "You're being naughty tonight."

He moved away from me just long enough to turn the lock on the door and then he was behind me again.

"I like it," he said as he tugged my little black shorts down to my knees.

I never even noticed it was cold in there.

Thinking about that night while I sat across from him at the patio table made me so hot that I looked over at the pool and thought about jumping in. I wondered if Jake noticed the color that crept onto my face or the beads of sweat that appeared on my forehead. Could he hear the sound of my heart pounding?

I was too afraid to look at him, afraid that I would give myself away, and he would know that I'd never gotten over him. I didn't want to be the one who cared more. No one ever wants to be the one who cares more.

I already made it clear that our sex life was stellar, but there was more to it than that. After our first snowball fight, when he told me his intentions, things were easier.

Being able to be honest all the time was a whole new way of life for me and I loved it. Saying what was on my mind without fear of judgment was so liberating. I don't think most people realize how much we keep to ourselves, either because we're afraid of what people might think, or we're afraid of hurting them.

Jake gave me the freedom to be me and he *still* wanted to hang out with me, which I thought was pretty cool. He made me feel comfortable and confident. If only every relationship could be that easy. Unfortunately, when you're that age, most of them are not. I was one of the lucky ones. For a little while anyway.

Just the thought of a snowball fight made me realize once again how much I had changed since I'd met Caleb. In the last few years I had stopped being honest, with other people as well as with myself. It was going to be hard for me to open up again. Opening up to someone would put me in a very vulnerable position, and that was scary. But Jake had never disrespected me, intentionally hurt me or made me feel like I didn't matter, so I was willing to give it a try. I was willing to trust him because I remembered how simple life had been as an open person and I wanted to get back to that simplicity.

"I can tell you're uncomfortable being here," Jake said.

I cleared my throat. "I'm sorry. My life has been turned upside-down in the past week. I'm not sure I feel comfortable with anything right now."

"Stop apologizing. That's what I'm talking about. It's weird."

I picked at the cuticles around my fingernails and avoided his eyes. "Okay."

He didn't say anything for a few moments. Eventually I looked up to find him staring at me like he was waiting for me to speak again.

"What?" I asked innocently.

"Are you gonna tell me?"

"Tell you what?"

"What the deal is. Why you're acting so weird."

"I thought I just did!"

He shook his head. "Come on," he coaxed. "Tell me the truth. What's happening in that head?"

I concentrated on my cuticles so I didn't have to look at him. And then I gave in. What did I have to lose?

I took a deep breath and began. "That day I got here, it wasn't a good morning for me," I started. "Leaving New York, not knowing what was going to happen to me. I was scared."

He nodded.

"But when you told me you bought me Cinnamon Toast Crunch, I felt so much better. You made me feel – I don't know – taken care of, I guess. Like you were trying to protect me and I thought that was really nice of you. Then I hugged you, but you didn't hug me back, and I got the idea that you didn't want me here."

"I understand," he said patiently. "I'm glad I was able to make you feel better. It was my intention. You caught me off guard with the hug but I didn't mean to make you feel unwelcome. I would definitely rather you were here with us than there with him."

"Why?" I asked.

He shrugged. "We don't need to get into it because it's not my business. But I *am* glad you're here. Even though we haven't talked in a long time, I've still got your back, okay?"

OMG! Is he the best or what? "Thanks."

"Do you want a redo on the hug?"

I laughed. "No. But since we're being honest, please don't pat me on the head ever again. It made me feel like a dog."

"Got it. So how'd the job search go?" he asked.

I leaned back into my chair and sighed. "Not great."

"Why not?"

"I went to apply at this little Italian place off South Main and you won't believe who the manager is there."

"Caroline Ganier," he said matter-of-factly.

"You knew that!" It was more of an accusation than a question.

"Yes," he said, as if I should have known he knew that. "I work right down the street. I pretty much know who works at every bar and restaurant down there."

I rested my chin in my hand. "I guess I'll ask you next time then," I said quietly.

"What happened? Did she see you?"

"Yeah! She was the one who answered the door."

"Oh man. What did you do?"

"I pretended I was there because I needed an event catered."

He nodded and looked impressed. "Nice."

"Yeah. So I hope you have a lot of friends. We're having fettuccine and lasagna for thirty people on Thursday."

CHAPTER TEN

Wednesday morning brought the moving truck with all the belongings I'd "won" in my discussions with Caleb. I'd also gotten the dining room table and chairs, the bistro set and patio furniture, and some nice artwork, but those had stayed behind to "stage" the condo. Caleb would eventually be taking the bedroom and living room furniture, and that was fine with me. They were ugly and boring anyway. I'd always thought so.

Jake woke up early (again) and helped me move all of the boxes up to my room. Just the shoes alone filled up twelve boxes! He put all of the incidental stuff, like my non-pink kitchen appliances, in the basement.

I made him breakfast to thank him for his help. We didn't have much in the house so I made him an omelet with bacon and Kraft cheese slices. It was probably the lamest thing I'd ever made in my life, but he acted like it was prime rib.

"You act like no one has ever made you breakfast before," I said. Then I felt stupid for opening my mouth because I was pretty sure his parents' versions of cooking breakfast consisted of pouring milk into a cereal bowl, and I hadn't heard anything about him having any serious girlfriends who might have cooked for him either. Jake didn't do relationships. He never had. He stuck to one-night-stands and quick flings instead. I was pretty sure the only reason he hooked up with me for so long that summer was because he knew there was a definite end. I'm no shrink, but my guess is he has a fear of intimacy and some abandonment issues as a result of the way his parents treated him.

"Not since your parents moved out," he said with a mouthful. "They were the only ones who ever cooked for me."

I poured myself another cup of coffee and sat down across from him at the island. "In that case I feel bad for not making you something better. Once we get to the grocery store I can make you all kinds of good stuff."

"Yeah? Let's go then."

I laughed.

"No, really, it's still early. Let's go out. We can look at some used car lots and go grocery shopping. We'll make a day of it."

Hmm, a whole day with Jake. That could very easily turn in to a whole day of blushing and stuttering and acting a fool ... or it could turn out to be a pretty good time. I decided to take my chances. Because that's what Michigan Roxie does.

First, we bought a car. I mean, *I* bought a car. Look at me using the "we" word like we're a couple. What's up with that?

It's nothing fancy. Just an older Chevy Malibu. Thanks to the income of my not-yet-ex-husband, I was approved for a used car loan immediately, and everything was pretty simple. I would just pay it off once my divorce settlement came through.

Then we went to the grocery store – AKA Meijer. It had been years since I'd done any major grocery shopping. In New York I always had groceries delivered. That sounded strange to non-New Yorkers, but it's pretty common there. Imagine carrying fifteen grocery bags on the subway or throwing them in the back of a cab and trying to carry them up to an apartment. Even if the apartment had an elevator and a doorman like ours did, it was still a huge pain in the ass when you've got milk and soda and other heavy items. If I only needed a few things I would go to a market, but for the heavy duty shopping, it was delivered.

Another thing different about Manhattan shopping is that there aren't any gigantic all-in-one mass merchandisers like Wal-Mart, Meijer, Target, etc. If you needed shampoo or Tylenol, you went to a drug store. If you needed lunch meat, you went to a deli. Bread – bakery. Produce – Farmer's market. And so on.

Walking into Meijer for the first time in many years was an experience. They had groceries, of course, but also toys, home goods, appliances, a nail salon, a hair salon, a fast-food restaurant, a deli, a bakery, a bank and even an auto department. An auto department in the grocery store! The whole thing blew my mind.

Jake thought it was funny I was so excited to be at Meijer. He also thought it was crazy to have groceries delivered.

"So you just call them up and read them your

list?"

"No, I ordered online. It's easier than talking on the phone. A lot of people speak broken English there," I told him. "Hey! Let's go to the toy department before the groceries!"

"Sure."

"I, um, I'm looking for a hula hoop." GLL Challenge #12 – Go into a toy store and hula hoop in the aisle for one full minute.

Jake didn't seem to think it was weird at all when I picked up the hula hoop but I made an excuse for it just in case.

"I heard about a new hula hoop workout that's supposed to get rid of love handles," I told him. "I'm not sure if I still know how to do this though."

I stepped into the hula hoop and wished I had chosen to complete this particular challenge when I was at the store by myself but I couldn't get this far and quit.

"I need to do this for a least one minute to see results," I told Jake. "Can you time me?"

"Yeah, I have a timer on my phone."

He leaned against the display on the aisle's end-cap and looked at his phone. *Perfect,* I thought. If he's looking at his phone, he's not looking at me.

Well, here goes nothing.

And I did it. I rocked that hula hoop! I felt a bit silly for the first ten seconds or so but after that, I started having fun. Being silly *was* fun.

Jake thought it was hilarious. He didn't even tell me when my minute was up because he said he was having so much fun watching me.

A little girl who was about eight came around the corner with her mom who looked about my age. When they saw me hula-hooping they decided to do it too. Then Jake said, "What the hell?" and picked up a hula hoop himself.

I've never had so much fun in a grocery store before. Thanks, Hope!

Thursday was the day of my catered "event." I'd decided to pick up the food and take it over to Allison's. I figured we could feed her family of five – three times – plus take some home for me, Jake, and Adam, and that would pretty much take care of it.

Was I ever surprised when I got to Allison's and found almost thirty people there! Well, there weren't that many, but Allison had rounded up about a dozen girls we went to high school with to throw me a surprise divorce party, which had been coordinated by Hope.

I saw these girls on social network sites all the time. I knew practically everything about their lives. I knew every time they took a nap in the middle of the afternoon, every time they bought a new handbag on their lunch breaks, and every time their husbands brought home flowers. I knew how wide their cervixes got when they went into labor, what they made for dinner and exactly how many minutes they spent at the gym each week. I mean, I knew everything. But I still didn't consider them my friends because I hadn't actually spoken to them in years. I was so surprised and touched that they came out to support me.

We ate Italian food first. Then Allison showed me the scavenger hunt Hope had put together for the night. It was going to be a competition to see which girl could get me the most phone numbers or introduce me to the most guys. It was just for fun. I definitely wasn't ready to start dating. But it was better than hanging out at home by myself.

Hope sent an outfit to Allison's house that I was

supposed to wear. It was a glittery halter top and a miniskirt so short it looked more like a thick belt. She also sent a temporary tattoo that said "Bad Kitty" which Allison applied to my cleavage. The tattoo I could deal with, but that skirt ... *um hell no.*

When I went into the bathroom to change into my outfit, I called Hope to protest.

"What are you wearing?" she asked when she picked up. Not even a hello.

"See, um, that's the thing," I said cautiously. "I really love it that you put this whole thing together for me. But, um, you're not supposed to wear miniskirts past the age of twenty-five."

"Uh huh," she said, "and who told you that?"

"I read it in a magazine."

"Was it the same magazine that claims to have discovered a hot new sex act on the cover of every issue and every month it ends up being something we've been doing since junior high?"

"Yeah. That magazine."

"You know I'd never make you look bad, girl. And remember, I'm in charge here. So stop arguing and put it on."

I sighed reluctantly and bit my lip. I really did want to be *that girl* again; the girl who wore a miniskirt as easily as a pair of sweatpants. I just wasn't sure I could.

"A few drinks from now and you'll feel like the hottest chick in the bar," she told me. "Until then, you're gonna have to fake it. Pretend you are confident and the confidence will come. Go on. Try it. Tell yourself you're the sexiest and most confident woman in Allison's house and watch how your whole attitude changes. Do it right now. For ten seconds. I'll count."

"Okay." I closed my eyes and did as she said. I

had to admit she was definitely on to something. Within those ten seconds I felt my chin rise and my shoulders push back as I stood up a little straighter. *Hmm, maybe this could work.*

I opened my eyes and saw that the face staring back at me from the mirror looked less scared and timid than it had a minute ago. I might be able to do this belt-as-a-skirt thing.

"Allison will be texting me pics all night," Hope warned me, "and they better be good ones."

"I got this," I said. And I believed it.

Hope's pep-talk experiment, along with the sangria that Allison served during dinner, helped me get the outfit *on,* but there was no way I was going without my underwear. I mean, at least until I had a few more drinks in me.

When the girls asked where I wanted to go I said The Bar because it was a mellow place to hang out and have some drinks and those were the kinds of bars I felt most comfortable in. Even though I've worked in a few of them, I'm not much of a bar person and I'm *definitely* not a club person. The Bar does have a dance floor and a DJ on weekends, but it's mostly just a place to chill out and have some beers with your friends or watch a game and have some wings – if you're into that kind of thing. I'm not. The sports I mean. Not the wings. Who doesn't love wings? Yum.

Last time I hung out in a bar for recreational purposes was in college. I hated it even then because I always seemed to be dressed incorrectly. If everyone was wearing denim skirts and white tube tops, I was wearing black. If everyone else was wearing black, I'd be in the denim skirt and white tube top. When everyone else had on heels, I was in sandals. When everyone was wearing sandals, I had on heels. It was pretty much guaranteed that I would be behind on the trends. By the time I figured out what was "in," it was already on its way out. It's not that I wanted to be like everyone else, I just didn't want to be so different from everyone else.

I could still remember the last time I was in a bar in Ann Arbor. It was the end of *The Summer of Jake and Roxie*. I was getting ready to start my senior year at UNC, and my friends from high school were all leaving for their respective schools. We had a bar-hopping going away party. I could still remember the inadequacy I felt when I showed up at the bar to see all the other girls had their hair pulled into high, bouncy ponytails (mine was down), faded jeans (mine were a dark wash), and one of those really long sweaters everyone wore back then that looked like a trench coat (I had on a tank top because – hello – it was summer). Where was the memo about the long sweaters, and why was I not on the mailing list? And what was it with girls wearing sweaters in summer and tank tops in winter?

Later on that evening, we moved to a karaoke bar and three of the girls put in a slip for the exact same song without knowing it ("Redneck Woman" by Gretchen Wilson). Like a parody in a satirical film, each one performed the song as if she was a hot country star on a world tour – complete with hip swaying, hair flipping and coy smiles at the audience. There were even a few winks involved. Maybe it was the lemon drop shot I'd just swallowed, but the whole scene was nauseating. If any of those girls ever went down south and saw what a *real* redneck was, they would not be acting like it was a cute thing.

We had ended our barhopping at The Bar and when Jake got off work, he drove my drunken ass to an empty parking lot by the airport so we could be alone on our last night together. I told him I was happy to go back to North Carolina because being around all of the clones in Ann Arbor was starting to give me a complex.

"Did you notice that every girl I was with had on a sweater except me?" I asked him.

"No," he said, thoughtfully. "I didn't notice anyone except you."

I didn't need to worry about being the outcast at my divorce party though. I finally fit in after all these years. Just about every other woman at The Bar was wearing a miniskirt. And mine was on the longer side compared to the others. I'm pretty sure I saw a couple of tampon strings.

Surprisingly enough, the fact that I looked like everyone else didn't make any difference to my inferiority complex. I still felt awkward for at least the first hour. But Jake kept giving me drinks, and pretty soon my panties were in my purse and I was leaning over the bar to tell him I wasn't wearing anything under my skirt.

"I see you haven't changed any," he said with a crooked smile, as he poured shots on the bar.

It was a simple statement, but it meant a lot to me because it meant Hope's experiment worked. She said I had to fake it. If Jake thought I was still the person he used to know, I was doing a good job. There might be hope for me after all because I felt fabulous. Or maybe that was the alcohol talking.

In one night I accomplished: GLL Challenge #8 – Wear a miniskirt in public with no underwear on; GLL Challenge #9 – Tell someone (preferably someone you're attracted to) that you're not wearing any underwear; GLL Challenge #20 – Get drunk; and

#24 – Make out with a stranger. I don't even remember his name. I'm not sure I ever knew it.

Even though The Bar didn't have karaoke, that didn't stop me from screaming, I mean singing, Pink's "So What" loud enough to be heard over the music from the jukebox. My friends joined in right away and then a few girls from the other end of the bar started singing with us. That was Challenge #18 – Start a sing-a-long in public, and get at least one other person, a stranger, to sing along.

I also crossed off #2 – Get thrown out of a bar. Even though I wasn't escorted out, Jake *did* cut me off at one point, and that's basically the same thing, right?

Things were a bit blurry after that. I vaguely remembered Jake asking if I was making out with guys to make him jealous. He said it with a smile, though, so I would know he was teasing me.

"Do I even have the ability to make you jealous anymore?" I asked. At least that's what I think I said.

I'm pretty sure he answered by saying, "You'll always be able to make me jealous, Little Girl." But, thanks to the alcohol, I can't be sure. Maybe I dreamt it.

I honestly don't remember a whole lot more than that. It's probably best if I don't.

I got pretty lonely after the divorce party. With the kids out of school for the summer, Allison had her hands full, and I had trouble dealing with the noise and commotion over there. Adam practically lived at the hospital. Jake was around for small pockets of time but he was usually on his computer working on his pictures and marketing his business.

I was supposed to be looking for a job, but I still felt scarred from the Skank Queen incident, and so I focused on volunteering to help others instead. I fulfilled GLL Challenge #25 by volunteering at a homeless shelter. I washed sheets and made beds and also donated a bunch of my expensive beauty products to the homeless women. I hoped to go a few times a month.

Even though it wasn't on the GLL, I'd also gone to Big Brothers and Big Sisters of America to request a little sister to mentor. Since I couldn't start my Social Work studies for another year, I thought a little sister would help keep me motivated. After a process of interviews, background checks, reference checks and drug screenings, they finally found me a little sister.

The info I was given was that she was thirteen, her name was Violet, she had been born to a teen mom, didn't know who her father was and had been raised by her grandma while her mom was off whoring around – under the pretense of trying to find a father figure for her daughter, of course. Seriously, I'm not making this up. Sometimes stereotypes exist for a reason.

The girl had started to act out by talking back to her grandma, getting in trouble in school and hanging out with the wrong crowd. Grandma was worried and contacted BBBSA. That's where I came in. I was supposed to hang out with her twice a month and try to show her different ways to enjoy life that didn't involve getting into trouble.

We'd already had one session together and I thought it went well. Since I knew she was in the art club at her school, I took her to an art gallery and then a carnival. I could tell she was a good kid, and my guess was that her bad behavior was influenced by this new group of friends she had. Saving Violet from a life of STDs, teenage pregnancies and drug use was my new goal for the summer.

Aside from saving Violet, I didn't do very much during my first few weeks back in Michigan. I sent in a few resumes via email for jobs that were way out of my league, just to say I was looking, but I wasn't putting any real effort into it. I wasn't putting much of an effort into anything. Most days I just hung around at home in my loungewear. My brother and Jake would make asshole comments about me wearing my pajamas all day but my clothes were from the "loungewear" section of the stores, and they were made specifically for laziness. There was no point in putting on cute clothes if I wasn't going anywhere, right? I knew people on TV were always dressed up with full hair and makeup when someone randomly and without invitation knocked on their doors. But in real life, people don't knock on your door out of the blue except Jehovah's Witnesses; therefore, in real life, people don't get dressed up and do their hair and makeup just to sit around the house. Correct?

Sometimes I stayed in my room all day and watched *Dawson's Creek* on Netflix. Every couple of days, when we were out of food, I'd put on some jeans, throw my hair up in a lazy ponytail (not the cool kind) and go to the grocery store. I didn't like using the oven in the summer, so I usually threw something into the slow cooker instead. The food would always disappear, so I was pretty sure the guys appreciated it. But even I knew my life had rapidly turned into a depressing scene.

It was nearing the end of June, the middle of the afternoon, and I was sitting on the couch eating ice cream directly out of the carton like a total cliché. I was watching a small-claims courtroom TV show about a pair of ex-roommates fighting over an electric bill. It had been at least three days since I'd washed my hair, and I was pretty certain that if I took the rubber band out, my ponytail would stay in place.

I was on the edge of my seat watching the judge yell at the two ladies on the television and hadn't noticed that Jake was in the room until he cleared his throat.

I looked over to see that he had taped a banner over the archway of the living room that said "Intervention."

I couldn't help but burst out laughing. There's an episode of *How I Met Your Mother* that deals with an intervention banner, and it's some of the funniest shit I've ever seen. Jake tried to hide his smile and look stern, but I could tell he thought he was pretty amusing too.

He pointed at me and twirled his finger around the living room. "This," he said, "has gone on long enough."

I played innocent. "What?"

"You know what I'm talking about," he said. "We're all worried. It's time for you to stop moping around, get off the couch, take a shower and *do* something."

"Do what? What am I supposed to do?"

"Show me your lingerie." He sounded dead serious.

"Huh?!"

"You need something to do, and I need a model. I tried looking on Craigslist but everyone I found was pretty trashy and wanted too much money up front."

"You want to take pictures of me in my underwear?"

"Yes."

"And what would you do with these pictures?"

"Put them on my website, blog and Facebook

pages."

I gasped. "Yeah right! I'm not an underwear model, Jake!"

He sat down on the ottoman in front of me. "Look, it is my job as a photographer to make you look good. I won't even show your face. But I wouldn't be asking if I didn't think you were good enough."

Hmm. If he could Photoshop me to look good and no one could see my face, what was the harm?

"For every boudoir session I book in the next two weeks I'll give you half the session fee."

Even better. "Okay," I said uncertainly. "Do I have time to get ready? I'd like to at least get a pedicure and a haircut." And definitely a wax, but I didn't mention that part.

He laughed a little. "Yes, please do. Because there isn't much I could do to make you look good right now."

I playfully punched his arm. "Thanks!"

"No problem. We'll do the shoot tomorrow. Indoor pics at seven and we'll go outside about eight. I get the best natural light an hour before sunset."

"I don't really have any lingerie though. Not like corsets or garter belts or anything like that." I threw away all of that stuff before I left New York. I didn't want to hang on to any reminders of how hard I had to work to get my husband to have sex with me.

"That's fine," he said. "Just some sexy underwear and stilettos will work – a few different sets. If you have thigh-highs or long necklaces we'll use those, too."

"I guess I better start making some appointments then."

I turned off the TV and stood up. He smirked at me and ripped the banner off the wall.

"See ya tomorrow, Little Girl."

I really got my ass into gear after he left the room, and I meant that literally. I showered, shaved and exfoliated. I then headed to a salon and got a Brazilian wax, a spray tan, a manicure and a pedicure.

The next morning I washed all my bedding and cleaned my room up just in case he wanted to use my room for the shoot. I got my hair cut, dyed and styled and had a professional smoky-eye make-up application done at the salon. Even though I did have some cute underwear of my own, I stopped at a sex store after the salon to pick up some *really* cute underwear with ruffles on the butt. I used to have a pair of ruffled underwear back during *The Summer of Jake and Roxie* and he had loved them so I figured he'd appreciate this pair too.

Jake sent a text that said he'd meet me in my bedroom at seven. I would be a liar if I said that didn't light the dynamite in my belly again.

I wore my kimono robe over my underwear. For my first outfit I wore a white bra and the white ruffled panties. I thought the color looked good with my tan. I added several long black necklaces of different textures and a pair of nude patent leather peep-toes. Even though he asked for thigh-highs I thought white would look too bridal and black would look tacky so I kept those in the lingerie drawer.

He arrived at seven as promised. He was very professional. He came in and started rearranging my furniture and bedding and curtains and setting up lights until he had the look he wanted. He took some test shots of me with my robe still on. I lied on the bed with my feet towards the window and he took the pictures from behind my head.

When I took the robe off he never missed a beat – just kept clicking away. There wasn't any eye contact between us because of the angles he was shooting from so, while I couldn't be sure, he didn't seem to be filled with desire. He could have been photographing a fruit bowl instead of a barely dressed person with whom he used to have awesome sex with.

There was a small, very tiny, like practically microscopic, part of me that was hoping he'd drop his camera as soon as I dropped my robe, throw me onto the bed and rip those ruffles right off my butt. And even if he didn't, I wanted him to *want* to. Just because it had been so long since anyone had wanted me. I thought it would be a nice feeling. But no, nothing like that happened.

When he was done with the first outfit, I went into the bathroom and changed into pale pink cashmere panties and a matching sweater. He said he wanted elegant and what's more elegant than cashmere? Besides, I paid a fortune for the set years ago and never had an occasion to wear it, so I was very excited to start getting some of my money's worth.

He took a lot of shots from behind in that outfit. Standing up in front of the window, lying on my belly, kneeling on the bed, all from behind.

"Try turning around and leaning back on your elbows," he suggested.

I did as he said and he took a few shots. It was the first time we'd been face to face since he'd arrived. I could tell he was really into his job because he had the most intense look in his eyes. For a second he even stopped clicking and smiled at me.

"How would you feel about taking off your shirt?"

I bit my lip. *If he wanted to touch me, then maybe.*

But for him to stare at me and take pictures that were going all over the internet, no way. "I'd rather not."

"Your face won't be in these shots. No one will know it's you – except me."

"No, it's not that. I just …"

"You just what?" He sounded patient as always.

The truth was no one had seen me naked in a long time. Except Caleb who wouldn't have noticed if I'd sat right on his face. There's a big difference between twenty-one year old boobs and twenty-nine year old boobs, and I wasn't ready for anyone to see my newer/older figure yet, *especially* Jake. He had seen the better version, and he would know what he was missing.

I knew nothing was less attractive to a man than a woman who lacked confidence in her body, however, there was something about Jake that made me comfortable telling him just about anything.

"I'm not twenty-one anymore, Jake." I bit my lip and looked down at the subjects of our conversation. "They aren't as perky as they used to be."

"Are you being serious right now?" he asked. His expression was one of disbelief.

I nodded shyly.

"You don't need to worry about that, Rox. Boobs don't start to sag until you're thirty," he said with a smirk. "You still have –" he paused while he silently counted the months on his fingers, "nine months left to show them off."

"That's nice you remember my birthday," I said honestly. "But I'm still not going topless."

He shrugged casually as he changed the lens on his camera. "All right. No big deal. Are you ready to go outside?" he asked. "You're gonna look great on a chaise lounge."

Mom and Dad called the next morning to check on me. I was surprised it took them so long. Hello, parents, my world was shaken up like a snow globe, thrown onto the ground and smashed into pieces and then ran over by an semi-truck and, besides the flowers they sent during my first week home, I hadn't heard from them in weeks.

"Hey Buttercup!" Mom said. She sounded way too cheerful for 10am. I was still in bed and she was probably on her third latte. "How's it going in A-Squared?"

Oh no she didn't. "Omigod, Mom! You know nobody says A-Squared except people who don't live here."

"I don't live there anymore, so I can say it."

True.

"How's it going?" she asked again.

"All right."

"Your brother says you've been doing a whole lot of nothing."

"Compared to a surgeon I guess I *am* doing nothing. I'm not saving lives. But yesterday I let Jake take pictures of me in my underwear."

"Well that sounds like a good time, dear," she replied. Either she wasn't really listening, or she wanted Jake to see me in my underwear.

"And what are you up to?" I asked.

"Oh you know, the usual," she said. "Just finished up some Zumba at the rec center."

Zumba? Isn't that some kind of booty-poppin' dancing? What has gotten into her?

"Any news from your lawyer?" she asked.

"Not yet. She hasn't been able to find any hidden assets but she sent over a counter-offer and we're waiting to hear back."

"Any offers on the condo?"

"No, not yet. We might have to rent it out until the market picks up. We've already lost money just having it vacant for one month."

"That's a great idea. Just like you kids renting our place. It's working out for the best for all of us. Are you looking for work?"

"Not too much. But I've been helping a girl named Violet through Big Brothers and Big Sisters of America. I've also volunteered at a homeless shelter and donated a bunch of makeup and hair stuff."

"Very good, dear. You sound like you're doing okay then. Hang in there. Your father wants to say hi. Here he is."

"Hi there, Sunshine," my dad said. "You doing okay up there? Adam said you've been feeling pretty down. He's got us worried."

"No, I'm okay, Dad. I got my hair and nails done and I'm feeling a lot better now."

"He said you've been watching too much TV. If you're gonna sit around, why don't you do it outside by the pool? A little sunshine can go a long way, you know."

"I know, Dad. I do try to get out there a few times a week."

"Every day, Love. You should be out there every single day. And on the rough days when the sun doesn't do the trick, well, you've got a professional bartender for a roommate. Have him make you a margarita. That always works for me. It's five o'clock somewhere."

Did my dad just quote Jimmy Buffet? I didn't know what had happened to the two of them. They used to be normal parents and now they were like ... happy all the time. Maybe the sunshine and waves really could change a person. Maybe I should have moved to Florida instead of "A-Squared."

J

There was a knock on my door. "I gotta go, Dad," I said quickly. "Love you guys. Talk soon."

I hung up the phone, got out of bed and opened the door.

Jake was standing there holding out an iced cappuccino from the coffee shop with his laptop tucked under the other arm. "I couldn't wait any longer for you to get up and see these pictures. I worked on them all night."

I opened the door wider to let him in, graciously accepted the delicious beverage and we sat down on my bed together. He opened up the files and started a slideshow. None of them showed my face straight on. There were a lot that showed my hair, but none of my face. He said it was better to show only the body because the women looking at the pictures (his target audience) could imagine themselves in the shot.

There were a lot of close-ups, too, especially of my butt and my shoes. But they weren't *Maxim*-style photos. They were classy and even a little innocent – as innocent as underwear pictures could be anyway.

"Your face is in the original pics, though, so if you ever want me to make you some prints or a book or calendar I can."

I snorted at the idea. I didn't imagine I would ever want a book or a calendar of myself in my underwear, and I knew for sure I wouldn't be putting a print over my mantle like Rebecca Dunbar. But I didn't say anything. I was too amazed by what I was seeing on the computer screen to even form a sentence.

I knew the girl in the pictures was wearing the same things I'd had on the day before but I still had a hard time believing it was me. He must be an amazing photographer because he really did make me look good.

"What do you think?" he asked.

"You must have edited the hell out of these."

He laughed. "Why do you say that?"

"I don't know. I mean, I actually look all right."

"I did edit the coloring on a few, but you looked good all on your own. Is it okay if I post them on my pages then?"

"Yep. As long as you don't tag me in any of them. It probably wouldn't look good if Caleb or his lawyer saw them."

"Good point. And for every session I book for the next two weeks I'll give you half of the session fee. That should help cover the cost of your recent, um, slothic behavior."

"Is slothic even a word?"

"I don't know, but I'm going to start uploading these," he said as he stood up.

"Jake?" I asked as he was walking out the door.

He stuck his head back in. "Yeah?"

"Thanks," I looked down, feeling shy again, "for making me feel better about myself and getting me off the couch."

"No problem, Little Girl."

After he left, I took my dad's advice, got into my bikini and took my drink and my tablet down to the pool. I'd finally given in to the tablet craze. I could play games, browse the web, listen to music, read books, and apply for jobs (if I was so inclined). I could even watch every single episode of *Dawson's Creek* right on my tablet through the Netflix app. It was a lazy and unmotivated person's dream, and I didn't know why I'd held out so long. Technology was my friend. And my dad might be onto something about the sunshine because I had a feeling it was going to be a great day.

CHAPTER ELEVEN

By the time Jake got back from his afternoon senior portrait session, he had messages from nine people wanting to book Boudoir sessions! At $200 per session that could mean an extra $900 for me to put toward my credit cards! And it was only the first day! Jake said he wanted to celebrate by taking me out to dinner.

"I know a lovely Italian ristorante we could go to," he teased.

"No thanks, smartass."

We instead went to a Japanese steak house. They sat us in this cute private room with curtains and a couch and we had steak, chicken, shrimp and sake. Even though it wasn't a "real" date, it was the best date I'd been on in years – maybe my entire life. When the bill came I tried to pick it up, but he wouldn't let me. I thought that was really sweet.

It started to rain on the way home. We both got soaked just running from the driveway to the house. It was so dark outside, even though it wasn't even eight o'clock yet. In the summertime, it doesn't get dark until about ten and Michigan had the most fabulous summer storms. They came in quick, and everything got pitch black, and they left just as fast and everything got bright and dry again, like it never even happened.

As I stood at the bay window and watched the storm, I remembered GLL Challenge #17 was to play in the rain. Maybe it was the sake, but I thought it was as good a time as any to complete that challenge.

"I'm going outside," I told Jake.

"Huh? What? Why?" He looked confused.

I shrugged. "I don't know. I've always wanted to play in the rain."

I ran upstairs and dug in my closet for the rain boots I'd bought years ago and hardly ever wore. Minutes later I was outside in the street splashing in puddles in my yellow rain boots before Jake even knew what to think. He followed me out and shook his head at me as I splashed in the puddles beside the curb.

"You're crazy!" he yelled over the sound of the rain. He had on a white t-shirt and the rain gave a whole new meaning to the wet t-shirt contest. I had a grainy view of the tattoos on his chest and the sides of his abdomen. I hadn't seen those particular tattoos in years and suddenly my mind was filled with flashes of images from *The Summer of Jake and Roxie*. I saw us in the shower, in my parent's pool in the middle of the night, laughing under the covers in his room, napping on the couch when no one was home, eating pizza in bed. I could still remember the very first time, that night I asked Jake to take me home with him. Getting his shirt off that night had been a struggle because he didn't want to stop touching me or kissing me for long enough to get it over his head. When he tried to take mine off, it was the same thing. I could still remember how good it felt once our clothes were finally off and we were skin-to-skin for the first time ever. *Sigh.*

The tattoos brought back many memories and so many feelings, too. I especially loved the tattoos on his side. They were tribal astrological symbols – one for Leo and one for Scorpio. Those were his grandparents' signs. His grandparents had raised him until they died in a plane crash when he was six. Those tattoos made me feel closer to him because nobody knew what they meant except Adam and me. Anytime I'd ever heard anyone ask him what they were for, he'd made up some silly story. But for some reason he didn't feel like he needed to be fake with me, and I loved that.

It was one of those ninety percent humidity days that begged for rain to put us out of our misery, and the rain finally breaking through was such a welcome relief. To have it falling directly on me was even better. It was the perfect ending to a pretty perfect day. There was only one thing that could make it better.

It wasn't like me to be spontaneous and reckless anymore. Everything fun I'd done all summer was because of Hope. But in doing so, I had rediscovered how fun life could be when I threw caution to the wind and did whatever the hell I wanted.

I didn't give it a few hours of contemplation or formulate a pros and cons list. I just did what felt right to me. I stepped closer to him, and he backed up until his feet met the curb. His hands were at his side and I reached down and lightly grabbed onto them so he wouldn't move any farther away. That was when he understood my intentions. But he still made me work for it.

Our faces were so close. I only had to move about an inch forward and our lips would meet, but I hesitated for a moment. It wasn't because I was unsure if I wanted to finish what I'd started. I definitely did. I just wanted to give him a chance to back away, to make sure that he wanted me too.

He didn't back away. Instead he tugged my hands to pull my body closer. That was when our lips met. It was just like in *Breakfast at Tiffany's*, minus the trench coat and wet cat squished between us. Seriously, the best director in Hollywood couldn't have created a better kissing-in-the-rain scene than we did. If I've done one thing right in my life, it was that moment right there.

Next thing I knew we were in the house. Up the stairs. In my room. He closed the door behind me and pushed us into it with all the passion and urgency I'd been looking for the day before. We couldn't get our clothes off fast enough. Just like that night so many years ago, neither of us wanted to let go of each other to get anything off. Even when we did try, it's very difficult to get wet clothes off wet skin. It was like trying to untie a knot in your shoelaces in the dark with one hand. With every second that went by, we got even more desperate and frantic to get them off.

Once our clothes were in a soggy heap on the floor, he stood back and looked at me. He had that intense look in his eyes again that I'd seen while he was taking pictures of me. I got the impression that he had stopped to give me a chance to back out, but I wasn't going to.

I knew it wasn't the brightest idea. There were so many reasons why we shouldn't do this. But I couldn't stop if I tried. The way he had bit my neck and sucked on my lips made me feel like a wild animal let out of my cage for the first time. There was no going back in – I was feral.

Once he seemed sure I wasn't going to change my mind, his urgency returned and he pushed me up against the back of the door by my shoulders. Wet skin smashing into wet skin. It should have been uncomfortable, but it was the opposite. Touching from head to toe, it felt like I was finally where I was supposed to be.

In one fluid move, he put a hand behind each of my thighs and literally picked me up and slid me down right on top of him. Just like that perfect kiss at his frat house so many years before, there were no injuries or "oops" moments. He got it right on the first try. I'm telling you, the guy is *smooth*.

Caleb and I had moved far away from passionate, I-want-you-so-bad-I-can't-wait-one-more-second-or-I'll-die, kind of sex. We had FWP during ovulation only. It was a lot like getting an oil change on my car; the free coffee was nice, but I was only there for maintenance and hoped the guy would do his job as quickly as possible so I could get back to Rachael Ray.

Being with Jake was so much better. Since I was using automotive analogies, I'd describe it as an expensive full-body exterior and interior auto detail that was about eight years overdue. Our hands and lips never left each other. I didn't want it to be over *ever* because I enjoyed falling off his cliff. Then again, when it's that good, it can be quick and still satisfying. By the time we collapsed onto the floor about ten minutes later, I'd already been satisfied twice.

We lay on the floor side by side and looked at the ceiling while we tried to catch our breaths and compose ourselves. I knew it was coming, that awkward OMG-WTF-did-we-just-do moment. We couldn't just cuddle and fall asleep and put the moment off until the morning. We weren't even on a bed. And even if we were, it wasn't even dark out yet. And how were we supposed to get dressed when our clothes were wet? As hard as it was to get them off, there was no way they were going back on without an even more embarrassing struggle. Oh, shit, this was bad.

After years and years of planning perfect moments and avoiding the awkward ones, I had developed a certain amount of skill in this area, and I couldn't help but give this one my best shot. When he seemed pretty much back to normal, breathing-wise, I sat up and silently held up my hand toward him for a high-five.

He turned his head toward me and laughed as his tired hand made its way over to meet mine. "Nice play, Rox," he said as he sat up, nodding his head in approval.

And that was it. Tension cut. Awkward moment avoided. I should seriously do this shit for a living.

"I've never gotten a high-five after sex before," he said. He looked pretty proud of himself, probably for earning the high-five.

"I've never been thrown up against a door before, either. With moves like that you should get a high-five every time."

"Ha. If you ever want to try it again, so I can really master the move, just say when."

Is it too early to ask? That's what I should have said. But I didn't. I bit my lip to keep myself from speaking and sounding totally desperate. He was probably only kidding anyway.

"I'm just messing with you," he said.

See?

"We both know this was just a fluke," he said as he dug through the pile of wet clothes, "so there's no need for us to have any weird conversation about it later."

"Excellent," I said, handing him his t-shirt. Weird conversations weren't on my to-do list either.

"I gotta get on the computer and start setting up appointments so we can make some money," he said.

He stood up and managed to get his wet boxers back on. The jeans and t-shirt, we both knew, were hopeless.

I remained seated on the floor and pulled my legs up to my chest just to stop being so exposed.

He kneeled back down to my level so he could look me in the eye.

"Can I kiss you one more time?" he asked.

Gosh, he made my heart melt. He could kiss me anytime he wanted. *Any. Time.* But I didn't say that. Another thing I should have said, but didn't. I smiled at him to let him know it was okay, and he kissed me once more before I scooted away from the door and let him out.

Once he was gone, I got up, threw on my robe and headed down the hall to the shower.

Jake sleeps in the master bedroom with his own bathroom, so I knew I didn't have to worry about running into him when I left my room. I definitely wasn't expecting to run into Adam, though. The guy had seriously been home a total of maybe five hours since I'd moved in but, of course, he was there now. He was just coming out of his room with a laundry basket of dirty scrubs when I walked out of mine.

"What's up, stranger?" he asked with a nod.

"Nothing, just getting ready for a shower." I tried

to act normal, but inside I panicked. *How long has he been home? Did he hear anything? Does he know? Omigod!*

"From what I hear, it's about time."

"WHAT?!" I practically screamed.

"Jake was telling me you had stopped showering. I'm just kidding, man. Relax."

Breathe out. What a relief.

"Lemme know when you're out of the shower so I can start my laundry," he said.

My afterglow started to fade once I got into the shower. I had so many questions in my head, bouncing around in there like it was a pinball machine.

What have I done? Are we ruined? After weeks of awkwardness and getting to know each other and being comfortable with one another again, it was starting to feel like we were really friends. Was that over now? He said we didn't need to have any weird conversation but things definitely wouldn't be the same as they were before tonight, weird conversation or not. I really liked having him back in my life, and I wasn't ready to lose him again so soon.

And seriously, what the hell *was* that? You'd think I'd have some kind of self-control at my age. I'm not some horny teenager, and this isn't an episode of *Jersey Shore* for Christ's sake! I'm still married. What a slutbag! We didn't even use a condom. What kind of person has unprotected sex with a random guy before her divorce is even final? Not a good person, that's for sure. In my defense, Jake was anything but random, and if it were that easy to get pregnant I'd be a mom of three in a New York City condo with five digits a month worth of child support right now. But what about STDs? He didn't look like he'd have an STD, but if people looked like they had STDs, STDs probably wouldn't exist because people would not have sex with those people. I mean, who would say to themselves, *that guy looks like a walking case of herpes and I totally want to do him?* Huh? No one!

I was ashamed of myself. I felt happy, refreshed and satisfied … all with a side of guilt. I needed to get my feelings under control because I was acting more neurotic than was acceptable for someone who was supposed to be only moderately inclined to neuroticism.

I decided to take my dad's advice for the second time that day and have a drink to calm my nerves. After my shower I put on some of my infamous loungewear and headed down to the kitchen. Adam and Jake were both in there as well. Adam was standing at the island digging through the drawer where we kept the pizza coupons and take-out menus. Jake was looking into the fridge. Neither of them felt the need to acknowledge my presence when I entered the room, and I took that as a good sign. That was normal.

"Is Carmen here?" Adam asked.

I didn't know who he was talking to or who Carmen was, but Jake must have known because he answered him.

"No," Jake answered. "I haven't seen her in awhile. She doesn't work at The Bar anymore."

"Oh. I thought I heard some, um, *noises* upstairs when I got home," Adam said.

Jake turned around from the fridge with a beer bottle in his hand and our eyes met. He gave me a wicked grin as he twisted off the bottle cap. Without missing a beat he said, "That was probably your sister watching porn upstairs."

I gasped.

"Damn, Roxie," he said to me with a gleam in his eye, "you could at least turn the volume down. You're not the only one who lives here, you know."

I probably should have been mad, but I laughed so hard I had to bend over and hold onto my stomach because I was afraid I might rupture something. In the middle of my laughing fit I snuck a look at Jake. I saw him bite his lip, probably to keep himself from laughing too.

"You guys are disgusting," Adam said sounding a little annoyed. "I'm gonna order take-out. You guys want anything?"

"No, thanks," we both said at the same time.

I pulled a bottle of Riesling out of the fridge and, without a word, Jake took it from my hand, opened it with a wine key and poured me a glass.

"Thanks," I said when he handed the glass to me.

Our fingers touched. I smiled. He grinned back at me. It was one of those sneaky half-grins, the kind exchanged only by two people who shared a secret. And I believe I've already mentioned how much I like secrets.

CHAPTER TWELVE

I took my wine outside to the pool and relaxed in one of the chaise lounges. The sun was about to set and GLL Challenge #13 was to watch a sunset, so it was pretty good timing.

Almost immediately the wine made me feel better about my *Jersey Shore* moment with Jake (um, not to sound like an alcoholic or anything). I had no reason to beat myself up over it. Yes, I was technically still married, but there was absolutely no chance of reconciliation between us. As for the lack of protection, well, I'd made a mistake, but I couldn't do anything about it now except learn from it and make sure I didn't repeat it. And as for ruining my friendship with Jake, that was silly to even think about. We were both grown-ups, even if we didn't always act like it. We were going to be fine. It wasn't the end of the world. So thank you, Dad, for encouraging me to have a drink and thank you, Barefoot Winery, for the Riesling.

Once the sun set and the wine was gone, I collected my tablet, wine glass and empty wine bottle and walked back into the kitchen with intentions to go to bed … alone. I set the wine glass in the sink and the bottle on the counter and heard footsteps behind me. I turned around. It was Jake. He was standing at the entrance to the kitchen holding an empty beer bottle.

I had read the term "smoldering look" before in cheesy romance novels, but I had never experienced one myself. Even during *The Summer of Jake and Roxie* I couldn't remember him ever looking at me quite like that. It was hot enough that I felt like I needed to shower again. I put my hands on the counter behind me and waited for him to speak because he looked like he had something to say.

"Hey," he said quietly.

"Hi."

He took a few steps forward, very slowly, until there was about a foot between us. He leaned forward to set his beer bottle on the counter behind me, pushing his chest up against mine in the process. When he straightened up and his eyes met mine again, they stayed there. He put a finger under my chin and tilted my face upward. A little sigh escaped from me. He tucked a piece of my hair behind my ear and then let his hand rest on my cheek. I leaned my head into his hand. He made me feel … and I know it sounds ridiculous, but he made me feel cozy. You know how good it feels to put on a pair of sweatpants straight from the dryer when they're still warm? Jake made me feel like *that*.

With no urgency at all, he brought his face toward mine and kissed me slowly and softly. I leaned back into the counter, glad I had something to hold me up since I felt dizzy again.

"I'm going to bed," he said quietly. His face was still so close to mine that I could feel his breath on my lips when he spoke.

"Me too," I told him, basically talking right into his mouth.

"But I don't want to go without you," he said.

Thud. Sleeping alone was overrated anyway.

A few hours later (we weren't in such a hurry this time), I was once again feeling satisfied, but ashamed. Jake was amazing. *We* were amazing. Together. But that whole I'm-a-married-whore thing kept nagging at me. What was I doing? I couldn't be with Jake in any kind of long-term way. I knew that. Why was I being so stupid as to start something with him that I knew couldn't last?

"Jake?" I asked quietly. I wasn't sure if he was still awake or not. He was lying on his back beside me on his bed. I had been lying toward him with my head resting comfortably in the crook of his arm. It felt like the spot was made just for me. And it was so hard to pull myself away. But I did. I rolled over onto my back as well.

He sighed loudly like he knew what was coming. "Yeah."

"Not that I don't want to, but I don't think we should do this again."

"No?"

"I had a lot of fun. I love being with you. It's just, you know."

"No, I don't know. What is it?"

"You know I'm still married."

He turned his head toward me. "So you're saying once your divorce is finalized, it's okay for you to be with me?" The tone of his voice sounded like he was challenging me, like he knew the answer to the question already.

I sat up and leaned back on my hands. "I can't say that. But I'm sorry about earlier. I shouldn't have kissed you. It was entirely my fault, and I take the blame. Can we pretend this day never happened?"

"I think we can handle it. We've had a lot of practice pretending things don't happen."

I stood up. "I'm gonna go back to my room then."

"No. Stay. You can go back to your room tomorrow."

"Fine." I lay back down and snuggled up against him. "I'll go back tomorrow."

Jake was right. We did have a lot of practice "pretending things don't happen" and that's probably why we managed to fall right back into our normal roommate routine without any glitches. He had a busier schedule than usual thanks to his blossoming boudoir business. He continued to give me $100 for every photo session like he had promised, and I was making quite a bit of money from them. I figured it was making up for my month of slacking.

I also stayed busy myself. The Good Life List Challenge #26 was to host a party where I made at least ten new recipes and The Fourth of July was scheduled to be the big day. When I wasn't designing invites and scouring Pinterest for patriotic recipes and creative decor, I was going over the remaining GLL Challenges and trying to figure out how I was going to complete some of the most difficult ones. Like #4 – Go skinny dipping in someone else's pool without their permission. How was a good girl like me going to pull off something like that?

Adam had miraculously been given the whole afternoon of the fourth off, so we invited over Allison and her family, some of the girls who had come to my divorce party, a few of Jake's coworkers from The Bar and a couple of people Adam knew from the hospital.

We had a piñata for the kids, red, white & blue martinis for the adults, a bonfire and a whole lot of fantastic food made by yours truly. I even built a make-shift tiki bar for the occasion. Jake joked around and told me I could forget social work and go into party planning or catering instead.

It was about an hour before the guests were to arrive. I was in the kitchen dipping strawberries into white chocolate and blue sugar when Jake came in and snatched one of the freshly dipped strawberries and shoved it into his mouth before I could protest.

"Hey!" I yelled. I tried to swat his hand but I was too late. "No eating until the guests arrive!"

"I needed to make sure they were good before you tried to serve them," he said with a smirk.

He didn't know it, but he was messing with the wrong person. GLL Challenge #16 was to start a food fight, and I just so happened to have a great weapon sitting on the counter right next to me: a bowl of white fluff salad that was going to go over the red and blue Jell-O. He was still chewing the strawberry and smirking at me when I picked up a spoonful of fluff and flung it at him like a slingshot. I had better aim than I thought and hit him right on his chin. Go me!

He looked startled at first, then surprised, but then his expression turned mischievous as he grabbed the spoon from my hand. I backed away from the fluff bowl in fear.

"Jake," I begged. "I spent an hour on my hair and makeup. Please don't."

He aimed it for my chest and a big glob of white fluff landed right in the middle of my cleavage and sunk down into my tank top.

"That was a three-pointer!" he yelled. "And the crowd roars."

"Okay, you got me. But let's play nice now. I really did spend a long time on my hair."

"Oh no," he said, shaking his head. "You can't start a food fight and wimp out on me."

He slung another spoonful and this time caught my shoulder, missing my hair by less than an inch.

"Seriously, Jake! Watch the hair!"

Before I could even clean up my shoulder, he hit me on my chest again. That was when I got pissed. I took the ponytail holder off my wrist and, very carefully, pulled my hair up, not taking my eyes off Jake for a second. I lunged for the spoon but I slipped on a bit of fluff and, like a total chick-flick cliché, went crashing into him, knocking us both to the floor. Jennifer Lopez would have been proud.

"Omigod!" I squealed, scanning his face and head for injuries. "Are you okay? Are you hurt? I'm so sorry!" I sat up, which was a bad move because it meant I was sitting right on top of him. And in my thin yoga pants I could feel *everything*. Damn!

Adam walked in the back door and saw us on the floor.

"What the hell?" he asked.

If my face wasn't already red from the food fight, it was definitely red after being caught in a compromising position by my brother. I was mortified, but Jake just laughed.

"Your sister started it," he said.

"Whatever," Adam said looking annoyed. "Just clean it up and get your shit together. People are going to be here soon."

When Adam walked out of the kitchen, Jake grinned at me. I tried to get up, but he put a hand on each of my hips to keep me in place. He pulled me down even closer to him and I could tell he was having as hard a time being in this position as I was. Pun intended.

"Your face is so red right now," he said with a grin. "Are you sure you want to get off me? Or would you rather get off *on* me?"

I gasped at his nerve. Then I bit my lip. He had a point. I did not want to get up.

"Since you're the one who doesn't want this," he said, "I'd really appreciate it if you stopped throwing yourself at me. Or on me."

I laughed, knowing he was only messing with me, and he smiled back.

I tried to get up again and this time he let me.

"Rain check?" he called out as I walked out of the kitchen.

Jake spent a lot of time at the party behind the bar making the martinis. You'd think he'd hate making drinks when he wasn't at work, but he loved it. I could tell he had a lot of fun. I could also tell things hadn't changed much since I'd worked at The Bar. A few girls he worked with showed up, and every single one of them flirted shamelessly with him. What is it about someone else wanting something that made me want it even more?

Allison's in-laws picked up the kids at about nine. That was when the real party started. Jake's martinis were a bit too tasty because I'm pretty sure I had at least two too many. By the time everyone left around 2am, I had enough liquid courage in me to do something I'd been meaning to do for a while.

"Jake," I whispered.

He was gathering the alcohol from the bar to bring back in the house. "Yeah?" he whispered back.

"I have a really good idea."

"What's that?"

"We should go skinny-dipping in someone else's pool."

"Why can't we just skinny-dip in our own pool?"

"Because that's boring."

"Whose pool should we use?"

"I was thinking the neighbor with the two boys would be a good one. You know how much she loves skinny-dipping."

He smiled and nodded. "You're right. That does sound like a great idea."

"I'll go get us some towels."

Jake and I walked next door in nothing but our towels. In my head, I had imagined a quiet, romantic game of cat and mouse, with steam coming from the water and maybe a kiss or two. But Jake ran into their backyard, threw his towel to the wind and did a cannonball into the deep end. I laughed hysterically as I tended to do when I was drunk. I barely had time to jump in before I saw a light come on in one of the second floor windows. We both scrambled to get out of the pool and grabbed our towels before we took off running.

We didn't get busted by the neighbor, but were not so lucky when it came to being busted by Adam. He was putting food away in the kitchen when we came barging in, dripping from head to toe and wearing nothing but towels.

"Seriously?" he said. "What is with you two? You're acting like teenagers!"

That made us laugh even harder.

It was approaching three, but I didn't feel tired yet. I was on a roll with my GLL Challenges and didn't feel like stopping.

"I think I'm gonna go dry off, put on my pajamas

and sleep outside tonight," I told them (GLL Challenge #19 – Sleep outside overnight). "It's so nice out. You guys wanna come with me? The fire is still going and we could make s'mores."

"I have to get some sleep," Adam said. "I have to be back at work by ten."

I looked at Jake. A sober me would have known that inviting Jake to spend the night with me wasn't a good idea, but the non-sober me was very naughty and had a habit of putting her hands up in the air and saying, "I just don't give a fuck." It's the reason I didn't drink often.

"I don't know if I want to sleep outside," he said. "But I'll make s'mores with you."

I'm not sure what all happened after that, but I woke up to the sound of the alarm on my cell phone going off at 6am. I must have set it to wake me up in time to watch the sunrise, GLL Challenge #14.

I was on one of the chaise lounges by the pool. I didn't know who did it, either me or Jake, but one of us had pulled another chair right up against mine and that was where Jake was starting to wake up from the sound of my alarm. We were both covered up by a quilt my mom had made years ago.

"What happened?" I asked him. I felt very groggy after only two hours of sleep and I thought I might still be a little drunk. I noticed a bottle of water and a bottle of Tylenol sitting on the plastic end table next to my chair. *Thank you, Magic Hangover Genie.* I swallowed two pills and handed both bottles to Jake, who gladly accepted them.

"Nothing," he told me. "You passed out as soon as you sat down." He took two pills and then stretched his arms and neck.

"I thought you didn't want to sleep outside."

"I wasn't gonna leave you out here by yourself."

"Did you bring the blanket?"

He nodded.

"And the water and pills?"

He nodded again.

"Oh," was all I said. Sometimes it was hard to believe anyone could be as nice as Jake. I knew bringing a blanket to a sleeping person was something a lot of people would have done, but having been with a man who wasn't very nice to me for so long, I just wasn't used to it. But I could definitely *get* used to it. "Thanks."

"No big deal."

"Want to watch the sunrise with me before we go inside?" I asked.

"I know a place where can get a better view," he said. "Let's go for a ride."

We grabbed the blanket and got into his Jeep. I knew where we were going, but I acted surprised when he pulled into my lot, *our* lot, with not a minute to spare.

I tucked my legs under me, covered us both up with the quilt, and leaned my head on his shoulder from the passenger seat. As we watched the stars vanish and the pink sun light up the sky, I truly realized how deeply I'd missed him these last few years. It felt more important than ever that I didn't lose him as my friend. I wanted to tell him then how much I'd missed him and how glad I was that he was a part of my life again. I should have. But I didn't.

CHAPTER THIRTEEN

A few days later I slept until 11am like the slacker I was. I did what I did every morning (or afternoon) when I woke up. I went downstairs for coffee. But when I walked into the kitchen I nearly screamed out loud.

There was a girl in the kitchen. She had her back to me and was standing on her tiptoes on one of our barstools, reaching into the top shelf of a cupboard. She had long, dark, wavy hair and was wearing what looked like a men's light blue button-up shirt with the sleeves rolled up to her elbows and no pants. Either she was wearing no underwear at all, or she had on a thong because her bare butt cheeks were sticking out from under the shirt. From the back she was perfection. It was as if a Dallas Cowboys cheerleader was standing in my kitchen.

She turned to look at me when she heard me come in and when she did, the front of her shirt opened to reveal some side-boob. No, she was not wearing a bra under her shirt. And yes, her face was just as perfect as her butt. Lucky bitch.

"Hi!" she said in a way-too-perky voice. She probably really was a cheerleader. "You must be Adam's little sister!"

Being called a "little sister" by someone who was probably a decade younger than me was a bit condescending and annoying, but I was so glad she was with my brother and not Jake that I let her comment slide and breathed a big sigh of relief. Not that I wanted to see my brother's sexual conquests naked in my kitchen and, trust me, he would hear about it later, but it was a billion times better than seeing Jake's sexual conquests, even if they were fully dressed in ugly, baggy clothes with dirty hair and no makeup. Because even *that* would suck. Seeing that Jake hooked up with a girl this hot in the same house where I was sleeping a bedroom away, would kill me. Just because I had stopped our sequel from happening, didn't mean I was ready to see him with someone else.

"Jake's told me so much about you!" she continued as she hopped off the stool (she was wearing a thong – thank you, God!) and held out her hand, which opened the shirt even more and revealed her perfectly perky C-cups.

Before I even knew what was happening, Jake stood up from behind the kitchen island and set his camera down on it.

"Good morning, Rox," he said, smiling like nothing was wrong with this scenario at all, "Or is it afternoon yet?"

I was so confused. Why was there a mostly naked girl in my kitchen? Where was my brother? Why was Jake hiding behind the island? What did I walk in on? Who the hell was this girl?

"I'm Carmen, by the way," Miss Perky-In-Every-Way said, as if she read my mind.

Carmen! Carmen was the girl Adam asked Jake about that one night! Carmen must be one of Jake's flings – one that began way before I arrived in Michigan and was apparently still going on.

I knew I wasn't Jake's girlfriend, but I never imagined I was merely a fling within a fling.

I'm so stupid! What was I thinking getting involved with him again? He's still the same different-DNA-on-the-sheets-every-week guy he's always been. I can't believe I was so effing stupid to think he ever cared about me!

I knew all along things would not end well. Jake was a dead-end road. He didn't do relationships. I was never going to be anything more to him than a convenient live-in lay, so it was a good thing I put an end to it. *Ugh, why do I have to be so stupid sometimes?*

I didn't say anything in the kitchen. I was speechless. I kept looking from one to the other, waiting for some logical explanation that had nothing to do with sex – an explanation I knew would not be coming, because there was no other explanation for this.

As irrational and childish as it was, I had the urge to pick up his camera and smash it on the floor. I wanted to throw something, and break something, and hurt something he cared about it because I felt so hurt inside.

I didn't shake the hand she held out. She eventually dropped it and used it to close her shirt. Then she also looked back and forth between Jake and me. She looked confused. *I bet.*

Confrontations were not my style. Even if I could've assembled some comprehensive thoughts and formed complete sentences at that time (and I couldn't), I wouldn't have started anything with either of them. As I turned around and walked out of the kitchen, I held my chin high, so as not to look like the desolate loser I felt like.

Once I was out of the kitchen and safe from their view, I ran up the stairs, into my room and closed the door before the tears began to fall.

Why did I ever think it was a good idea to come here? I was looking for a fresh start but all I did was move backwards! I've been here a month, and I'm no closer to a so-called better life than I was when I got here. I have no job, no life, and no purpose. I'm like a waste of space on the couch. In fact, if Jake and Adam threw a piece of leather over me, I could BE the couch!

I'd only met with Violet twice, but didn't seem to be making a difference to her since she had just been caught stealing lip-gloss from CVS. I couldn't go to school for another year. I was too embarrassed to get a job because the only job I knew how to do was one that I was ashamed of. I never saw my brother because of his work. My BFF had a life of her own. And the cherry on top of this shit-sundae was that I'd had sex – unprotected sex – with the biggest player in Ann Arbor who had just made a fool of me in my own house! One thing I probably had was an STD. One thing I definitely did not have was a future here in Ann Arbor, and there was no reason for me to be here. No reason at all.

I pulled a weekender bag out of my closet and started mindlessly throwing things into it as tears fell freely down my face. As much as I would love to go back home to NYC, I knew I couldn't afford it. There was only one place I could think to go – Florida. Maybe my dad could pull some strings and get me a late acceptance into the MSW program at his school … if they even had an MSW program. I knew my parents would let me stay at their condo until I could get on my feet and get my own place. I wouldn't mind being a barmaid on a beach. For some reason serving drinks on a beach seemed a lot more sophisticated and respectable than serving drinks to a bunch of drunk and arrogant college kids in Ann Arbor. Yes, I could totally do this. I could move and get a real fresh start, not just an opportunity to remake mistakes all over again. Not a re-do, but a clean slate.

"Rox?" Jake tapped on the door.

No. He couldn't see me crying. He couldn't know how hurt I was about the cheerleader in the kitchen. I couldn't let him see how much I cared. He could never know. I took a deep breath and tried to keep my voice steady.

"I can't talk right now, Jake," I said. "I'm not dressed."

"It's not like I haven't seen you naked before."

Don't remind me, asshole! What a jerk thing to say right now!

I took another deep breath to keep my voice from wavering. "Please get away from my room, Jake. I do not wish to speak with you."

"You do not wish to speak with me?" he mocked me. "Why are you talking like a robot? Are you okay? You know that wasn't what it looked like."

If I wasn't so upset I would have laughed out loud at that overused line. "I'm fine," I said in my calm robot voice. "Please let me be alone right now."

I didn't hear anything else after that so I figured he'd gone downstairs. I stayed in my room packing, crying, sniffling, and texting Hope and Allison, who both said I should talk to him before I moved to another state.

Once I was all cried out and had a full set of luggage packed, I went into the bathroom to put some cold water on my eyes and apply some makeup so it wouldn't look like I'd been crying.

When I felt composed enough, I held my head high and went downstairs. I didn't know if Jake was around, but I was going to have to take my chances because I needed coffee even more after all of that crying.

The kitchen was empty – score! I walked over to the Keurig and pushed the power button. It whirred to life as I selected a K-cup of blueberry-flavored coffee from our carousel and stuck it in the machine. I thought I was in the clear, but as I was getting the coffee creamer from the fridge, Jake came in from the patio carrying his laptop under his arm.

I ignored him and continued with my coffee. He set the laptop on the island and flipped open the screen.

"It's not what you think," he said quickly.

I stirred my coffee, still ignoring him. I looked up at the ceiling to avoid any tears from escaping. I still felt extra sensitive.

"I was just taking pictures," he explained. "She's engaged. She wanted to have some pictures taken to give to her husband on their wedding night. She wanted some pics taken in a kitchen and asked if we could do them here because she liked our bar stools and the glass cabinets."

I put the creamer back in the fridge and avoided his eyes.

"Here, I have them on my laptop if you want to see. I should have told you, but I just wasn't thinking, and that was stupid of me."

I picked up the coffee mug and took a quick, nonchalant glance at the thumbnail photos on his screen that Jake had clearly taken while lying on the floor. Looking at her perfect butt and her coy smile as she glanced over her shoulder, ugh, it made me want to throw up.

I tried to exit the kitchen, but he stepped in front of me and blocked the door.

"I'm sorry, Roxie. I mean it."

I looked at the floor to avoid his eyes. I wasn't ignoring him to be a brat. I was worried that if I tried to talk, my voice would crack, and the last thing I wanted was to stand there and cry in front of him.

"Hey," he said, his voice soothing. He rubbed my arms just under my shoulders. It felt comforting and his voice was caring and kind. His apology was genuine. Damn him! "What's happening?" he asked. "Why are you so upset? I told you it was nothing, and that's the truth."

"It doesn't matter," I said, trying hard to keep my voice steady. "You can do whatever you want."

"I know I can do whatever I want, but I'm not going to bring some girl home a couple of days after you slept in my bed. That would be a dick move and you have to know I have more respect for you than that."

I did know that. And his story made sense. He really was taking pictures of her. Why else would she be reaching into the top shelf of our cupboard? There wasn't anything up there but some Tupperware from like 1985. But sometimes when I get really mad, I don't want to stop being mad, so I find more reasons to stay mad. Does anyone else do that? Or is it just me?

"My brother asked you about Carmen," I said quietly. "When he heard us upstairs. He asked you if Carmen was over."

Jake let out a long sigh, walked into the living room and sat down on the couch. I sat down, too, curious to hear the rest of this story.

"You're right," he started. "There was a time a while back when her and her boyfriend broke up and she came over after work a few times. But now they are back together and I am not at all interested in her."

I thought about this ridiculous scenario for a few moments before I spoke.

"So she wants to give her husband, on their wedding night, a bunch of pictures of her that were taken by some guy she hooked up with when they were broken up?"

"Hey, I never said she was the brightest crayon in the box. That's why there's no way I could ever seriously date her. But she paid me like everyone else; the shots I took of her are going to add a lot of value to my portfolio because she has a great body, and the prints she orders are going to make me even more money. So I really don't care what she does with the pictures."

As another woman, I was able to see through her façade more so than Jake. She was probably trying to seduce him, and I doubted if she even had a fiancé, but it wasn't really my problem anymore. I'd be moving out anyway.

"Do you forgive me?" he asked.

"You're forgiven. But I think we both know this roommate situation isn't going to work out. We can't be having conversations like this every time one of us brings a date home."

"You're right. We should probably just keep having sex with each other then. And that way we wouldn't need to bring dates home, and we'd never have a conversation like this again." He gave me a cocky, but hopeful, grin as he waited my response.

To be honest, that sounded like a super idea. But how long would it last before he decided he was bored with me and traded me in for another one of his cheerleaders?

"Or," I said, "I could just call it a loss and move down to Florida with my parents."

"Are you serious?" he asked quietly. His silly smirk was gone.

I nodded. "I've already packed."

He took a deep breath. Then he stood up and shook his head at me. "You're seriously going to run away again? God, that is so like you. I don't even know why I'm surprised."

I stood up, defensively. "What do you mean run away again? When did I run away before?"

"How about going to North Carolina instead of going to school in Michigan? Your hockey player boyfriend humiliated you, so you ran away."

"I applied to UNC before that even happened!" It was true. I had. I might have chosen the school afterward, but I had already applied.

"And why'd you move back here? Because you were running from your problems in New York."

"NO!" I shouted. "I wanted to stay in New York! I just couldn't afford it!"

"So you came here? To Ann Arbor? It might not be New York City, but it's definitely not cheap to live here. Try again."

"It's a lot cheaper than New York. And why wouldn't I come here? When something bad happens to a person, they're going to go to the people who love them for support."

"So what are you running from this time then?"

"I'm not running! I'm fixing a mistake I made."

"What was the mistake?"

"Moving here!"

"Why was it a mistake?"

I sat back down on the couch and studied the

fibers in the living room carpet. "You guys," I said quietly, "you, Adam, Allison – you all have your own lives, and I need to find a life of my own too. There isn't anything here for me. There's no school that will take me on such short notice, and there's no job I can get where I won't be serving people who are going to look down on me. All I do is watch TV, drink wine and lay out in the sun. That's not normal."

"What are you going to do in Florida that's so much better?"

I couldn't really think of a good answer. If there was any way to start my Master's sooner that would be a good reason to go, but I should probably find out for sure if that could happen before I moved over 2000 miles away.

Jake sat down next to me again. He seemed calmer, less agitated. "I agree that you need to get a job; if not for money then just to get out of the house. But there *are* things for you here. You've got that little sister to keep out of trouble. You promised you'd take Allison's kids to Cedar Point. I can even get you your old job back at The Bar. You used to make tons of money there."

"That's a nice offer, Jake, but there's so many people I know that go in there. I don't think I could handle having them laughing at me."

"Yeah, there are people we went to high school with who go in there, but they are just regular people with regular jobs. It's not like they are all millionaires or anything. You're the one who's been living in some penthouse suite in New York all this time. You're the one with a bedroom full of shoes that are probably worth more money than I've made in my entire life. No one is going to look down on you for having a job, and it's ridiculous that you even think that."

"It wasn't the penthouse," I mumbled.

He stood up. I could tell he was angry again.

"And you know?" he asked, as he paced in front of me. "It really pisses me off that you think working in a bar is so shameful. *I* work in a bar, Roxie. Does that mean you look down on *me*?" He stopped pacing, stood in front of me and pointed at his chest. "No, wait. Don't answer that question. Of course you do. That's why you left me and got engaged to some rich asshole a week later."

I gasped and looked up at him. Was that the way he saw it? Was that what he'd been thinking all this time? That I was ashamed of him for being a bartender? That I married Caleb for money? *Is he right?*

I touched my cheek because it felt like I'd been slapped, even though he hadn't touched me. And since I was still in an uber-sensitive mood after crying all morning, that was all it took to get the tears behind my eyes again. I blinked away what I could, but there was really no way to hide them this time.

"Never mind," he said. "I shouldn't have said that."

"I wasn't ashamed of you," I said quietly.

"That shit doesn't even matter anymore."

"It seems like it kind of does, or you wouldn't have said it."

He sat down next to me again and looked at me seriously. "Look, staying and trying to make this work for you, that's nothing to be ashamed of. Running away after barely giving it a chance, *that's* a reason for people to look down on you. *That's* something to be ashamed of. But you go ahead and leave if you want. I've gotten used to it."

And with that, he left the room. A few minutes later I watched through the bay window as his Jeep pulled away from the house.

Jake's comments gave me a lot to think about, but I didn't have the time to think about them at the moment because I was supposed to meet Violet for our afternoon outing in an hour, and I looked like a train wreck.

I ran upstairs and washed my face *again*, put on some of my Benefit Eye Bright *again* and took another chance on mascara – except I used waterproof.

I wasn't in the right mood to be trying to encourage or inspire anyone, but I told her I'd be there today, so I was going to be there.

I was sitting on a park bench, lacing up my roller skates, when her grandma dropped her off in the parking lot. When Violet told me she liked to roller skate, I'd been super excited about it because I hadn't done it since I was a kid. I had to buy myself a pair of roller skates but I bought them at a discount sporting goods store instead of an expensive designer. At least one thing about my life seemed to be changing for the better, eh?

Violet got out of her grandma's car and headed toward me with a surly look on her face. Don't tell anyone, but I kind of wished I had gotten a younger little sister, one who was too young for attitude problems and backtalk. I could tell by the look on her face that she wasn't happy to be there. She'd rather be hanging out with her hoodlum friends and stealing makeup from drug stores. Maybe I didn't have to feel guilty for not particularly wanting to be there either.

She was a pretty girl, with her thick brown ponytail, big blue eyes and petite frame, but she wore way too much makeup for anyone to tell. Also, attitude was worth a lot more than a pretty face, and she had a serious problem in that department.

As her grandma's car pulled away from the park, Violet turned and held up her middle fingers on both hands towards the car like she was some kind of gangsta. She sat down next to me on the park bench, looked at her watch and said, "One hour. Starting now."

Umm, okay. I was suddenly kind of scared.

She had the kind of skates that attached to the bottom of her shoes. Once she had them on she stood up and said, "Come on, lady. I'll race you to the concession stand."

I was still fuming over being called lady as she raced off like some kind of speed skater. I wasn't foolish enough to try to beat her so I skated over at a slower pace that was just fast enough to keep my eye on her in case she tried sneaking off. By the time I made it to the concession stand, she was literally skating circles around the small building, and I was clutching my sides in pain. I needed to work out more.

She laughed when she saw me. "I was going to say we should get an ice cream, but it doesn't look like you need one," she said with a smirk.

Was she calling me fat? That little bitch! I was too out of breath to reply, and for that I was lucky, or I might have been banned from the BBBSA forever.

She giggled, and her eyes danced as she skated around me. I was still trying to catch my breath.

"Water," I gasped. I sat down at one of the picnic tables and pulled a plastic Victoria's Secret Pink water bottle out of my bag. It was gigantic. It didn't fit in the cup holders of my car or any piece of exercise equipment in our basement. It took up practically all of the space in my bag and I needed two hands to drink from it. But it was a free gift with purchase, and it was cute and girly, and said Drink

Pink on it, so how could I resist?

Violet laughed even harder. She sat down across from me at the picnic table. "You need some help with that?" she asked snidely.

What is this girl's problem today?

She pulled a water bottle out of her backpack. It was yellow and had a smiley face on it.

"You couldn't find one with a frown?" I asked.

For a second, she looked pissed that I had given her some of her own crap. Then she smiled and I could tell she appreciated it.

"What's this I hear about you stealing lip gloss from CVS?" I asked her.

She shrugged. "I stole lip gloss from CVS."

"I heard. But I don't understand why you did it. Your grandma told me she gave you twenty dollars, and the lip gloss was only like three dollars."

"It wasn't about the money," she said. "It was about the thrill."

"You think getting arrested is thrilling? You think having to go to court and possibly being sent to a juvenile jail is thrilling? You think your grandma having to pay your fines and court costs is thrilling?"

"No," she said seriously. "Not that stuff. I really do feel bad about the fines."

"You should. Especially since she was nice enough to give you money to shop. A lot of kids your age don't get an allowance."

"I know," she agreed. "None of my friends ever have money. That's why they steal."

"Did they know that you had money that day?"

She shook her head.

"Why didn't you tell them that you didn't need to steal makeup? That you could buy it?"

She shrugged and looked at the ground. "I don't know. I guess I wanted them to like me. To think I was brave."

Oh dear ... she reminded me so much of myself for saying that.

"Violet," I started off cautiously. "Being a follower is not brave. It's weak. The brave person would be the one who said to all her friends, 'Hey, we have enough makeup and stealing is for losers. Let's take my allowance and get a pizza instead.'"

She shook her head. "You don't understand," she told me. "There are two kinds of people at my school – rich ones and poor ones. I'm like the only one in the middle. I can't pretend to be rich but I can pretend to be poor."

"I understand wanting to fit in. But stealing doesn't make you poor; it makes you a criminal. You really have to stop worrying about what people think before it takes over your life, and you don't even remember who you really are anymore."

She snorted. "That's great coming from you."

I was shocked at her audacity. "What do you mean?"

"Look at you with your Kate Spade bag and your Victoria's Secret water bottle that probably weighs fifteen pounds. You didn't bring that to the park because it's a practical way to stay hydrated while you're roller skating. You brought it because other people would see it and think to themselves, oh how cute is that? I wish I had a water bottle like her."

Hmm ... she might have a point. I could have easily brought a plain looking and easier to carry water bottle with me.

I guess today is the day for everyone to call me out on my character flaws.

"And," she continued, "didn't you tell me last week that you didn't want to get a job at the bar you used to work at because you were afraid people you knew would see you working there and think you were a failure?"

Umm, yes I did say that.

"Yeah," I said quietly. "And you don't want to end up like me when you're older."

"Maybe not," she said honestly. "But I *would* like to have a Kate Spade bag someday."

We both laughed. I pulled some things out of my bag. I took out my wallet, my gigantic water bottle and my keys. I left the expensive mascara and lip-gloss inside and handed her the bag.

"Here," I said. "You can have it."

She looked stunned. "Really?"

"Sure," I told her. "I have enough bags."

"Wow," she said as she put the shoulder strap over her arm and stared down at it in awe. "That's really nice. Thank you."

"You're welcome," I told her.

"I can either use it to fit in with the rich kids or tell the poor kids I stole it," she explained. "Either way, it'll give me some clout."

I smiled and said a silent prayer. *Thank God it wasn't my Chloe bag.*

CHAPTER FOURTEEN

After my visit with Violet I started replaying the argument with Jake and thinking about all of the things he said. What was that crap about me choosing Caleb over him because of money? That may be how it looked to Jake, but that was not how it went down. Caleb came from an upper-middle class family. They had more than some but it took almost everything they had to put him through school. There were times in the beginning of our marriage when I didn't even have quarters for the laundry machines. Jake was way wrong. I wasn't a gold-digger.

He wasn't wrong about everything he said though. When I started thinking back, he was right about me running away. That day I'd caught Skank Queen in bed with Riley, I ran off to CMU instead of facing my friends at his birthday party that night. Originally I had only applied to UNC because I liked their school colors (I know, I know; I tend to make decisions for very random reasons), but when I got my admission letter shortly after Riley's birthday I accepted because I didn't want to go to U of M where most of my classmates were going, just to deal with the same looks of pity every day. I wanted to go where no one would know about my rise and fall in the high school hierarchy game. I thought, to hell with Riley and his homies. And I left. I guess I did run away.

When I found out about Destiny's child, I ran to Jake to keep my mind off it.

When Caleb told me he wanted a divorce, the first thing I did was run off to the beach only to run even farther to Michigan.

I went for one job interview, saw someone I didn't want to see and basically gave up job searching all together.

Jake was right. I *had* been running. Every time things didn't go my way, I left. Even if it was just going to the mall, I always left to find a distraction. And poor Jake, he'd basically been the distraction a number of times. It was like I'd been using him, and he didn't deserve that. He deserved someone who wanted to be with him always, even when times were great, not just when they'd been dumped. It suddenly occurred to me that I was a total jerk. All this time I'd been using him and abusing him, and he'd let me do it. I didn't know why he'd put up with it all this time, but I made a promise to myself that it was going to stop.

I had to stop running. I needed to face the fact that I hit the bottom and start climbing my way back up. I would get my job back at The Bar. The summers weren't as busy, but during the school year I could easily make several hundred a night, and if someone wanted to think I was a loser for that, screw them. I couldn't tell Violet to stop worrying about what people thought if I wasn't going to take my own advice.

I picked up my phone to call Jake, to thank him for pointing out a huge problem and to tell him about my new attitude. That was when I saw I had a missed call from my lawyer.

I called Jake twice and he didn't answer. That was fine. He had to come home eventually, and I'd be waiting for him when he did. I knew he wasn't bartending since it was a weeknight, so I figured he'd be home when he was done making his statement.

I had thrown some pulled pork in the slow cooker before I left for the park. I mastered the pork butt while I was at UNC. They call it "barbeque" down in North Carolina, just barbeque. Once that was ready, I "pulled" the pork and shredded carrots and cabbage for the cole slaw.

I spent the evening unpacking the bags I'd haphazardly packed that morning and repacking them in a neater way. I brought them downstairs and put them by the back door when I was done so they'd be ready to grab when I left in the morning.

And then I waited … a long time. I was watching *Chelsea Lately* in the living room when I finally heard his Jeep pull into the driveway. I got up and went into the kitchen to greet him at the back door. I felt like jumping into his arms and wrapping my legs around his waist like I'd seen people do in photos a lot but never in real life. But he wasn't alone. My brother walked in behind him.

Oh yeah. They were friends after all. I guess they would hang out together every once in awhile. But this really wasn't something I wanted to talk about in front of my brother so that meant I had to wait until Adam went to sleep. Oh well. At least he didn't walk in the door with Carmen or some other shooter girl with perfect legs.

"I made some barbeque," I told them. "And homemade slaw."

"Fantastic!" Adam said and grabbed a plate right away.

Jake looked less enthusiastic, but even a guy who is mad at you doesn't turn down food. Throughout getting his plate, filling it up and eating, he avoided my eyes the entire time. I didn't like it. Not one bit. He was making me angrier every second. And the strangest thing about it was that I wanted him more the madder I got.

I told them I was going to bed, but I really just wanted to get away so I could wait for Jake to come upstairs and ambush him. That doesn't sound totally stalker-esque does it?

I played some apps on my Kindle while I waited. *Grrr ... hurry the hell up already!*

Finally, FINALLY, I heard a beep on my phone.

JAKE: Are you awake?

Just seeing his name made my stomach feel like I was going downhill on a roller coaster.

ME: Yes
JAKE: Can I come in?
ME: Of course

I got out of bed and opened the door so Jake wouldn't have to knock, and Adam wouldn't get suspicious. When Jake reached the top of the stairs he slipped into my room like a snake, and I quickly closed the door behind him, leaving us in darkness except for the light on my Kindle Fire screen.

I hugged him because I'd really hated our argument earlier, and I was glad he was home. He smelled like beer. I know this is weird, and I'm pretty sure it has something to do with all of the sexual experimenting I did when I was in high school, because beer was usually involved, but the scent of beer on a guy's breath was a huge turn-on for me. And being in the dark, and so close ...

But I made a promise that I wouldn't use him as a distraction anymore, and I wasn't going to break it on the first day. At least, it wasn't my intention to. But Jake didn't pat my head this time. He hugged me back. Tightly, too.

"I've been waiting for you all night," I whispered into his neck.

"Me too," he said quietly. "I'm sorry."

"Me too."

Then he kissed me. It was rougher than usual. He was aggressive.

He wrapped his hands into the bun on the back of my head and held my face so tightly to his that even if I'd tried to pull away, I couldn't. Not that I tried to pull away. I had enough self-control not to start anything with him. But once he started it, it was over. I wasn't trying to stop him. The only thing I tried to do was catch my breath before he took it from me again.

He snapped my head back with a quick pull of my hair and I gasped. He kissed my shoulder, my neck, and just under my chin.

"Why?" he asked quietly when his mouth was right by my ear.

"Why what?" Why was he talking? I couldn't even think, let alone form words.

"Why are you sorry?" he asked.

"We'll talk later," I told him. "Right now I just want you to fuck me."

"Yes, ma'am," he said. He threw me onto the bed and, not long after, he ripped those ruffles right off my butt. Better late than never.

"We seriously have to stop doing this," I said quietly. We'd been quiet the whole time since my brother was home. There was something seriously hot about quiet sex in the dark. It's way underrated.

But my inability to keep it in my pants was not as hot. I was beginning to sound like a broken record. If my life was a movie, the viewers would be throwing popcorn at the screen right now. I was even annoying myself. Make up your damn mind!

He had been lying next to me but sat up in self-defense. "You're the one who told me to fuck you!"

I sat up, too, and pulled my comforter up over my chest to keep warm. "Shhh! That's because you're the one who got rough with me and kissed my chin. You know you can't pull my hair like that and kiss my chin and then *not* fuck me! It wouldn't be right!"

"What did you think I was going to do when you pulled me into your dark bedroom? Don't act like you're innocent in all this. You even had on those ruffles. But I'll take the blame if you want. I'm not the one who keeps saying we need to stop."

I smiled and shook my head at him in disbelief. "This. Is the best argument. Ever."

"I agree."

"At least we agree on one thing."

He lay back down, got comfortable and patted the bed beside him for me to lie down with him. So I did. I crawled under the covers facing him and enjoyed the comfort of being close to him.

"Why were you waiting for me all night?" he asked.

"I wanted to say thank you," I said quietly.

"For what?"

"For telling it to me straight."

"About the running?"

"You were right," I said. "I have been running. I just didn't realize it. No one ever called me out on it, and I'm glad you did. Now I can stop running and learn to deal with things instead."

"You're welcome. I guess. But if you're not running anymore then why are your bags sitting by the back door?"

"My lawyer called. We're going to have a face-to-face with the other side to see if we can work something out." I sighed because all of this divorce and lawyer stuff was annoying. "My lawyer thinks I should get more than fifty percent because I've been a homemaker all this time, and I'm the one who is going to have to get a lower paying job and get used to a lower paying lifestyle. Caleb's not agreeing on the bigger settlement, so we're having a sit-down. I don't care either way. I just want it over with so I can move on. But when someone says to come to The City, I don't argue."

"When are you leaving?"

"Tomorrow," I told him. "The meeting is Wednesday morning. I was gonna ask if you could drive me to the airport so I don't have to pay for parking. Adam has to work."

"I could just drive you to New York."

"You ... want to come to New York?"

He shrugged. "I don't bartend until the weekend, and I can reschedule some photo shoots. I've never been there, and I'd love to get some shots for my portfolio."

I sat up, suddenly not tired anymore, and clapped my hands together in excitement. "Omigod! You have to come then. I can buy you a plane ticket with all the money I made being your underwear model!"

He looked away from me. "I can't fly. You know."

I'm such a douchebag! How could I forget?

Jake's grandparents, his mom's parents, died in a plane crash when he was six. He and his mom lived with them so Jake was super close to them both.

After the accident, he was plagued with nightmares for many years, and refused to ever set foot on a plane. I thought it was weird that he would come to the lot by the airport with me if he was so afraid of them. I guess they didn't bother him as long as he was on the ground. But he swore he would never, ever step into one. Being on an airplane was his worst fear.

I lay back down and reached for his fingers next to mine on the bed. "I'm sorry. I wasn't thinking."

"It's fine. You up for a road trip?"

"Always," I said, eagerly. "But there's one thing you should know."

"What's that?"

"I am not going to have sex with you."

He laughed.

"Ever again." I said, determined.

"Please, Roxie, don't challenge me. It's only going to make me want to prove you wrong."

"I mean it!" I said, even if I knew he could easily prove me wrong if he tried. Especially with that take-charge-and-throw-me-around shit.

"Does that mean you want me to leave?" he asked.

NO! Never! I shook my head.

"And by the way," I said to change the subject, "that stuff you said earlier, about me being a gold digger-"

"I didn't mean it like that," he said. Even in the dim room I could tell he looked pained and annoyed. "I told you I didn't mean it. There's no reason to go over it again."

"No, there is," I said. "You don't know how it was. Caleb wasn't rich when I met him. He was a normal college guy. We really struggled in the beginning. I got my wedding dress at," I coughed because it was so hard to get the horrible words out, "David's Bridal on clearance for ninety-nine dollars!"

I waited for him to scream in horror or give me a look of disgust after I revealed that shameful secret, but his expression didn't change. Must be a guy thing.

"When we first moved to New York," I continued, "we were so broke we ate meatless pasta for dinner nearly every night, and I had to wear my jeans like three times in a row because we didn't have quarters for the laundry machines."

"I was wrong."

"And I have never been ashamed of you."

He groaned. "I take back everything I said earlier! Can you drop it?"

"No, I want to explain this to you," I said. "Bartending is a respectable profession. It requires a lot of skill."

He sighed and rolled over to face the ceiling. I guess he was giving up on getting me to drop it.

"Serving food and drinks is not as cool of a job," I explained. "It doesn't require any skill, except patience. And the ability to smile in someone's face when you really want to squeeze lemons in their eyes. It's a fine job for someone in school, someone younger. I just feel that, at my age, I should be able to get a more professional job."

"I get it," he said through clenched teeth.

"The reason I have been too embarrassed to get my job back at The Bar is because I feel like working where I worked eight years ago is moving backward, ya know?"

"If you were moving forward in the wrong direction, maybe moving backward isn't a bad thing," he said.

"No, maybe not," I said thoughtfully.

We were both quiet for a few minutes. Long enough for him to relax again. He took my hand in his and started running his finger up and down the inside of my palm.

Then I remembered something else he said yesterday.

"And one more thing," I said.

He dropped my hand and groaned. He knew where this was going. "Just let it go."

"I didn't choose him over you."

He took a deep breath. I could tell that my usually calm and patient friend was starting to lose that infamous patience. He sat up again. "I'm going back to my room."

"No," I said, pulling him back down. "I won't talk about it again. Just have your facts straight. I didn't choose him over you because I didn't have you to choose. You told me long-distance relationships were stupid. You said it was best for us both to move on. So I did. And there is no reason to talk about it again."

"Agreed."

I have always been a huge fan of road trips as long as the weather was nice. Winter road trips were awful, sucky, nuggets of crap. Summer road trips were the most fun to be had in a car.

Never mind. What was I saying? Jake and I had plenty of fun in cars during *The Summer of Jake and Roxie*. Most of the time when the car wasn't moving … if you know what I mean. And a few times when it was, wink wink. I know, it's totally juvenile, but I mentioned before that we had to get creative at times. I had more fun with Jake in cars and trucks that summer than I ever had in my Manhattan bed, even with the best sheets and comforters money could buy.

Anyway, I'm digressing. Our first stop was McDonald's because both of us had a few drinks last night and stayed up way too late. Everyone knows a McDonald's Coke is the best hangover cure you can get through a drive-thru. Knowing I was about to set out on what I hoped would be a great adventure, I was in a fantastic mood. When we got to the window to pay, I told the girl working the drive-thru that I was going to pay for the order of the person behind me, too.

"What'd you do that for?" Jake asked.

I shrugged. "It's the little gestures that can really make a person's day." I didn't mention that GLL Challenge #3 was to do something nice for a stranger.

After McDonald's, we stopped at the gas station to fill up … on candy. It would be criminal to go on a road trip without gummi bears.

Jake did most of the driving while I was in charge of entertainment. The eight hour drive went by quickly, thanks to my expertise in road trip playlists and conversational games. He was so easy to be around, especially when we were just hanging out and acting like friends and not having any dramatic meltdowns.

We arrived in NYC (aka My Soulmate) at around 4pm. I moved to the driver's seat to give him a drive-by tour of some of Manhattan's most popular spots. We drove through Times Square, downtown and the former site of the World Trade Center, as well as Battery Park and the Statue of Liberty, Grand Central, Rockefeller Center, and Central Park.

Being back in The City made me feel like a completely different person. In Ann Arbor I was pathetic and whiny, but NYC gave me a confidence I'd never been able to find anywhere else. No job? Big deal. No husband? Big deal. New York does that to people. It's like a drug. It makes people happy.

Jake was having a good time too. He did non-stop clicking on his camera during the drive-through tour and also had a permanent smile on his face.

By the time we'd driven around the island, I was starving and ready to get out of the car. We had a double room reserved at The Plaza Hotel. I'd tried getting us a room at the Soho Grande or Tribeca Grande, but they were booked. The Plaza would have to do (sniff sniff). It was probably better that we stayed on the Upper Side anyway – less chance of running into Caleb up there. The last thing I wanted was for Caleb or his lawyer or any of his friends to see me with Jake. It wouldn't look good, especially since I was there to try to get more money from him.

I was used to being a spoiled princess, so I walked into the hotel with my head held high and acted as if I belonged there. When we got into the room, I lay down on my stomach on one of the beds and checked out the room service menu.

"What do you feel like for dinner?" I asked him. "We can go out, eat downstairs or order room service or delivery."

"Um ..." he looked dumbstruck by all of it. He

wouldn't have been any less obvious if he had the word "tourist" tattooed on his forehead. "You're the one who knows what you're doing. You decide."

I rolled over onto my side and propped my head up on my wrist. "I'm way too hungry right now to bother getting ready to go out so I vote for room service."

He agreed to room service for dinner as long as we could go out later on so he could take some pictures of the city at night. We were driving home tomorrow after the meeting so he only had one night in New York. I wanted to stay longer (like forever), but I was only supposed to use Caleb's travel expense account for divorce-related stuff, like meetings and court. I didn't think it would be right to stay longer than I needed to and bill him for it.

***

"I love room service," I told Jake once the food arrived and I was digging into a bunch of yummy carbs. We each sat cross-legged on our own beds while we ate. "Sometimes it's nice to be able to enjoy a fine cooked meal while wearing cutoff shorts, yesterday's makeup and a ponytail. Don't you think?"

"I would rather die than wear cutoff shorts," he said like a smartass. "But yeah, this steak is great. I can see how you got sucked into this world."

"I didn't get sucked in," I said, defensively. "It's not some kind of cult, Jake. I chose to live here. And even though my marriage didn't work out, I don't regret moving here. This is where I belong."

"I didn't mean the city sucked you in. I was talking about all of the rich people stuff. Like this hotel. And room service. You seem like a completely different person when you're here. I feel like I don't even know you right now."

Hmm. He was right. He really didn't know this version of me. "Do you want to know me?"

He set his fork on his plate and looked at me thoughtfully and then shrugged. "I'm not sure." That's Jake. Always honest.

When we were done getting ready for the night, I took Jake on a photography/barhopping night in NYC. My annoyance with him and the comment he'd made about not wanting to know me left me confused and frustrated. I took my frustrations out on my hair and face. A person can always tell what kind of mood I'm in by the amount of makeup on my face. If you see black eyeliner, walk the other way.

I put on my new hot pink peep-toes, the ones I'd bought at Barney's the day Caleb told me he wanted a divorce. I hadn't been able to wear them yet, and this city was made for shoes like these. People in Ann Arbor wouldn't know the difference between a Louboutin and a Balenciaga while some women in New York could name your shoe designer from three blocks away.

I introduced Jake to the world of NYC transportation by using both taxis and the subway. I also showed him all about overpriced drinking. We went to bars in Chelsea, Murray Hill, the Meatpacking District and waited thirty minutes to get up on the garden rooftop bar at 230 Fifth where he *oohed* and *ahhed* and snapped like I knew he would.

By the time we got downtown to see Hope at her martini bar, we were both pretty buzzed. She didn't know I was coming and screamed out loud when she saw me.

"Who is this stunning young man you've brought into my bar?" was the first question. No hi, how are you, what are you doing here – just who is the guy.

"Hope, this is Jake. Jake – Hope."

"Oh," she said with a nod of recognition. "The roommate slash ex-boyfriend slash lifelong friend of the family who you accidentally had sex with?"

"Yeah," I replied. "More than once."

"Nice going!" she said in approval. Jake was standing right next to me and even though the music was loud, Hope was also loud, so I was pretty sure he could hear the conversation. Especially when he looked at me with that shit-eating grin I loved to hate.

"Come on, I'll buy you a drink," she said, pulling me over to the bar. "You look great. You look young and happy, like the old fun Roxie again. How's the list?" she asked while she shook up some watermelon juice martinis.

"It's fine," I said. I gave her a look that I hoped she would understand. It meant not to talk about the list right now.

She looked back at me like she didn't understand. "There's a photo booth over there," she said. "You know, in case you need one."

Ah ha. GLL Challenge #6 – Get your photo taken in a photo booth … Topless. And GLL Challenge #7 – Give the photo to someone.

"I got this," I said. "Take care of my guy for me, will you? Don't let him get lost."

For the first two shots in the photo booth I tried to look sweet and innocent. For the third one, I flashed the camera and gave my best supermodel expression. In the fourth one, I was sweet and innocent again. *Jake is going to love it,* I thought, as I stepped out of the photo booth proudly. He loves the sweet and innocent girl turned naughty kind of stuff.

I handed it to him at the bar right in front of Hope who gave me a knowing smile. "I wouldn't go topless for all of Facebook," I told him, "but I'll go topless for you."

"You're a tease," he said smiling. "You can't tell me you never want to have sex with me again and then give me a picture like this."

I took it from his hands and stuck it in my purse for safekeeping. "I never said I didn't want to. I just said I wasn't going to." Were we really having this discussion in public? In a loud bar where I needed to raise my voice to be heard? *I must be drunk.* As if passing around a topless photo of myself wasn't my first clue.

"Maybe you can explain the difference to me later," he said with a smirk. "After sex."

I playfully punched him in the arm. "Not happening. Can we stop talking about it?"

He laughed out loud. "You're opposed to uncomfortable conversations when you're on the other side of them, huh?"

I rolled my eyes. "Are you having fun?"

He smiled at me and took my hand in his. "You know I am."

I pulled my hand away. Being drunk around him was no good. When I was sober I could try to keep myself in check, but when I was drunk, the game was over. We needed to sober up a little before we went back to the Plaza, and we weren't going to do it in a bar. Air. We needed air.

"We should probably start heading back," I yelled over the music. "I've got that meeting in the morning."

He nodded and took my hand again. I let him keep it this time since it was easier to get out of the crowd that way.

When we were back on the street I asked him if he got the pictures he wanted.

"I would have gotten better ones if I'd had my

tripod, but I didn't want to carry a bunch of gear around all night."

I got an idea. "Hey, I know where we can go! The condo is only a few blocks away. You can set the camera down on the balcony and get some awesome pics. I still have my key and we haven't rented it out yet."

I started walking faster out of excitement. I couldn't wait to show Jake my beloved terrace and its incredible panoramic views. Maybe then he could get to know the New York me.

He kind of pulled my hand back a little though.

"What?" I asked him.

He shrugged. "I don't know. Are you sure? It won't make you upset or anything?"

"No way," I answered quickly. "I love my condo. I can't wait to show you the views."

I realized as soon as I opened the door that someone was living in the condo, the condo that I was still paying half the payments for each month. The empty beer bottles on the coffee table and dirty dishes on the counter gave it away. My first thought was that Caleb had rented it out and forgotten to tell me, in which case I intended on leaving immediately and praying that the tenant never found out I'd walked into his or her apartment, especially since there were noises coming from the bedroom that were of a private nature, if you know what I mean.

Caleb was as anal-retentive as they came. He wouldn't ordinarily leave beer bottles and dirty dishes around. He preferred neat and orderly to chaotic and disorganized. Every night when he came home from work he took off his shoes, polished them with a special rag and lined them up evenly and neatly next to the other shoes on the mat. When I looked down, there they were; shiny and sharp and lined up as always.

I should have left. But I didn't. I headed toward the bedroom. Jake put a hand on my shoulder to stop me but my adrenaline had kicked in and there *was* no stopping me. I moved fast and burst into the bedroom without warning. Afterward, I really wished I had knocked.

The first thing I saw was a blonde head, a cheerleader's uniform and some pom-poms. Next, I saw a person sitting on the bed wearing nothing but a black, furry bear mask.

It all happened so quickly, but I *really* thought I had walked in on Rebecca Dunbar going down on my husband while he sat on our bed dressed as a bear. I mean, *that* would be kind of weird, right? And most likely traumatizing. And certainly vomit-inducing to the current-but-soon-to-be-ex wife who drank seven cocktails in the last four hours.

Except that's not what I saw at all. It was way worse than that.

When the cheerleader turned around I saw that it was Caleb – wearing a cheerleader's uniform and a wig – not Rebecca. And when the bear stood up and took off the mask, I saw it was Rebecca Dunbar ... wearing a strap-on.

I am not a prude. I can handle a little bit of freaky shit. But that was the melting pot of freaky shit. It was a pot of Freaky Shit Stew and they had thrown in a little bit of everything.

I didn't make it to the toilet. I tried and I even covered my mouth but I didn't make it. Oh well. Let them clean it up. I took off running, grabbed Jake's hand and pulled him out the door with me. I was too scared to wait for an elevator because they'd likely be dressed and running after me before it arrived. I ran for the door to the stairs and slammed it open.

I quickly removed my heels and ran down the stairs, totally expecting Caleb to chase after me with a chainsaw and then throw it down at me like in the movie *American Psycho*. I had never been more scared in all my life.

I ran down four floors and when I didn't hear anyone following us, I thought it was safe to leave the stairwell. I pulled Jake back into the hallway, closed the door to the stairwell and leaned against it so they couldn't open it if they tried. It was now time for me to slide down the wall and put my head in my hands like they do in the movies.

"I don't want to leave for awhile," I whispered to Jake. "Just in case they come after me."

"I'm starting to feel like I'm in a James Bond movie," he whispered back.

"I'm starting to feel like I'm in a Tom Cruise movie," I said. "A horror film starring Tom Cruise."

He looked alarmed. "That does sound scary," he said seriously.

I shook my head slowly. "You don't even know, Jake. You don't even want to know. I won't even scar you for life by telling you."

"That bad?"

"Worse."

He sat down next to me on the floor and turned on his camera. "Then I won't show this to you. But you might want to let your lawyer know you have it on camera."

We waited in the hallway four floors down for about thirty minutes before I felt it was safe to take an elevator. I worried they'd be waiting for us in the lobby, but they weren't. We escaped the building safely, and I found a cab right away, even at the late hour.

It wasn't a surprise to me when my cell phone rang right after Jake and I got back to our hotel room.

"I just got an emergency call from the other side," my lawyer told me. She sounded raspy, like she'd been woken up. "The meeting tomorrow morning has been postponed. He said he and his client have a lot to discuss before we meet. Do you have any idea what this is about?"

"Unfortunately," I said gravely.

"Do you want to tell me?"

"I caught him doing some pretty twisted stuff with his coworker's wife. I really don't want to get into detail because it's pretty, um, disturbing. But I have a picture."

"Okay," she paused. "This could be really good news for us, Roxie. He said he'd call me by tomorrow afternoon to reschedule. Why don't you sit tight for one more day and I'll see if we can get this taken care of quickly."

"Sounds good. Talk to you tomorrow then." I hung up and gave Jake a small smile. "I guess you get to spend some more time in New York."

He put his hands just under my shoulders in that calming way he's done before and looked me in the eye. "How are you feeling? Are you okay? I don't want to be happy about staying another day if you're miserable."

I shook my head. "I actually feel kind of relieved because this explains so much." I paused. "I wish I hadn't had to see it firsthand, though. And how did you get the picture? I thought you stayed in the living room. I never saw you follow me."

He shrugged. "I'm quick."

I showered to get the smell of vomit off me, put on my pajamas and then came out to the sink to brush my teeth. Jake came over and started brushing his teeth right beside me. He gave me that "let's fuck" look in the mirror. I just laughed and showed him a mouthful of toothpaste.

"I'm going to bed," I said when I was done. "Think about some places you want to see tomorrow."

I got into the bed closest to the window and turned away from him. *Mmm, aren't hotel beds the best?* He turned the lights off, and I heard him get into his bed, too.

It was about ten minutes later when he said, "You awake?"

"Yeah."

"If it wasn't money, then what was it? When I thought he was rich I assumed that was your motive. But now, with you telling me he was just some regular guy, I'm even more confused because the guy is a dick. He's a sick dick. A sick dick who likes dicks. On chicks."

I started laughing so hard I nearly peed myself. I knew it wasn't funny, but I was glad I was able to laugh about it. I was laughing too hard to answer the question. I didn't even know if there was an answer to the question. Why had I married Caleb? Why had I ever even gone out with him?

"I just can't believe that's the guy you chose over me," Jake said quietly.

I turned around to face his bed. The room was not completely dark, but merely dim, thanks to all of the lights on the street. I could see the outline of his face. "Jake, stop saying that. I didn't choose him over you. It's not like someone said 'do you want Caleb or Jake?' I didn't have you as an option. You weren't there."

"No, I wasn't there. I was at home waiting for

you to come back. I figured I'd been waiting for you for like ten years so what was nine more months?" He rolled onto his back and faced the ceiling. "I thought you were coming back. You know, *just so you have your facts straight*," he mocked me. "And I was fine with you meeting someone else and falling in love—"

I snorted from the other bed at the thought of being in love with Caleb.

"—and getting engaged. I was too young to think of anything that serious. But I hated it that you never talked to me about it. You just sent me an invitation to your wedding. You weren't just some chick I hooked up with one summer. You and your family were the only people I'd ever really had in my life. And you acted like I was never anything to you but a wedding gift. It was pretty shitty. So forgive me if I keep bringing up the past or asking you questions. I'm just trying to understand why it happened."

Could this night get any fucking worse? A winter storm advisory would have been appreciated. At least then I could have brought a jacket. I was totally not prepared for this snowball fight. It wasn't like I'd had eight years to prepare or anything.

I rolled onto my back and sighed. Jake was right. The way I'd handled it was wrong. Even if he had told me he didn't want a long-distance relationship, he had been my closest guy friend. We had been friends since I was three years old. He deserved a phone call or, at the very least, an email.

I turned over to face his bed again. "You're right. It was shitty the way I did things. At first I thought it was too soon to talk to you about it. Then my mom sent the invitations out and I thought it was too late. And so much time kept going by, and I thought about you a lot, but I was too scared to talk to you because I thought you'd be mad. You know I don't like confrontations. When even more time went by I figured you'd forgotten all about me by then."

He didn't say anything so I continued.

"And I can't really explain what I was thinking when I started seeing Caleb. I was young and stupid, and here was this guy telling me he was moving to New York and taking me with him. He was so sure of himself, and in control, and I listened to him. You know I'd wanted to move to New York since I was little. And it was everything I thought it would be. Even when we were struggling, I was happy to be here. But I never meant to hurt you or screw things up with us, and I'm sorry for that. Do you think you'll ever be able to forgive me?"

Even in the dark I could see him smile. "Of course, Little Girl. I already did. I just always wondered if maybe I did something wrong, if it was my fault. But I'm not holding it against you."

"It wasn't your fault, Jake. I promise."

I heard his breathing change a little while later and knew he had fallen asleep. If only I was so lucky. I was too tired to deal with this, but I couldn't seem to fall asleep. I kept imagining Jake getting that wedding invitation without hearing a word from me. He must have felt like part of his second family had abandoned him. He probably felt like he didn't matter at all. I had felt like that before, several times, and I knew from experience that it was the worst feeling.

Knowing I was responsible for hurting him like that made me so angry with myself. I felt awful. I swear I could spend whatever I had left of my life making it up to him and I'd still feel bad about it.

It was hard to be so far away from him after what he'd just told me. I needed him to know how sorry I was. And that he *did* matter. *A lot.* That was why I crawled into his bed with him. I had no trouble falling asleep after that.

The next thing I knew, I was waking up to a bright and beautiful Manhattan morning. The sounds of traffic instantly made me feel at home. Jake was next to me in the bed – shirtless! – awake and smiling at me from under the comforter. I could smell coffee. I was pretty sure he'd been up for awhile which made me a little nervous. I liked to be the one who woke up first so I didn't get caught drooling or farting in my sleep or anything embarrassing like that. But it was too perfect of a scene for me to care. The way his tan skin contrasted with the pristine white bedding, the way his 500-watt smile lit up the room, and the way the sun beamed in through the windows, it was like I was in my own fabric softener commercial.

There was a time when I didn't think life got any better than drinking coffee on a beautiful summer morning in NYC. That changed when my coffee was poured by a smiling and shirtless Jake. This was the apex of mornings right here. There was no way it could get better – unless he kissed me good morning.

I couldn't stop the images from running through my mind. Jake, me, soft fluffy comforter, two cute kids bouncing around on a huge bed; two cute kids climbing the *Alice in Wonderland* statue in Central Park while I freak out that they might fall and Jake laughs at my anxiety and takes pictures of us; the four of us plopping down on a blanket and having a picnic in the park. It was nice. I didn't want to turn the reel off, but I had to.

"I hope you don't mind," he said, as he handed me the coffee, cream and sugar already mixed in the way I liked it, "but I ordered some breakfast from room service."

I graciously accepted the mug and laughed. "Who is getting sucked into this world?"

CHAPTER FIFTEEN

Insert: Central Park Montage.

This is the part of my movie that could be summed up in an assortment of nice clips of Jake and me enjoying a beautiful summer day in Central Park. We played a game of Checkers, swung on the swings at one of the playgrounds (GLL Challenge #21), explored the Belvedere Castle, took a walk through the Shakespeare Garden, ate hotdogs from a vendor, walked through the most photographed area of the park, the Mall, and lounged on the infamous steps of The Met.

Jake was beyond happy with all of the photo ops. A few times during the afternoon he took my hand. I let him. It was okay for friends to hold hands, wasn't it?

We were both exhausted when we finally collapsed on the lawn of Sheep Meadow with all of the other sunbathers. We lay on our backs with our hands behind our heads and gazed up at the view of the skyline above the trees.

"This is incredible," he said.

I turned my head to look at him and smiled. "It really is." Remembering GLL Challenge #15 was to take a nap in a park, I pulled my cell phone out of my purse and set my alarm for thirty minutes from now. "We're taking a nap," I told him.

He pulled me over toward him, and I rested my head on his shoulder and fell right asleep.

My lawyer called shortly after my alarm went off, while we walked back to the Plaza. Caleb and his team had done some brainstorming and would be ready to see me in the morning.

I had so many reasons to be nervous about it. What was he going to be like? Would he be sorry about what he had done or only sorry he got caught? Would he be mad at me for catching him or mad at himself for not changing the locks? Would he be embarrassed and lash out at me as a result? Would he yell at me for throwing up all over the place? Would it be like in the movies where a bunch of stuffy people in expensive suits argued with each other across the table right next to a window with amazing views of the city?

I wasn't looking forward to seeing Caleb's face again – that was for sure. Just thinking about what I had seen might make me throw up right in front of him. I was curious how long he'd been engaging in such extracurricular activities, but then again, I didn't want to hear his answer. Ugh, so not looking forward to the meeting. I really wished I could bring Jake along for support, but I knew that would look bad. I had to stop acting like he was my lifeline anyway. I'd lived without him for eight years. I could go to a meeting without him.

"You okay?" Jake asked when we walked into our room. I had been quiet ever since the phone call.

"Just nervous," I said with a shrug. I lay down on my bed and curled into the fetal position. "I've never gotten divorced before so I'm not sure what to expect from this. I'm afraid he might be mean to me."

I saw his body tensed up as he sat next to me on the bed. "Is he usually mean to you?" he asked. He looked very concerned. Way more concerned than I deserved.

"No, no," I said quickly. "He was never mean to me in a bullying kind of way. He was never abusive, if that's what you think."

I could actually see his body relax right in front of me.

"You haven't seemed very upset about this," he said. "Even after what we saw last night, you seem to be handling it pretty well. I thought maybe that was because he'd been hurting you and you were happy it was over."

"No, no, nothing like that. He just worked a lot, and I was lonely. But there was no abuse. I promise." I paused. "And if I'm handling it well, it's because of you."

"Really?" he looked pleased. "What did I do?"

"You did the same thing you've done after every break-up I've ever had. You distracted me and made me feel better. Does that make you feel used?"

He looked surprised. "No. Isn't that what friends do?"

"I think friends bring over cookie dough, funny movies and tequila when their friends are sad. I don't think most friends use sex as a distraction."

He smiled. "Hey, I don't mind. I'll gladly distract you any time. If you're worried about the meeting tomorrow, I can distract you right now."

I smiled and shook my head. "I'm being serious. After what you said last night, about how my family were the only people you had – "

"Hey," he interrupted. "Don't even think about that. I said what I had to say. I asked what I needed to ask. It's over now. Don't over-think it. Don't think about it at all. It doesn't matter anymore."

I sat up next to him on the bed. I needed to be close to him. I needed him to know how much he meant to me. I had the sudden urge to tell him I loved him. I'd been saying "I love you" to Jake since I was a kid. But something felt different now. I couldn't get the words out. I felt like they were suddenly going to mean too much. My chest tightened up like someone was sitting on top of me, and I felt like I was going to suffocate.

Our faces were only inches apart. He looked at me like he was waiting for me to say something. And he had a reason to think that because I did have something I wanted to say, but I couldn't get the words out.

Don't tell my girlfriend about this.

It was that image again. The one I'd had that afternoon in Mount Pleasant twelve years ago. I couldn't do it. I couldn't let that happen. I could say "I love you" to Jake right now and mean it with every piece of me. He could say it back, and maybe he would even mean it too. We could make love on the fluffy Plaza bed and have a romantic night together in the city. We could go home tomorrow and have a blast finding secret places to rendezvous at the house whenever Adam was home. We could sneak kisses in when no one was looking and do a little bit more than skinny-dipping in our neighbors' yards in the middle of the night.

Fall would come and we could rake the leaves

into piles and jump around in them and go to the apple orchard for cider and carve pumpkins together to put on the porch.

During the holidays, we could hang mistletoe in the archway between the living room and dining room and then hang out underneath it so we would have an excuse to kiss. We could hide secret presents around the house for each other to find.

I had no doubt we could have a few wonderful seasons together. But I also had no doubt it would one day end. I know people say it's better to have loved and lost than never to have loved at all. But I have loved and lost – three times now. And I disagreed with that proverb wholeheartedly ... I mean broken-heartedly.

I stood up and walked over to the sink. I took a few deep breaths and blew them out to try to calm myself down. *I'm in love with Jake,* I suddenly realized. *My safety guy isn't safe anymore.*

Don't panic, I told myself. Nothing has to change. We can still be friends. The "benefits" couldn't happen anymore, but everything else could stay the same. I just needed a distraction – again. I needed to be distracted from my distraction.

"You wanna go shopping?" I asked.

He was still sitting on the bed where I'd abruptly left him. He looked confused. "Not really."

"You don't have to. You have a GPS on your phone so you can do something on your own and we can meet up later if you want."

He stood up and walked over to the sink. He stood behind me and looked at my face in the mirror. "Why do I feel like you're trying to get rid of me?"

I gave him my best fake smile in the mirror. "I'm not trying to get rid of you. But I want to make sure you get to do the things you want to do while you're here, and I know Chanel and Marc Jacobs probably aren't on your list."

They shouldn't be on my list either. Michigan Roxie doesn't spend three months of rent money on one handbag.

And come on, Roxie. Could you maybe try to act normal? I wouldn't normally tell my friend to basically screw off and do his own thing in a place he's never been. Just because I was in love with him didn't mean I needed to be mean. *This isn't kindergarten. What the hell is wrong with me?*

I turned around. That was probably a mistake because now I was facing him head on. His face was about two inches from mine, and he was looking down at me. His eyes were focused on me intently, like he was searching for an answer to my sudden change of behavior. I looked down because the eye contact was too intense for me, and what was below the eyes? His lips. Ugh, not good.

I turned around again and kept busy by applying some mascara. "I'm sorry, Jake. I don't need to go shopping. You're the tourist here. Is there something you want to do?"

My phone beeped in my purse. I was thankful for the interruption. He backed away from me, and I went back over to the bed and reached into my purse to grab the phone. It was a text from Hope.

HOPE: Dinner tonight?

"It's Hope," I told Jake. "She wants to know if we want to have dinner later, but we don't have to if you don't want to."

"Dinner is fine, but we need lunch first. And please don't say another hot dog."

I laughed and texted her back.

ME: How bout lunch first? PB & Co?
HOPE: Super.

I threw the phone back into my purse. "Let's have lunch," I told Jake.

We took a cab to Peanut Butter & Co by NYU. Jake loved it, as I knew he would. He had the peanut butter, banana, honey and bacon sandwich, and we all shared the eight different varieties of peanut butter in the sampler platter.

After lunch, he let us show him around The Village, Soho and Tribeca. I managed to keep my cravings for shopping at bay, but when we walked past the Marc Jacobs store, I couldn't help but open the door so I could smell it. I know. I'm lucky I didn't get arrested.

We took a ride on the Staten Island Ferry so Jake could get some pictures of the skyline and the Statue of Liberty. Then it was time for some cocktails and tapas for dinner.

It was nice having Hope around the whole time because I was a little apprehensive about being alone with Jake. I could tell by the little glances I kept getting from him throughout the night that he was suspicious of me. He could tell something was different. I was hoping to avoid that conversation until I got my feelings into check.

At one point, when Jake had gone to the bathroom, Hope said to me, "I would've told you to fall in love this summer, but I thought that was too ambitious."

"No way," I said. "I haven't even had a chance to fall in like. I've been too busy moping around to meet guys."

She smiled and shook her head. "Really, Roxie? You didn't let me finish. I was going to say I didn't think you could fall in love so soon, but I underestimated you."

"Oh, you mean Jake?" I flipped my hand and blew my bangs out of my eyes. "That's just a childhood crush. I have love for him, but it's not something that could work out in the grown-up world."

"Why not?"

I shrugged. "I don't know. Too much history. Too much family involvement. He being a Casanova. Me being a flake who never knows what I want. Lots of reasons."

"I'm adding an amendment to the Good Life List," she informed me. "It's called Take a Fucking Chance!"

"I took a chance on Caleb, and where did that get me?" I asked.

"It got you a lot more than you realize," she said seriously. "It got you to New York. It got you to me. You lived in an apartment I would give my arm for. Like, I would seriously let you cut off my arm with a dull steak knife to live there. And Caleb used to be an okay guy. You had some good years together. It wasn't a total waste. It just didn't work out. He changed. You changed. Things happen. But you can't use that as an excuse to give up something that could be great. Don't let him get away again."

I was glad Jake came back to the table then, and I didn't have the opportunity to argue with her. My feelings for Jake were too personal for me to discuss. With anyone. That was why, when we got back to the hotel, I feigned exhaustion and went straight to bed.

I let the hotel know we needed a late checkout

since my meeting wasn't until ten, and I wasn't sure how long it would last. I didn't want poor Jake to have to sit on top of our bags in the lobby.

The meeting was over before noon and as soon as I got outside I checked my phone and saw I had a text from Jake.

JAKE: Going to see Times Square. Meet me for lunch when you're done.

ME: Last time I ate in a restaurant in Times Square, I got food poisoning. There was so much power in my diarrhea, it propelled me off the toilet seat like a torpedo taking out a submarine.

JAKE: LMFAO! We can go somewhere else.

ME: I know a place more authentic. Go to the subway on 42nd and take the One train to W 79th. ONE train. I'll meet you.

JAKE: One train. Got it.

Since my meeting had been held on the Upper West Side, I arrived at the intersection of West 79th and Broadway before he did. I waited at the top of the stairs where he would exit the subway. After a few trains' worth of people walked past me, I finally saw him. The fact that he had been able to navigate the subway system with only a little instruction sent sparks over to my dynamite stick. He didn't help matters any by smiling that smile that made me want to tear his clothes off right in the middle of the busy intersection. I waved and watched him walk up the stairs toward me.

If I had been a stranger watching the scene unfold, I would have wondered who that smile was for. I would have waited to see which one was "that girl." I would have wondered if she knew how lucky she was to be loved like that. Sometimes you can see love in a person's eyes and, in that moment, I saw it. It was hard to believe it was looking at me. It might not be there forever, but right now I was "that girl." *I* was the lucky one.

When he reached the top he hugged me, and it wasn't a friends-only hug either. He wrapped his arms around my lower back and pulled my whole body into his, and I let him. I knew that anyone who was looking at us was probably envious. To the outside, we probably looked like a perfect couple.

I took him to Zabar's for lunch.

"How did the meeting go?" he asked for the second time while we stood in line at the deli.

"I'll tell you about it when we sit down."

It was crowded. The tables inside were already taken so we took our pastrami sandwiches outside and found a bench on the median.

"How'd the meeting go?" he asked for the third time.

I had just taken a huge bite of my sandwich so I pointed at my mouth to let him know I couldn't speak at the moment.

"You're doing this on purpose aren't you?" he asked.

I shook my head innocently and finally answered him when I stopped chewing.

"It went well. He was embarrassed and apologetic and looked like a dog with his tail between his legs."

"Good. So you got what you wanted then." It wasn't a question, but a statement. I knew him better than to think he would be nosy and pry.

"Yeah," I said. Truth was I could've gotten more. My lawyer wanted to push him and bring up the picture, but I was satisfied with their offer and didn't think it was necessary to embarrass him any further. Being a trophy wife was fun while it lasted, but I didn't want to be the girl who lived her whole life off of her ex's money like a bad sitcom-in-syndication. I didn't want to be a cast member on any *Ex-Housewives Who Took All His Money* reality shows. I wanted to find a way to make my own money and take care of myself. My student loans were paid off during the marriage and now he was taking care of most of my credit card debt. He was also buying me out of the condo, which ended up being worth a little more than we thought.

Considering all that, plus two years of maintenance and health insurance and his offer to pay part of my schooling in the future, I would have been one greedy ass bitch to pull that blackmail card out of my pocket.

"Does this mean it's officially over?" Jake asked.

"No," I explained. "Officially we have to wait for the judge to sign, but unofficially it's done with."

"Good," he said.

I was relieved the meeting was over and even more relieved that he'd offered so much without any issues. There had been no yelling, bitterness, or even a need for my trademark sarcasm. It was amicable. We both acted like adults. Even so, it didn't feel right to be jumping for joy over the end of my marriage. I knew reconciliation between us was impossible. I knew there was nothing I could have done to make things work (except maybe strapping on a you-know-what). And I truly believed I'd be happier and more fulfilled in the future than I'd been in the past. All this considered, though, there was still a part of me that felt like a failure, not just because of my marriage, but because of the time wasted.

When we were done eating we balled up all our garbage and I walked it over to the trash can on the corner. Jake looked at his phone to check the time.

"Are you ready to get our bags and get on the road?" he asked when I sat back down.

No! Never!

When I was a little girl, my parents went out with their friends every Friday night and left Adam and me with a babysitter – some teenager who lived down the street. She was nice and all. She let us stay up late to watch the entire TGIF lineup on ABC and never made us eat veggies. But she wasn't my mom and dad, and every time they tried to leave I would fling myself onto one of my parents' legs and wrap my little arms around them and scream and cry and carry on like I was gunning for an Academy Award.

At the thought of leaving NYC, I felt like doing the same thing.

This is my home. Just sitting here in the sunshine – watching the yellow cabs and buses go by, listening to the sirens and horns, the smell of my coffee mixed with the scent of hotdogs and sauerkraut coming from the vendor on the corner, the family of tourists on their way to the museum, the speed-walking business class trying to grab a quick bite on their lunch breaks, the woman wearing a pin-striped suit with purple Chuck Taylor shoes – it was all so New York. With Jake sitting right beside me, it was absolutely perfect.

I sighed and stood up. "Yeah, I guess we have to." I tried to disguise the disappointment in my voice, but I doubted Jake missed it. He never missed anything.

The drive home was never as fun as the drive there. He did most of the driving and I played with the music, just like last time. But the atmosphere wasn't the same.

When you begin a road trip there are so many possibilities and places to explore and get lost in. But when you have to go home and return to your normal not-on-vacation life, you can't expect everyone to be filled with cheer.

Even so, something wasn't quite right about us. Knowing that, though, didn't make me want to talk about it. I did a lot of fake sleeping to avoid conversation.

After a very long eight hours, we finally made it home and dropped our bags in the living room. Jake said he was tired and going straight to bed.

I yawned. "Yeah. Me too."

"I don't know how you could be tired since you slept practically the whole way home."

"Oh, well, you know," I explained. "It's like when you're super tired and you can't sleep – except it's the opposite. I'm so not-tired that I can't stay awake."

He gave me a sad smile and shook his head as though he didn't believe me. "Whatever you say, Roxie. Goodnight."

"Jake," I said as he started to walk away.

He turned back around.

"Umm," I began. Suddenly I felt shy and insecure. "Thanks for coming with me. It was nice to have a friend there."

He nodded slowly, like he was letting my words marinate for a minute. "No problem," he said and then paused before adding, "friend." The word sounded a bit harsh. "Glad I could help."

"Are you mad at me?" I asked. Ugh, I hate it when my insecurities speak without my permission. Jake seemed to have a bit of aggression in his voice, and he probably *was* mad at me, but I was supposed to be playing the-girl-who-didn't-care. Blurting that out pretty much gave me away.

He shook his head slowly. "No. I'm not mad at you. I'm confused. You clammed up, and you've been acting weird since yesterday."

I understood what he was saying. He was right. I had been acting weird.

"I thought you were worried about the meeting," he continued, "but you said everything went well. Except you looked sad when you said it, so I don't know what that means."

He was right again. I *was* sad. I was sad because I knew I had to move out. The reason I had moved in with Jake and Adam was because I didn't have enough money for my own place. That wasn't the case anymore, and it only made sense I would get out of their way. Except I didn't want to go to all the trouble of packing my things and loading a moving truck just to move a mile away. If I packed, I was going home to New York. It was the only thing I could do. It was the only thing that made sense to me. But how could I tell Jake without upsetting him?

I put a hand to my forehead and scrunched up my eyes. My head was killing me. "It's just that a lot of things happened today in that meeting, and now there are things that will change and it's a lot to think about right now."

"What happened?" he asked. "Are you guys getting back together? Is that why you're acting weird?"

"God, no!" I said quickly. "No. Absolutely not. Never."

"Did he give you the condo? Is that was this is about? Are you moving back to New York?"

I sighed and sat down on the couch. I put my

head in my hands because I hated having to tell him I was leaving again.

"No," I said quietly to the carpet. "He didn't give me the condo. I would never be able to afford it."

"But?" His voice was already getting louder. I was glad Adam wasn't home because I had a feeling this was going to be a blow out.

"But he's giving me half of what it's worth. Well, minus what we owe."

"And?"

"And he's paying off most of my credit cards."

"And what does that mean?" he asked, even though I knew he knew what it meant.

I shrugged and looked up at him with tears in my eyes. "I'm sorry, Jake," I whispered. "Being there, it's the only thing that feels right to me. I'm not running away. I'm only going back home."

"So what you're saying is you're moving back to New York?"

"Yeah," I whispered and looked back down again. And I waited. I waited for the explosion of accusations, for the psychoanalyzing, for him to tell me how crappy of a person I was to be leaving him AGAIN.

But it didn't happen.

He was quiet for a minute before he walked toward me on the couch. I felt a teardrop dangling from my chin and watched it splat onto the toe of his Adidas shoe. He patted my shoulder.

"If that's the only thing that feels right to you," he said quietly, "then you *should* go."

He left the room. I heard him walk up the stairs to his bedroom. Then I cried some more.

CHAPTER SIXTEEN

I was certain that I wanted to move back to the city, but that didn't mean I was going to pack up, take off and hope for the best. I needed a plan this time – a good solid plan.

I needed an apartment, of course. I could look on the internet, but I would need someone in New York to help me out too. A lot of listings on the internet were spam and scams and sometimes the best apartments were the ones with the inconspicuous For Rent signs in the windows.

I needed a job. Hope assured me that I could have a job at the martini bar, but I was going to look around a little on my own as well.

Most importantly, I needed to become self-sufficient. I could use Caleb's money to get by for a little while, but I needed to figure out a way to take care of myself before all of that money ran out. That was the tricky part because I was still unsure how to do that. Did I still want to pursue my MSW? Working with Violet had me doubting my abilities to change the world. I didn't feel I was in a position to mentor teenagers when I was such a mess myself. I was starting to wonder if social work was the wrong type of work for me. If that was true, what was the right type? Jake had joked about me starting up a catering business or party planning company. That sounded like something I'd enjoy doing a lot more than social work, but that kind of stuff only happened on TV. I'm not Bree Van de Kamp. I can't flitter about Wisteria Lane with a basket of muffins and all of a sudden be running my own empire. But even Rachael and Martha had to start somewhere. Maybe culinary school? Or public relations?

Whatever it was, I needed to stop screwing around. Now! No more wine or whining. No more roommate sex. No more TV series on Netflix. No more lounging around by the pool. *Mission: Back in the New York Groove* had begun.

Step One: Find a liaison in NYC. I called Hope and told her I was coming back. She agreed to be my apartment scout.

Step Two: Pack. Most of my things were still in boxes in the basement so all I really needed to pack were clothes, shoes, other accessories and beauty products, which I had in abundance. I set some things aside to take to the women's shelter too.

Feeling inspired, I went down to the basement to see what all I had down there. When the moving truck had arrived earlier in the summer, Jake and I threw everything down there, and I had never bothered to open any of the boxes to see what was in them. If I hadn't needed any of it in two months, I probably didn't need it at all. I might be able to donate more to the shelters than just shampoo and lotion. The less crap I had to haul back with me, the better.

I've never believed much in destiny. I always felt my life, and the way it turned out, was up to me. But of all the boxes down there, I do believe I was meant to open one. Lying right near the top of the only box I opened was a clock my mom had given to me when I graduated from UNC. It was engraved, "Your future is an unwritten script. Make it award-worthy. Love, Mom."

I kneeled down on the floor with the clock in my hands and let her words marinate for a minute. I thought back to the time in my life when I also believed my future would be award-worthy. During my marriage to Caleb, this clock had sat on my nightstand. Nearly every day I would glance at it and a little wave of disappointment would ripple through my mind. Why had I waited so long to realize my mistake? Why had I let him make the decision to save me? I should have had the courage to save myself! My mom had never said anything to me about it, but looking at the clock, I knew. I knew I hadn't achieved the greatness, or even the happiness, she had hoped for me. I'd let her down. I'd let everyone down.

But the clock was still ticking. I had time to make it right.

I knew what my mom had really been hoping for when she'd had that clock engraved. She didn't care about financial success. She didn't care if I married an important man or had an important job. She only wanted me to be happy.

I took another look into the box, and the next thing I laid my eyes on may have also been placed there by destiny. It was an expensive knife set I'd bought for myself a few years back, when I'd taken some cooking classes. The set of high quality cutlery even came with a carrying case.

I had signed up for those classes as a way to get out and be social and maybe make some new friends. I had gone once a week for ten weeks. Those classes were some of the most fun I'd ever had without alcohol.

Even though my decision-making record was pretty bleak, I was confident the one I made then was the right one for me. It was so right for me that I was surprised I hadn't thought of it sooner.

Step Three: Research. Feeling very accomplished, I took my tablet out to the pool to look for apartments, jobs, and culinary schools. I figured lounging by the pool could be permitted as long as I was doing something productive regarding my mission.

I did a lot more research throughout the next five days. I took back control of my life and ended up with some impressive stats.

Number of apartments looked at by Hope: 2
Number of gigantic decisions made: 1
Number of fantastic meals prepared: 12 (As if I even needed schooling).
Number of boxes donated to the homeless: 6
Number of schools applied to: 1
Number of times I saw Jake: 0

How is it possible to share a house with a person and not see him once in five days? Either he was super busy or super skilled at avoiding roommates. I was pretty sure it was the latter, but either way, his absence was driving me nuts.

When I made the decision to go to culinary school, I'd instantly felt inspired and determined and, for the first time in what seemed like years, I believed in myself. As soon as I clicked the send button on my online application to the Institute of Culinary Education (ICE), I felt like my imaginary audience was applauding. The people in the theater even stopped throwing popcorn at me and nodded in agreement as if to say, "Yeah, that's totally what she should do." I was relieved, happy and even proud of myself ... but without Jake to share it with, I'd only enjoyed it about half as much as I should have.

I tried not to be angry with him. I knew he was allowed to be upset with me. I didn't call him, go out of my way to find him or send him any texts. I let him deal with whatever he had to deal with and hoped when he reared his head around me again, we could skip right over the argument and go back to being friends.

That was why I didn't give him any attitude when he finally came around on the sixth day.

I was in the kitchen cutting up veggies for kabobs when he casually walked in from the living room. He was carrying a bottle of water, and the way he was twisting the cap back and forth in his hands showed me his casualness was just an act – he was nervous.

"Hey!" I said cheerfully. "I'm glad you're here."

"Why's that? You need some help?"

"I do," I admitted. "You wanna skewer the meat?"

He shrugged and sat down on the bar stool across from me.

I grabbed two bowls from the fridge; one with steak and one with chicken, both marinating in different sauces. I set them down on the island, and he started threading.

"You've been doing a lot of cooking lately," he observed.

"Yeah," I said cheerfully. "I've decided to go to

culinary school."

"I see."

"I wanted to tell you, but you were off somewhere avoiding me." I smiled to let him know I wasn't mad.

"I wasn't avoiding you," he insisted. "I just needed some space to get you out of me."

"Get me out of you?" I repeated.

"Like a detox," he explained. "Or I guess a de-Rox."

I laughed and looked up from the peppers on my cutting board. "That's funny. But you don't need to de-Rox just because I'm moving. It won't be like last time. We'll still be friends, and you can visit whenever you want."

"It was more the *idea* of you I needed to get out of my head," he said honestly. "Ever since you came back, I've been thinking we might get a second chance. I thought once everything was done with your divorce, it would finally be the right time for us. Now I know it's not happening. So I took a few days off, got rid of the idea and I'm ready to help you pack. What is this steak soaking in? It smells good enough to eat right out of the bowl."

My stomach turned at the thought of eating raw meat and possibly e-coli. Or maybe it was him telling me he'd help me pack that made me feel sick. "What do you mean you're ready to help me pack?" I was officially in defensive mode. "You're in a hurry to get me out of here? It's going to be a few weeks. Maybe more."

He shrugged again and looked nonchalant. "I'm not in a hurry. I'm just over it. Stay as long as you want. All I'm saying is when you're ready to go – as your friend – I'll help you."

Maybe he wasn't trying to start a fight. Maybe I

was being too sensitive. But he was pissing me off. I set my knife down on the cutting board with enough force to make my peppers jump a little.

He sat up straighter and stopped threading. "Something wrong, friend?" he asked.

"Stop calling me that!" I ordered. "And I'm glad you're over it because there was never going to be a right time for us anyway!"

"Dude," he said calmly. "Chill the fuck out. I'm working with what I have here. Do you want me to be friendly, or would you rather I stay upstairs and cry into my pillow?"

I scowled and fought the urge to pick up the knife again because an angry woman should never hold a knife. "No, Jake. I want you to be friendly, not sarcastic. And I don't believe for a second you would cry over me because you'll move on to the next girl like you always do. There's always going to be a next girl, and that's exactly why there's NEVER going to be AN US!"

I looked up toward the ceiling and took a deep breath. I hadn't meant to raise my voice and get all out of control. Now I was embarrassed and wished I could take it back because I revealed way too much in that dramatic outburst.

Jake looked stunned for a second. He dropped the piece of steak and wooden skewer he'd been holding.

"What do you mean, baby?" His face looked wounded and his voice sounded just as hurt.

He called me baby. I could tell he hadn't meant to. It was a slip, but it sounded like he was my boyfriend or something. I really liked it. If I could close my eyes and pretend for a few moments there *was* an us – that Jake only wanted *me* and I would never have to worry about a pretty Shot Girl catching his eye and pulling him away – in those few moments I would be happier than I'd ever been. But it was a fantasy world, not the one we lived in.

I bit my lip to distract me because I could feel tears starting to form behind my eyes.

I shook my head and went back to cutting the peppers before I changed my mind and grabbed the onion instead. I could use the onion as an excuse if the floodgates cracked.

"Nothing," I said quietly. "I can finish this if you have something to do."

"What are you talking about? Why did you say that?" He wasn't going to let it go.

I rolled my eyes at his playing-dumb game. *Good, get mad again,* I told myself. Mad is a better weapon than sad. "I'm not blind, Jake. I watched you move from fling to fling all through high school, all through college, and I know you were the same after I moved. You don't do relationships. When it comes to anything serious, you're a dead-end road. Forgive me if I'm not willing to change my entire life to be your flavor of the month so you can toss me aside as soon as someone dumber and blonder comes along."

He was quiet for what seemed like a really long time as he stared into the bowl of steak. "Is that really what you think?" he asked quietly. "Or are you using that as an excuse to push me away?"

"I don't think it. I know it."

"You know for sure what I'm going to do in the future? How is that possible?"

"What is it they say?" I asked him. "A leopard doesn't change its spots, right? Look, I don't blame you for the way you are. I think it's probably because of your parents that you have a fear of intimacy but-"

"A fear of intimacy?" he asked loudly. "Are you fucking kidding me right now, Roxie? Did you seriously just accuse *me* of being the one in this room with a fear of intimacy?" He threw his head back in angry laughter. "Oh, God. That's rich."

He pushed off the island and turned to leave the room.

I set the knife down again, wiped my hand on my apron and went after him. "I'm over it too!" I yelled. "We can't even be in the same room for five minutes before we're taking off our clothes or arguing. Or both at the same time. That isn't normal. It's fucked up!"

He turned around so fast I bumped into him, and we collided in the hallway. But I didn't stop yelling.

"This isn't an Eminem video!" I continued. "Maybe you like the drama, but I'm done with it! And you better believe I'll be out of this house as soon as I can! And I WON'T need help packing, but thanks anyway!"

He put his face so close to mine our noses almost touched. "Good," he said. He touched the corner of my bottom lip and traced it with his finger. Then he traced the top lip. When he was done, he raised his eyes to meet mine.

The intensity in his eyes made me hope he would kiss me. *What the hell is wrong with me? How can I be turned on right now?*

"Good," he said again. "Then you can marry another guy you don't love because you're afraid of being hurt, and you can live the rest of your life in mediocrity."

That was enough to clear away my desire. I pushed him out of my way and ran up the stairs to my bedroom. *I hate him.*

A little while later I heard the patio door below my bedroom window open and close. I peeked out and saw Jake in the backyard turning on the gas grill. The SOB was going to cook my kabobs without me. UGH, whatever. I wasn't hungry anymore anyway.

I changed into my pajamas, climbed into bed and crawled under my down comforter where I was safe from Jake and his insults.

I was just starting to drift off to sleep when I heard music from out back. "In Your Eyes" by Peter Gabriel.

I heard my phone beep. I figured it was Jake, and I wanted to ignore it, but curiosity got the best of me, and I looked at the text.

JAKE: Look out your window.

I got out of bed and did as he said, expecting to see him standing out there with a boom box held up over his head like the popular scene from *Say Anything*.

I was close. There wasn't a boom box, but he was holding the speaker from his phone out to me as an olive branch.

It took everything I had in me to keep a straight face. If I laughed, he would think I'd forgiven him, and that was far from true.

When he saw me looking, he put the speaker down and started texting

My phone beeped again.

JAKE: Have dinner with me?

I didn't want to have *anything* with him, but I couldn't let someone else eat the meat I'd been marinating for an entire day.

I closed the curtains, put on a zip-up hoodie and left my room. I stopped in the bathroom and looked in the mirror. My hair was a mess and my mascara was smeared from crying; I didn't even have a bra on. I went downstairs anyway. Why? Because fuck him, that's why.

He was standing at the grill, placing the kabobs onto a plate, when I stepped outside. The patio table was set up very nicely. There was a candle in the center, a glass of wine for me and a bottle of beer for him. The volume on the speaker was turned down, but still played eighties music. It was all a sweet gesture. But he was still a jerk.

He looked up from the grill and waved his hand at the plate of kabobs and said, "I cooked."

"Thanks," I said, my voice as flat as could be. There was no emotion left in me. I was tired of the emotions - tired of this whole screwed up relationship. I thought I could move back to New York, and we could still be friends, but I knew now I'd thought wrong. Jake and I couldn't be friends. Not in any city.

I walked over to the table and sat down. He had made a simple salad to go with the kabobs. I was impressed.

He brought the plate over, set it on the patio table, and sat down across from me.

I tried the chicken first (incredible), then the steak (unbelievable), then the veggies that Jake had finished on his own. They were also good.

"I'm gonna miss this," he said as he licked his fingers clean.

"Yeah, I guess it's back to frozen pizzas for you two," I said dryly.

"Guess so," he agreed. "But I was talking about hanging out with you, not the food."

I didn't know why he'd want to hang out with a gold-digger who ran away from her problems, tried too hard to impress people, cared too much about what other people thought and had a fear of intimacy that would lead her to a life of mediocrity ... but I didn't say that. I didn't have any fight left in me. I wanted to eat and get back in bed.

"Tell me about this cooking school," he said to break the uncomfortable silence.

"I'm not going to sit here and talk to you like everything is normal, Jake. Not anymore. I'm tired of pushing things aside to try to get along with you. We shouldn't have to try this hard."

As soon as the words left my mouth, I wished I could grab them and reel them back in. The look on his face left no doubt I'd hurt him, and I felt bad about it, even after the things he said earlier. The two of us had issues, but Jake was truly a good guy and didn't deserve any of this.

He swallowed like he was getting ready to say something important, but I think he changed his mind. "Okay," he said. "We don't have to pretend anything, but I didn't want this food to go to waste."

"Thank you for finishing it for me," I said quietly.

"Sure."

We ate the rest of the meal in an awkward silence. When we were done I stood up and started clearing our dirty plates, and we both went inside. While he wrapped up the leftovers and put them in the fridge, I rinsed our plates and put them in the dishwasher.

"I'm going to bed early tonight," I told him when I was finished. "But thanks again for dinner. I really mean it."

He closed the refrigerator door and turned around to look at me. "I'm in love with you, Roxie."

I didn't even know what to say to that. I just shook my head.

"The reason I didn't have girlfriends was because I didn't want to waste my time on the wrong ones. I've known who I wanted all along. If you think I'm some kind of womanizer, you're wrong. I don't want an endless string of one night stands. I want you. Only you."

I sighed. Those were nice words and all. He may even mean them right now. But that's the thing. People always want what they don't have and when they get it they're like, *what the fuck is this shit?* I couldn't fall for that.

"Jake, you can't want me," I insisted. "You don't even know me. You said yourself you don't know the New York me, and this me is a phony."

"That's an ironic thing to say. I was thinking it was the other way around."

"I have to go upstairs and get something. I'll be right back."

I ran up to my room and pulled my folded up Good Life List out of my purse and ran back down to the kitchen. I unfolded it and handed it to him.

I watched his face as he read over the now wrinkly and check-marked piece of notebook paper. He didn't seem surprised or mad. He actually seemed a bit entertained.

"Everything I did this summer," I explained, "was on the list. It wasn't really me. All the fun things I did, they were Hope's ideas, not mine. You don't love me, Jake. That girl that hula hoops in the grocery store is not me."

"You think I'm telling you this right now because you played with a hula hoop?" he asked, like it was the most obscene idea I'd ever had. He set the Good Life List down on the island and touched the side of my face with his hand.

Why does he have to do that? It makes my heart fall

straight to the floor every time.

"I've loved you since I was ten," he explained, "and you found me under that table in your living room – the one with all of the plants. Remember?"

I nodded slowly.

"Girls were gross back then, so I thought I loved you like a sister. It wasn't until we were in high school when I realized you weren't gross. You were actually kind of amazing. But at the same time, you were too important for me to lose. I knew I couldn't tell you how I felt until I was ready, really ready for you. And that's why I'm telling you now."

This was it, the climax of my movie. Those were the words I'd been waiting to hear since I was a little girl. I didn't know what to say to him. I sighed again and closed my eyes so I could really enjoy the moment.

Jake slowly traced his finger down my neck, past my collarbone and then across the top of my shirt. I squeezed my eyes shut and hoped I wasn't literally melting.

"Do you remember that summer?" he asked, and I knew then that he remembered everything the way I did. I knew he had all kinds of images from that summer flashing in his head, just the way I still did – all the time.

"That summer," he said again, "when you were finally mine, I knew you were the only one I'd ever need."

"But you said –" I interrupted.

He put his finger on my lips to quiet me. "I know what I said. I said I didn't want to long-distance it. Nine months wasn't a long time for me. I'd already been waiting so long, nine months was nothing. I didn't want to turn what we had, which I thought was pretty fucking awesome, into something that caused us both stress. I didn't want to be that 'boyfriend from home,' like I was a liability to you."

I'd had a few friends in college that had a "boyfriend from home" and Jake was right – they were a liability. My friends had to make sure they called every night by a certain time or the guys would freak out. If the boyfriends didn't call by a certain time, my friends would freak out. It was just another task to check off the list. Paid the phone bill – Check. Studied for Psych test – Check. Called the boyfriend – Check. Those girls had very little fun when they were being good girlfriends, and nothing but grief when they were bad. I totally understood what Jake was saying. All this time I thought he didn't like me enough to deal with it, but he had been trying to spare me the bullshit.

"I still don't really understand why you didn't come back to me," he continued, "but I forgive you for it. Maybe this was how it was meant to happen. Maybe we weren't ready then. I don't know. But I do know I love you. Whether or not –" he picked up the Good Life List again and scanned it quickly, " –you play in the rain or wear underwear."

If this was a movie, there would be no questioning. I would jump into his arms, and we'd share a really gross kiss. Our mouths would be wide open like we were trying to eat each other's faces off, and our heads would move from side to side every two seconds. The credits would roll to the tune of a dramatic, but catchy, love song performed by the runner-up of the latest reality show talent competition.

It would be assumed we lived happily-ever-after, but no one would ever know for sure. Because the movie would be over. The movie always ends when the characters finally get together. There's a reason for that – it's because nobody wants to sit in a theatre and watch petty arguing and boring sex scenes (ahem, Jason Segal and Emily Blunt). If the real Hollywood screenwriters couldn't come up with something good, and some of the best actors couldn't make it entertaining, how could we?

I started to feel like I was being backed into a corner. All this time I had been able to scurry on by and pretend this thing between us was just for fun. I could pretend I didn't love him, and that I couldn't tell he loved me back. But when he said it out loud like that, there was no way I could pretend anymore. If we were still kids, I could put my hands over my ears and sing lalalalanotlisteningtoyou. If we were drunk, I could pretend to black out and not remember it tomorrow. But I wasn't a little kid, and I only had one glass of wine, and even I couldn't think of a way to avoid this conversation without being painfully obvious about it.

That was probably exactly what he was expecting me to do, right? That's what the girl who runs away would do. Should I do what was expected of me because it was the easiest way out? Or punish myself by sticking around just to prove him wrong? Was the risk worth the reward in either scenario?

He lifted the few strands of hair that fell in front of my eye and pushed them to the side. "I know what you're doing," he said with a crooked grin.

"What am I doing?" I asked. I wasn't even sure what I was doing.

"You're trying to figure out a way to get out of this conversation without putting me in a position to say 'I told ya so,'" he replied.

He was right.

"Look," he said. "Baby, you don't have to say anything, okay?"

He called me baby again. Damn he was making this hard on me.

"You can run if you need to," he continued, "but I let you leave before without telling you how I felt. When you didn't come back, I wondered if things could have been different. I don't want to have to wonder again if I didn't do enough. Know what I mean?"

I nodded.

"I saw how happy you were in New York," he said, "and I want you to be happy. I really do want that for you. If you think you'd be happier there than here with me, I understand. As long as you leave knowing how I feel, that's enough for me."

He was giving me a way out. He was telling me it was okay for me to go back to bed and pretend this never happened. But it wasn't okay with *me*. I couldn't do that to him. I cared too much to walk away and let him think I didn't love him back.

But asking me to choose between him and New York wasn't fair. That was like choosing between chocolate cake and apple pie. I could pick one tonight if I could have the other tomorrow, but to let one go permanently? How could I? And what if I picked the wrong one, and by the time I realized my mistake, it was too late to change my mind? *Ugh, why couldn't we just keep on pretending?*

"Jake," I said quietly. "I ..."

"You don't have to say anything," he repeated.

"I think you're kind of amazing too," I blurted out. "Not even kind of. You're all the way amazing. But I ... it's just ..."

"I know, baby." He put his arms around my neck and pulled me into a choke-hold kind of hug. He rested his chin on the top of my head, and I wrapped my arms tightly around him. The soft worn-out cotton of his t-shirt felt comforting on my cheek as I pressed it into his chest. His familiar smell put my mind at ease, if only for a moment. I clenched my fingers into a fist around his shirt like I was holding on for my life.

"I know," he said again and I felt his breath on my neck. "But it's really not that serious. Just relax. I can take it from here."

"Are you going to take it all the way to New York?" It was the first time the idea had occurred to me. If Jake came to New York, I could have my cake *and* my pie. If he loved me enough to come with me, I would owe it to him to give him a chance. I would feel a lot safer putting my heart on the line like that if I knew for sure he loved me *that* much. It was easy to love someone who was right in front of you. But to move to another state, you've *really* got to mean it.

I didn't have to wonder for very long. He pulled apart from our hug and held me at arm's length.

"I wish I could. But my business is here. It's taken me ten years to get this far. I can't just throw it all away and start from scratch, Rox."

That was all I needed to hear. He loved me ... just not enough. And that was okay. At least he was honest.

"How about we compromise?" he asked.

I crossed my arms in front of me. "How would that work?"

"You'll go to New York," he said. "I'll stay here. Maybe one day you'll miss me enough to come back. Or maybe half of my clientele will move to New York too, and I can follow them."

"Or maybe you'll find someone else."

He smiled. "My *entire* clientele moving to New York is more likely."

You know the way the vampires' faces sparkle in

the *Twilight* movies? I felt like my heart was sparkling the same way.

"How long until you go?" he asked.

I shrugged. "I'm not sure. Two or three weeks. Could be less."

"So how about for the next few weeks we stop pretending?"

"We take it day by day?"

"I was thinking more like lay-by-lay, but I guess either term is acceptable."

"I can do that," I said.

"That means you're mine until you leave, right?"

"Yes," I said with certainty. "I'm yours. And that possessiveness is getting me hot, so hurry up and stake your claim on me."

I'll remember the way he kissed me then for the whole rest of my life.

CHAPTER SEVENTEEN

Honesty really was the magic answer. *The Summer of Jake and Roxie – Part Two* was a spectacular, 5-star, A+, top-of-the-box-office hit. There was the kind of romance that created butterflies in my belly, laugh-out-loud comedy, edge-of-my-seat excitement, porn star quality sex scenes and a great soundtrack as well. We both knew this romance had an expiration date, but we didn't talk about it. We were too obliviously happy to think about anything except when we could touch each other again.

It was nearing the end of August when I got The Phone Call. Jake and I were entwined on the couch watching a Tigers game and trying to throw popcorn into each other's mouths when Hope called.

"Listen," she said.

"Listening."

"J.D.'s cousin's boyfriend finally asked her to move in with him."

I sat up straighter. This was intriguing. That kind

of scenario could mean a hand-me-down apartment, and those were the best kind to get.

"Listening more closely."

"The Village. Rent-stabilized. One block from subway."

This was good. This was *very* good. The most important thing about any Manhattan apartment was its proximity to the subway. The Village was an excellent neighborhood. Rent-stabilization was just a cherry on top.

"How long do I have?"

"Ten minutes?"

"Shit."

"Tomorrow morning."

"Okay. I'll call you."

I hung up the phone and saw that Jake was giving me a suspicious look.

"That was a vague conversation," he pointed out.

"Yeah."

"And a vague response."

"Yeah."

He sat up straight, which caused me to fall off of him and onto the other end of the couch.

"Something you need to tell me?"

"Hope found an apartment."

"Oh," was all he said. He looked disappointed, and I felt a little bit of disappointment myself. "You sure you can't go to school here?"

I fought the urge to laugh at his question. I could probably find a program around here, but I don't need a culinary education to work at Olive Garden.

"Are you sure you can't take pictures in New York?" was my rebuttal.

He didn't reply. I don't blame him. That was kind of a shitty thing for me to say.

"It doesn't mean we can't still do our day-today," I said hopefully. "I can be done with school in less than a year. I can visit. It could be like a month-to-month lease. I promise you won't be a liability."

He patted my knee. "Sure, we'll figure it out."

"I need to see the apartment first. It could be infested with cockroaches the size of baseballs, and the toilet could be in the shower."

"Then find a different apartment. I don't want to be the reason you are stuck in Ann Arbor. I said I want you to be happy, and I meant it. I'm not gonna be mad at you. I promise. Do what you need to do."

"I need to see this apartment."

"Okay then."

"I'm going to look up flights for the morning."

"If you wake me up, I'll drive you."

I didn't wake him up to drive me because I'd booked a return flight for later that evening. I drove myself and left my car at the airport. I did leave him a cute little love note on the nightstand though, letting him know I'd be home later.

I took a cab from LaGuardia straight to the apartment where Hope and J.D.'s cousin met me. When I walked in I knew I had to have it. It was tiny, as most of them are. But it was a cozy, homey kind of tiny and not a buried alive in a wooden coffin kind of tiny.

It was neglected. The hardwood floors were scuffed and dull. The paint was peeling and stained with cigarette smoke. The small kitchen counter was probably older than my parents. But all I saw in it was a blank slate. I could make it beautiful.

As is the norm for me, I got a little ahead of myself. As I stood in the doorway I was already imagining myself doing homework in the galley-style kitchen like a scene from *Julie and Julia*. I could speak with a French accent and boil lobsters, and Jake could laugh at me when the lid popped off and I went running from the kitchen ... oh wait, Jake wouldn't be there. And if I went running from the kitchen, I'd trip over the couch or run straight into a brick wall. But the point was that this apartment could be my future. My life was like a brand new notebook and this was the first page. This little apartment in The Village would be where my story began.

I celebrated my new apartment with a shopping trip down Broadway. J.D.'s cousin needed a few weeks to get completely moved out, but she said I could start bringing things in right away. I spent the afternoon at Crate and Barrel, Urban Outfitters and Anthropologie. I was so excited to have an apartment of my very own for the first time ever. Being able to buy window treatments and placemats and a shower curtain without having to ask anyone else's opinion was fun and liberating.

Not that I wasn't thinking about Jake. It bothered me he hadn't called yet to see how things had gone, but I hadn't called him either. It was probably for the best if we distanced ourselves a little now so when the time came for me to move - and for us to distance ourselves a lot - it might be easier. I knew I was going to miss him like crazy, but I kept telling myself if it were meant to be, it would be.

This was New York, my soul mate. I belonged here. And that was what I kept telling myself. Any time I felt a fresh batch of tears coming to my eyes, I put another item into my shopping bag. It's not called retail therapy for nothing.

Once I lugged all of my shopping bags back over to the apartment and stored them in a closet, I took a walk to explore my new neighborhood. The apartment was two blocks from Washington Square

Park, in the same area as NYU and Peanut Butter and Co where we'd had lunch last time.

I made my way over to the park. It was a beautiful day and, just like last time I was here, the ambiance of the city made me feel at peace. I sat on a bench near a dog run to people-watch for a bit and enjoy the sunshine.

I felt good to be home, but I couldn't deny the fact that something wasn't right. A few weeks ago, when Jake and I had sat on the bench outside of Zabar's, I'd had one of those rare moments in life where everything was perfect. The sun was shining. I was in my favorite place in the world. There was great food in my hands. I didn't have to worry about money for a little while. I knew I had people in my life who loved me. My split with Caleb had ended up amicable. And to top it all off – I was drinking a Zabar's coffee!

Theoretically, I should have been feeling the same thing in Washington Square Park. The sun was still shining. People still loved me. My divorce was completely over and no hard feelings were left behind. I had my own apartment. I was starting school to do something I really wanted to do. I was in my favorite place in the world. There were even puppies around! Puppies! But it wasn't one of *those* moments, and I knew it wasn't the absence of coffee. It was the absence of Jake. It couldn't possibly be one of *those* moments without him in it.

My phone rang. *Finally*, I thought, thinking it was Jake. But it was my dad's number on the screen.

"Hi, Sunshine," he said cautiously. He sounded sad. My heart started beating faster at the sound of his voice.

"Is something wrong?" I asked, my voice shaking a little.

"It's your mom," he said. His voice squeaked a little at the end, which scared the shit out of me. "She's being prepped for emergency surgery in a few minutes. She has an aneurysm in her aorta."

I wasn't sure what an aorta was, but I thought it had something to do with the heart and I knew for sure than an aneurysm was a very bad thing. I stood up and started walking quickly toward the street to look for a cab.

"She only has a few minutes and wanted me to call you and Adam. I'm putting her on," he said.

"Hi, Buttercup." It was Mom. Oh my God! Could this be the last time I ever talked to her? It was so sudden. I wasn't prepared! This was one of those things I hadn't prepped for. Not that I'd never thought about it happening, but I'd be a seriously crazy person if I had a speech prepared.

Even so, you'd think with my expertise I'd be able to come up with something better than a high-pitched, "Hi, Mommy."

"What are you doing?" she asked, like it was a normal day and a normal phone call.

"I'm, um, in the city," I told her. "I found an apartment of my own."

"Excellent news!" she said, sounding genuinely happy about it. "I knew you'd be better off without him."

"What did they say about this surgery?" I asked. My voice sounded like that of a little girl. I got that panicky feeling in me again where I wanted to kneel down and cling to her legs and beg her not to go. "Is it risky?"

"Well," she said with a sigh, "not having the surgery is a sure death, so whether it's risky or not, it's the only option. They're coming in just a minute, and I've still got to call your brother."

"Okay, Mom," I said breathlessly as I was still running toward the street. "I'm on my way to the airport right now. I'll probably be there by the time you're in the recovery room."

"Okay, love, I'll see you then. And just in case I don't –"

"No!" I interrupted. "You will!"

"I'm really proud of you, baby girl."

I couldn't even say anything because I was crying. It was the face-all-squished-up kind of cry.

"I love you, Mom," I managed to squeak out before the call ended.

Oh God! What do I do? LaGuardia, JFK or Newark? Who had the next flight to Fort Myers? Why didn't I just buy one of those phones that I could talk to and ask questions?

I sat down on another bench to gain composure and search for flights on my Blackberry. My fingers were shaking as I tried to type in the search bar. Then I had to watch the hourglass go round and round and round as my dinosaur of a phone took its sweet time to load a page. *Damn you, hourglass! I hate you!* I wanted to take my phone to a field with a baseball bat like they did with the copy machine in *Office Space*.

Once I knew which airport to head to, I stood up, signaled a cab and climbed in. All the way to the airport I searched on my phone for aortic aneurysms and felt worse by the second. Most of what I read was probably a bunch of nonsense, but I wasn't thinking clearly enough to realize that. All I was seeing were words and phrases like "50% mortality rate" and "highest cause of death" and "one of the riskier surgeries."

By the time I got to the airport, I could hardly breathe. Everything seemed to happen in a blur. The lovely people of JetBlue got me a seat on a flight that started boarding about five minutes after I arrived at the ticket counter.

In line for the security check I bit off every one of my fingernails.

Once I was on the plane I Googled more about Abdominal Aortic Aneurysms until it was time to put my phone into airplane mode.

It wasn't until after we were in the air when I realized I hadn't called Jake or Adam. I didn't know if my parents had been able to get in touch with Adam, or if he'd been in the operating room at the time. I didn't know if he would go to the airport straight from the hospital or go home first. I could have called him to bring me some clothes since all I had with me was my purse.

I should have called and let Jake know what was happening and that I wasn't coming home tonight. Not only because he was almost like my boyfriend, but also because my mom was almost like his mom. But it was too late for any of that now. I was not about to use one of those airplane phones.

I tried reading on my Kindle to pass the time on the three-hour flight, but I was too worried about my mom to concentrate. Once I reread the same paragraph four times and still had no idea what I'd read, I gave up and ordered a drink instead. It was too bad the flight attendants didn't serve Ambien. All I wanted to do was close my eyes and not open them until I was in Florida with my mom.

Three hours and three cocktails later, I landed in Fort Myers. I took a cab to the hospital and found my dad in one of the waiting areas. The poor guy looked like a deflated balloon in his button-up tropical print shirt, khaki cargo shorts and flip flops, with his messy hair and red eyes.

I ran into his arms and he hugged me tightly. I didn't know what he would do without Mom and I tried not to think about it.

He told me he'd talked to Adam for a while on the phone, and Adam had calmed him down by telling him how advanced this procedure was. It used to be a very risky surgery, which is probably why I'd read all that terrible stuff during my Google search.

Once at the hospital I didn't know what to do with myself. They didn't serve alcohol in the cafeteria (I asked). My fingernails were already bitten down to ugly little nubs. I tried calling Jake to tell him what was going on, but his phone went straight to voicemail. All I could think to do was look up viral videos on my phone to show Dad. We watched about ten videos just of cats. Cats can be pretty funny.

Adam arrived about an hour after I did. What a relief! He was much better in stressful situations than I was. He was the calm and reasonable member of our family, and also the one most likely to take charge. I felt relaxed just by his presence. The fact that he was calm made Dad and me calm too. Right away Adam took control and said he was going to the cafeteria to get us snacks and drinks. *Why didn't I think of that?*

Shortly after Adam left the waiting room, I caught a glimpse of a guy in the hallway. All I could see was the back of him, but I could tell he was built like Jake. I felt a stab of pain in my heart.

I *so* wished Jake were here. Even if he left today, though, it would take at least a full day to drive down, and that was if he didn't stop at all. He would have to stop and sleep at some point. The earliest I could hope to have his arms around me again would be two days from now. And that was only if he was willing to make the trip. He might not even want to.

For the first time in my life I truly understood the meaning of the word "yearn." I had always thought of it as being a lame word used in romance novels by virgins with tiny boobs or men with six-pack abs who wore cowboy hats. But nope, it was me; former bad girl, lover of high heels and frozen Cokes, who still had a crush on Pacey Witter and had never had sex with a sexy stranger in front of a fireplace while snowed-in at a log cabin in the woods. It was I who felt the pain of *the yearn*.

Another thing that caught my eye about the guy in the hallway was that he was carrying a black tote bag that said Love Pink in big fuchsia letters. I recognized the bag because I had the same one – yep, another free gift with purchase. It took a real man to carry around a Victoria's Secret tote bag, and I thought to myself that whoever he was carrying that bag for was one lucky chick.

When the guy poked his head into the waiting room and smiled at me I nearly peed my pants! He looked identical to Jake! I wondered if he'd let me take a picture of him so I could show Jake his Florida doppelganger but I didn't have time to ask him.

"Hi, baby," the guy said softly. He set the tote bag down near my feet. "Sorry it took me so long. I couldn't find a parking spot. We left in a hurry, but I packed a few things for you."

It *was* Jake!

I jumped out of my seat and grabbed onto him and held him tighter than I have ever held onto anyone before – even tighter than I held my parents' legs when I was little.

"How did you get here so fast?" I asked while my arms were still wrapped around his neck in a choke hold.

"I came with Adam," he said into my shoulder.

"But Adam, he came on a plane, right?" It was a stupid question. It's not like he borrowed George Jetson's car or arrived in a spaceship.

"Yeah."

I let go of him and stood back to get a good look at his face. "You got on a plane?" I still needed clarification.

He shrugged like it was no big deal. "Some things are worth facing your fears for," he said quietly as if it was the most simple and obvious answer.

"You did that for me?" I asked sheepishly.

"Of course."

I hugged him again as the tears filled my eyes. "I love you, Jake. I've loved you forever and I'm sorry I didn't tell you." I didn't even care that Dad was sitting right there, and Adam had just walked into the room with fountain sodas, candy and snack-sized potato chips. I didn't need to keep him a secret anymore. Why would I ever want to keep such a sweet thing a secret anyway?

"I love you, too, Little Girl."

The surgery was a success. The doctors said my dad saved her life by making her go to the doctor for her back pain. They never would have found the aneurysm otherwise, and they were certain it would have burst had they not repaired it. I could have very easily lost my mom without warning.

We were allowed to see her once she was out of recovery and, besides being a little groggy from the medications, she seemed like her normal self.

When she saw Jake she asked, "Did you fly here?" Ha, I guess I get it from her.

"Yes," he answered.

She looked at me and smiled because she knew he hadn't done it for her.

Dad and Adam stayed to help her eat dinner but they didn't need four people in that tiny room so Jake suggested we go get something to eat.

Everything I was feeling for Jake was suddenly so strong. I was overwhelmed by the amount of love I felt for him, but underwhelmed by the various ways I knew how to express it.

I wanted him to know, to *really* understand, how much it meant to me that he'd come to Florida. But I didn't know the right words to say. It seemed like so many adjectives and phrases were overused these days. I was one of the guilty over-users.

I went over some words and expressions as Jake drove the rental car down the coast. Amazing was definitely overplayed, that was out for sure. Fabulous reminded me of a commercial for gum. Outstanding, super and excellent were all words a teacher would write on a well-written term paper. Magnificent made me think of shopping in Chicago. Phenomenal was the way I would describe a red-carpet look at the Golden Globes, and he was way more than a pretty dress or a classy up-do. Extraordinary was a word I'd used just last week to describe a flourless cake I'd made. He wasn't even on the same planet as those words! I needed something more. I needed a word used to describe something that couldn't be described.

I was seriously going to invest some of my divorce money in Google.

We were seated at an outdoor table at the nearest sports bar and had just ordered beer and wings when I told him about my problem.

"I want to tell you how much this means to me,

you being here. But I don't know how to say it. Every word I can think of doesn't come close."

"Don't worry about it. I know you were happy I came."

I shook my head. "See? That's the thing. I am happy a lot of the time, and for the most simple reasons. This day, and what you did for me, made me way more than happy. I can't even say it. It's like not describable."

"It's really okay," he said.

"I found a word. It means something incapable of being described in words."

"What's the word?"

"Ineffable."

"Ineffable," he repeated. "Okay."

"I thought it could be a special word that we reserved for only the most special of times and this is definitely one of them."

"You say that like there's going to be other special times."

"I hope there are," I said.

"Those are big words for a day-to-day girlfriend to say," he said.

I looked down at our hands on the table. "I don't think day-to-day is enough for me anymore," I said honestly. I nervously bit my lip and only slightly glanced up at him. "I need more. I need," I paused because, even though I knew for sure it was what I wanted, it was still difficult for me to say, "I need forever."

"You and me?" he asked. "Forever?"

I shrugged, feeling shy and fearing rejection. "I mean, if it's too much for you we can do day-to-day still. I don't want to scare you off or put too much pressure on you."

He laughed out loud. "It's funny how you think

I'm the one who is scared. You and me forever – I can do that."

"You think I'm the one who is scared?" I asked.

I was thankful he didn't say "duh." I'd always hated that expression. He just smiled.

"Maybe I am," I said thoughtfully. "But some things are worth facing your fears for, right?"

He smiled and nodded. "So? Are you ever going to tell me about this apartment?"

The apartment! I had forgotten all about it. How crazy that I woke up this morning in Michigan, flew to NYC, found an apartment, went shopping, and had dinner on the Gulf of Mexico. All in one day.

I shook my head. "My mom almost died today. Life is too short to be selfish. I spent way too many years without you, and I don't want to spend another one. I don't even want one minute without you."

I laced my fingers into those of my best friend and knew *he* was where I was supposed to be. New York was just a city. I could visit it often if I needed to. But my heart was with Jake, and that's where it needed to stay.

"I'm not moving to New York," I said firmly.

"Yes, you are," he insisted.

"I'm not. I can take cooking classes at a community college or something. I don't need New York. I need you."

The waitress dropped off our wings and the conversation stopped as we started eating.

"Do you want to know a secret?" he asked, a few wings later.

I nodded.

"I heart New York," he admitted.

I smiled. It was a very easy place to heart.

"And the truth is," he said, "I haven't been able to stop thinking about that pastrami sandwich."

I laughed out loud.

"You might need me, Rox. But I need to live by that deli. For at least one year."

I dropped the wing I'd been holding. The bone made a clink on the ceramic plate. I knew I had buffalo sauce and bleu cheese dressing on my face, but I was too stunned to grab my napkin. I knew what he was saying, that he was willing to come with me, to leave his jobs, his business behind, to be with me. I loved him for it, but I couldn't let him do it. I shook my head. "I can't let you give up everything for me."

"I'm telling you the truth. I loved being there. I can take a sabbatical. We'll give it a year and see how it works out. If it's not working, we'll reevaluate. Now tell me about this apartment. How close is it to the deli?"

Very slowly, a smile started to appear on my face. First, it was just the corners of a slanted grin, but soon it morphed itself into a huge toothpaste-commercial kind of smile. "Really?"

He nodded. I was so happy I accidentally let out a sound I hadn't heard since I was eleven and my parents took me to the set of the *All New Mickey Mouse Club* during our vacation in Orlando. (Yep, Justin and Ryan, I saw them first).

"This is going to be …" I paused while I thought of a word that was good enough for us, "epic."

EPILOGUE

I stayed in Florida for a week to help Dad take care of Mom while Jake tied up his loose ends in Ann Arbor and finished packing all of our things. Once we were ready to go, Adam took a few vacation days to drive the moving truck. He helped us unload, clean up, repaint and refinish the place. By the time the three of us were done, I had the apartment of my dreams. Well, at least a tenth of the apartment of my dreams, but that was a good start.

Adam wasn't surprised to find out about Jake and me. He said he had known the whole time, but he pretended he didn't because he appreciated our subtlety. He was more than happy to leave me in Jake's care, and Mom and Dad felt the same way.

Jake found a job at a bar in the Meat-Packing District within a week. We didn't want his business in Ann Arbor to suffer too much, so the plan was for him to schedule shoots on every third Tuesday and Wednesday. He would fly back and forth now that he had overcome his fear of flying. It would be costly, but if it kept his business afloat for a year while I was in school, it was worth it.

I thought he had a good enough portfolio to start his business up in NYC as well. He just needed to advertise. That was why I secretly had some business cards and flyers printed to surprise him. He was good at his job, and I had no doubt he would find success in The City.

Jake loved our apartment, he was happy with his new job, he felt right at home in New York, and he loved me. Everything was falling into place.

The day before school started I made it my goal to have every single box unpacked. There wasn't enough room in our place to have a bunch of boxes hanging around. I spent the day hanging photos and shelves, organizing drawers and cupboards, and scouring the Ikea website to make room for our things without having our apartment look like a cluttered hell. It was when I got to the last box labeled "bathroom" that everything in my world changed.

In spite of donating a bunch of beauty products to the homeless shelter, I still had enough to make my bathroom look like the basement of Barney's. I was trying to figure out where to put everything when I saw a familiar pink box. Tampons.

I pulled out the box and looked at it strangely as I tried to remember the last time I had seen them or had any use for them. It had been an unusually long time.

I pulled up the calendar on my phone to see if anything triggered my memory. Nope, I couldn't remember my last period. *What are you, twelve?* I scolded myself as I grabbed my purse and flew out the door toward the nearest drug store.

Jake was working the lunch shift at the bar. I sent him a text while I walked. It said to come straight home after work.

Once at the store I couldn't decide what kind to buy. There were vertical lines, perpendicular lines and the digital ones that actually spelled out the word or words. The digital one was least likely to be misunderstood, but a photo of the plus sign would look better in a pregnancy scrapbook. Ah, screw it. I bought both and hurried home.

As I waited for Jake to walk in the door, I paced the five feet of empty space in the apartment - back and forth, back and forth. I bit off the nails that had finally started to grow back after Mom's surgery

When I heard his footsteps coming up the stairs, I ran to the door and threw it open just as he was approaching. He looked startled.

"Everything okay?" he asked.

I pulled him into the apartment, closed the door and headed straight for the bathroom. He followed me.

"Do you remember that time we used a condom?" I asked him.

He put a finger to his chin like he was actually trying to remember. A few seconds later he shook his head.

"No, I really don't," he answered.

"Me either," I replied, nervously.

He slanted his eyes at me in a curious way. "What are you saying?" he asked cautiously.

I held up the boxes I'd bought at the store.

"Oh," he said. I couldn't tell if that was an *Oh, yay!* Or an *Oh, fuck!*

I went into the bathroom and shut the door (Hope taught me well - no more peeing in front of anyone).

I tried the plus-sign one first. Once the stick was lying flat on the sink, I opened the door to Jake's stunned face, his mouth still in the "O" form. He came into the bathroom like he was in a daze. We both stared at the test on the sink as a horizontal blue line appeared in the window. Then we watched a perpendicular line appear shortly after.

No doubt about it. It was a Big Fat Plus. A BFP!

I knew it was early in our relationship for this to happen, and it certainly wasn't part of my plan just yet. But I hoped he would be as happy as I was to see this plus sign. Who knew? Maybe things were better left unplanned.

"What do you think?" I asked him quietly.

"I think this is …" he stopped as he searched for the right word. "I think it's ineffable."

THE END

Thank You

I have to first give many thanks to the other half of me, my husband, Brian. You encouraged me when I wanted to give up, you reminded me to keep writing when I got distracted, you took on most of the housework and never complained about the piles of dishes in the sink, or the fact that we were having hot dogs for dinner again. I know this is so sickeningly sappy, but you really are the Wind Beneath My Wings.

Ian, if it wasn't for you I would have been perfectly content as a career waitress. You made me want to reach higher. I couldn't encourage you to be the best person you could be if I wasn't going to lead by example. I'm sorry for being a "couch-mom" while I was writing this book, but I promise to make it up to you.

My parents, thank you for believing in me more than I believed in myself, not only while writing this book, but always.

The rest of my family and friends: I can't name them all because I am lucky to have so many. I have been truly blessed to have the most supportive and loving family. From my nucleus (my parents, step-parents and brothers), to my extended family (grandparents, aunts, uncles and cousins), to my chosen family (my friends), I will NEVER forget how much you all encouraged me. Thank you, thank you, thank you!

My beta-readers: Beth Ehemann, Jamie Sager Hall, Chrystle Woods and Lisa Stallmann – Thank you all for taking the time to help me and for making The Good Life a better book! Oh, and thanks for all the gushing and pimping too.

Thank you to Sarah Hansen at Okay Creations for the cover. It's even better than the one I imagined. And thank you even more for the recommendation!

Thank you to Kim for the clock; Julie at JT Formatting for taking on the last minute job; the bloggers and readers who helped spread the word; the independent authors who helped pave the road; Melissa Brown for helping a total stranger; One Republic and Katy Perry for the inspiration; and thank YOU for reading this!

My last bag of props, and it's a *really* big bag, goes to my fabulous editor, Madison Seidler. What a sparkly gem you are! I felt like you really "got" me right from the start. You have been so much more to me than an editor. You've been my personal cheerleader, publicist, therapist, tour manager. You've introduced me to so many great people. You taught me the difference between farther and further, towards and toward, and you broke the news that it is no longer acceptable to add two spaces after a period. I will never be able to say or type enough thank-yous to you!

FIND ME. STALK ME.

Please visit me on Facebook
www.facebook.com/sweetbutsnarky

Follow me on Twitter
https://twitter.com/GoodLifeList

Become a fan on Goodreads
http://www.goodreads.com/JodieBeau

Email me
booksbyjodiebeau@gmail.com

Or check out my blog
http://jodiebeau.wordpress.com/

Made in the USA
San Bernardino, CA
21 April 2014